Out of Sight, Out of Mind

Elle Ann Brown

Published by Brown Creative LLC

Cover design: joshandrewbrown.com
Author Photo: Bre Hargrove

ISBN: 979-8640081268

To my readers:

because you asked for more.

1

My hands pushed the cold metal drawer shut with a *whoosh* and *bang* as a proud smile graced my face. Another account balanced to perfection. I walked away from the wall of cabinets taller than me in the accounting office, mentally high-fiving myself. As I sat back down, I straightened the nameplate on my desk. Something I did multiple times ~~an hour~~ a day, even though I'd occupied the space for one month. The newness of my impressive role as CPA for a major oil company at only twenty-four had yet to wear off; empowering and equally confounding. The enormous accounts I kept tabs on contained more money than would ever pass through my bank accounts in this life.

The knock on the open door pulled me out of my victory party-of-one.

"Who has Seymour?" Donald, our top company-buyer-outer, asked Steve and me from the doorway. His odd smile pulled his face into something like a kid's drawing.

There weren't many people in the office I connected with yet, but I for sure wasn't keen on Donald. His smiles were a tick under candid, and his eyes always squinted a smidge. Further annoying, the slew of nicknames he spit in my direction were never the same twice. Needless to say, I kept our conversations brief.

"Me." I reached for the file he offered. Opening the folder, I buried my face inside so I didn't have to look at him.

"Pack your bags then. We're headed to Illinois."

Um, what?

I looked up, abandoning the file on my desk. Donald scratched his chin. The sound of the short hair succumbing to his fingers was the only reason I knew a short beard matching his blonde hair covered his face. It was so light, I couldn't see the facial hair against his fair skin.

"We, as in...?"

"You and me, Star."

Star. That was a new one. From what I could remember, I had been called Queen, Penny, Wonder Woman, Number Whiz, New Kid on the Block, and Bubblegum. I despised the nicknames. Make that loathed, whichever word was stronger in hatred on a scale of go-away to I'd-rather-eat-a-live-scorpion-than-talk-to-you. But had I asked him to simply call me Londyn? Of course not. Not until I filled this role a few more months and didn't feel the looming possibility of getting fired. Donald, our company's Merger and Acquisitions Advisor, was responsible for bringing in most of the massive accounts I managed after all. Not to mention, this company wasn't booming with ladies like it was oil. All I needed was to be called Nag.

"Turns out, Seymour sits on top of a major reservoir," he continued. "Ralph wants to keep the office there but make sure it's up to par with Aspire quality. So you, Lucky Lady," *add that one to the ever-growing list*, "get a two-week paid work-cation to beautiful St. Louis. Before you get too excited," *I doubt my face looks excited*, "we aren't going *to* St. Louis, but who's heard of its less popular sister, Belleville, twenty minutes down the road?" Donald pulled his suit coat together and fastened a button.

What I wanted to ask: *Do I have a say in this? Want to trade accounts, Steve? Is there* anyone *else in the company who can go with you? Or go with me?*

What I asked: "When do we leave?" My mouth in a pursed line.

"Sally's booking our tickets as we speak. We leave in two days." He meant Sammy, short for Samantha, but I didn't feel like correcting him. She was the *one* co-worker I connected with — being female and all. And not a decade, or more, older than me like the majority of employees.

Splendid. "Okay. I've got a few things I need to finish before then. Better get back to work."

"Of course." Donald turned to walk away but leaned back in the doorway. "Oh, and uh, bring business and recreational clothes. Apparently, there are some local outdoor sites worth seeing. We might even check out Saint Louie."

I'd rather stare at the St. Louis sun for a minute straight than tour sites with Donald. I raised my hand in a thumbs up, acknowledging I heard him, but never took my eyes off the laptop screen so he wouldn't stay in our office.

"How much would it cost me to convince you to take the Seymour account, Steve?" I asked louder than the radio playing on my fellow CPA's desk, hoping I wasn't too loud to be heard down the hall.

"My wife would kill me if I left her with the kids for two weeks."

"So, your life?"

Steve chuckled. "Yeah, and I quite like living."

"This is going to be the longest fourteen days of my life." I dropped my head onto the keyboard until a warning beep filled the air.

———————

"You're leaving me alone tonight?" my roommate asked, throwing herself on my bed.

"Guilty." I grimaced as I sat at my vanity and let my long hair out from its work bun.

"Well, that explains you actually doing something with your hair."

I looked at her via the mirror and stuck out my tongue. "We can't all have effortlessly flawless hair like you, Cam."

She flipped her dark wavy hair in an arch, framing her face with perfection. "Your hair could look like this, too, you know? Only takes some training and less shampooing." Camilla sprang up with excitement in her eyes. "How about you let me do your hair and makeup tonight?"

"Uh-no."

"Oh, come on, Londyn! You know you want to."

"I'd rather try your vegan cheesecake."

"You don't trust my abilities?" Camilla placed a hand on her chest.

"When was the last time you did your own makeup? You leave here looking like a disheveled, and hungry might I add, college student, and come back ready to have tea with the Queen of Aldovania."

"This is true." Camilla huffed and fell back onto the mattress, looking every bit the professional model she was.

"Get on the app and find a date of your own."

"I don't know. I'm pretty tired. I feel a long bath calling my name. Who are you going out with tonight?"

"Roman," I responded.

The answer had been the same for me for the last several weeks. I hadn't gone on a date with anyone else in months. Camilla, in contrast, seemed to be stuck in a revolving door of first dates. Though she could have a date any night she wanted, she was far too high maintenance to keep them around. There weren't many areas our lives overlapped other than our gender, age, and address.

"The business guy you see when he's in town?"

"That's the one." I rolled some nude lipstick onto my lips.

A few months ago, while trying to amp up my love life via a dating app, I swiped right, he swiped right. It wasn't that deep of a connection or anything. One thing I seemed to neglect in my drive for success was my love life, giving me a new goal to aim toward in the near future. Technically, I was still in high school the last time I had an *actual* boyfriend.

Roman, a venture capitalist, worked almost anywhere but here in our city, rarely home before hopping onto the next plane. I saw him twice a week tops in the beginning, even less now. I got cute gifts almost every time he saw me, though—like the necklace I clasped behind my neck before finishing my look. Not that I asked for them.

The buzzer filled our condo, drawing me to the intercom to respond. Camilla followed me out of my bedroom like a sulking puppy and made a pit stop at the fridge.

"Hello?" I asked with a smile on my face.

"I'm here." Roman's charming voice came through the speaker.

"Be right down." I turned to Camilla, "Do something productive while I'm gone."

"Mmmm, like relaxing and sleeping. Then again, I don't know?" She waved the long celery stalk in her hand around, then took a bite, filling the air with a crisp pop. "Maybe I'll get out and find me a man too."

"You are *such* a rabbit."

"Better than you, carnivore." Camilla pointed her zero-calorie snack at me.

I rolled my eyes; she rolled her eyes. We actually worked well together, but had we been dinosaurs a couple millenniums ago, she would've eaten leaves, and I would've eaten her. Which was ironic, seeing as how Camilla was the bossier one of the two of us.

"Goodnight."

"Have fun," she added. Another snap of celery sounded before the door closed behind me.

"If you aren't the prettiest thing I've seen all day." Roman greeted me when I opened the glass door downstairs.

"You don't look so bad yourself there." I touched the lapel of his suit coat and leaned in for a greeting kiss. His five o'clock shadow hair tickled my face—something I was still getting used to. "Where are we headed?"

"There's a new place my partner told me about that would be good to take potential clients. So," he fixed his high-dollar glasses on his face, "I figured I should get familiar with the place, know the menu, meet the manager. You know, those kinds of things. And I couldn't think of a better person to check it out with than you."

"Lead the way then, beau."

Roman chuckled.

Upon arriving, a host in a tux opened the door for us. A thick, plush carpet runner greeted our feet as soon as we stepped inside, quite the variation from the hard cement outside. I was more than a hint intimidated Roman would frequent such a lavish location for business meetings.

All throughout the night, Roman held himself with a confident demeanor as he asked for details of the menu and even acquired the manager's personal cell phone number. He never came off as arrogant or prideful, more like the poised type who allowed you to know he was probably more important than you.

Wait. Important wasn't the best word. I wasn't supposed to think like that anymore.

My brain was just as impressive as his, maybe even more so. *I'm a CPA.* Which reminded me, I had some impressive news of my own.

"I have something to share with you," I said while cutting into my immaculate steak, revealing the juicy rose center.

"Shoot."

"I'm joining the cool-people-club and traveling for work."

"Are you now? Tell me more." Roman smiled, swirling his glass in his hand, and took a swig of red wine.

"We bought out a company in Illinois, but Ralph, my boss, wants to keep the office open. I'm on the rebranding team. It's prime. Oil. Real estate." I uttered the words like they were romantically charged and popped a small bite of steak into my mouth. He laughed.

After swallowing, I continued. "Usually, we buy the rights to the pumps and shut the local offices down. So these people really lucked out on keeping their jobs." My heart tensed for a beat at my confession. I was one of the lucky people when my former employer's company was absorbed by the Aspire conglomerate.

"And you're the accountant guru who's going to blow their minds with your number tricks."

"Something like that." I downplayed my valuable brain, not ready to be so ~~conceited~~ confident.

"When do you leave?"

"Tomorrow."

"Oh. When do you get back?" Roman asked before taking a bite of his salmon.

"In two weeks." Would Roman miss me? We probably would've seen each other at least once in the next two weeks.

"Wow, okay. That's a longer trip than I expected. Talk about go big or go home. You better bring me back something really nice."

"Ah! Is that how it works? Teaching me your methods now?"

"For sure. Considering I'm well-seasoned, and you're a beginner here, it's the gentlemanly thing to do."

"Hold on, let me grab my notepad." I pretend-searched in my purse. "What else do I need to know, Sensei?" I licked the tip of my phantom pin and took fake notes on my air-pad.

"There isn't enough time." Roman played along, patting a yawn. "It seems you'll have to learn this one on your own."

"Drat. I so looked forward to learning *everything* you know, too."

"You couldn't handle it." His words pooled my insides like the butter on my steak.

Our relationship—whatever title it did or didn't have—was an easy one. Lord knows I wouldn't put up with someone I rarely got to see if we didn't mesh well.

"You're probably right. Any tips on traveling with co-workers, at least?" I worked on cutting another bite.

"Oh, you aren't going alone?" Roman asked.

"Nuh-uh. This guy Donald is going." I didn't intend to, but saying my co-worker's name puckered my lips as if I ate something sour.

"Even worse, a guy."

"Trust me, you have *nothing* to worry about."

"You know what they say, 'What happens in Illinois, stays in Illinois.'"

"Pretty sure that's Vegas."

"Right! *That's* what they say." Roman pointed my direction.

Our food was long gone, even dessert. My date already added his signature to a hefty tip on the tab twenty minutes ago. I tried but didn't succeed, not to glance at the total. Conversation grew thinner.

"I should probably call it a night so I can finish packing."

He nodded and escorted me out.

I thought about *us* on the drive back to my place.

Roman stopped telling me over the weeks where he was off to each time he was about to hop onto a plane. Or maybe it was me who stopped asking? His job was kind of like the annoying uncle you put up with because he gave you a hundred bucks every time he saw you, sometimes more than once if he was tipsy. Roman liked his job, though, and I enjoyed the time we did have together when we had it, so the situation was what it was. If he was in town, I heard from him.

"You don't have to park and walk me to the door. I know you want to, and that is gesture enough. Dropping me off at the entrance is fine."

"You sure? It's dark and late."

"You can wait until I'm safe inside." I covered his hand, resting on the console with mine.

"Sounds good. Don't go silent on me."

His request to not go two weeks without talking to him made me grin. That meant something, right?

"I won't. Talk to you soon."

"Until then."

I closed our night with a simple kiss.

If he said something along the lines of "See you later, babe" or "honey" or "baby girl" or "yes-I-do-consider-you-my-girlfriend," that would've been more helpful, though.

Not wanting to mess things up, because they were good, really, I still had a small desire to ask Roman where we stood in his mind. I mostly wanted to know so I wouldn't be ahead or behind, but how was I supposed to know where my position was when I didn't know his?

Maybe this time, since I was the one to leave, we'd both have a better gauge on our status. Two months hadn't been a waste of my time, but I didn't want the months to morph into a year at this same pace, which probably *would* feel like dozens of equity-less dates.

Everything else in my life was great, except for not having anyone to spend it with. Putting myself out there and asking Roman for clarity, and possibly losing whatever we did have, equally didn't sound appealing. He was my first good romantic lead in years, so I hoped he'd make it clear before too long.

Tomorrow would be good.

Camilla was full-on snoring when I walked down the hall toward my room. Never had I heard such a flimsy thing make so much racket. I seriously wanted to debrief with her and get her opinion on my thoughts concerning Roman and me.

However, if I took a minute and thought of the exact opposite of what I'd do, there was about a seventy-five percent chance that would be the advice she gave me.

I could almost hear her saying—over her motorboat snore— *Stop trying to 'Define the Relationship.' Just have fun with the guy! Let him take you out on fancy dates. Eventually, you'll feel how you fit.*

But since the condo was silent after I shut her bedroom door, I reflected alone as I packed.

More times than I could count, I asked a date if he was dating anyone else, if I was his girlfriend, or what our title was. Maybe not in those exact words, but the desire to "Define the Relationship"—DTR—was ever-present. Cue the ghosting. How relationships and dating worked seemed to have changed while I buried my head in my studies for the last few years.

Unlike most of the other men I dated in the last year, I managed to get past the third date with Roman by denying my desire to know our status, but that didn't mean the question didn't continue to resound like a gong in my head.

2

If I made it through this trip, I deserved a raise. No one technically asked me if I wanted to travel for work. Everything happened so quickly, I didn't even think to ask questions. I hoped against all the odds, Donald wouldn't make me want to pull my hair out one strand at a time until I was bald. Facts were, most of our days, we'd be working, and I could easily call it an early night. There shouldn't be too much alone time with Donald. Except for the airplane.

Oh, the airplane.

This is not fun. How much longer until we land?

I lost track of how many times his elbow bumped mine from the armrest during our two hours of close proximity.

One thing I absolutely did *not* forget to pack in my carry-on bag was my headphones. It made sense to me and my calculated brain that even if I wasn't listening to anything, the mere sight of the buds in my ears would encourage Donald to leave me alone. A plan that worked until he breached the imaginary border.

"Whatcha listening to?" he asked as he pulled the earbud out and stuck it into his ear. *Gross.* "You don't have to pause it for me. Play it again."

"Uh, I'm good." I took the other bud out, hiding that I wasn't listening to anything, and gave my sore ears a break.

"Are you going to be this fun the whole trip?" If he was attempting to be friendly by joking around, he wasn't very good at it.

"Probably. I've never been the party type, if that's what you're asking. Besides, I still need to prove myself in this company."

"So, you're saying no dinners with me after work?"

"Not a single one." I held out my hand for the right side of the headphones with the fakest smile I could muster. My eyes squinted so much they were basically shut. I wasn't intentionally trying to mock Donald's unique eyes, so I quickly returned my face to normal.

He dropped the earbud in my hand. "Guess I'll just have to convince someone at the new office to take me up on that offer."

"Not a bad plan."

"Ladies and gentlemen, we're coming over Illinois MidAmerica airport, but word from the tower is we need to circle a few times until a terminal opens up. Hopefully, we'll get you landed for any connecting flights shortly." The pilot brought closure to our conversation.

Graciously, ten minutes later, I felt the pull in my stomach. I looked forward to having more than a few inches of space between my co-worker and me.

The taxi took us to our hotel, one of the handful in the city. With every passing minute, I grew closer and closer to some alone time. I could already feel the sheets on my bare feet, a book in my hands, and nothing but the sound of the air conditioner running. Glorious.

Donald passed the pre-checked-in paperwork over to the receptionist, who greeted him with a smile.

Moments away, I reminded myself. Looking across the lobby, I got lost in thought. *Is Roman thinking about me?*

"Hear that, party animal?"

"Huh?" I turned back around because I hadn't heard what he referenced.

"Your room isn't ready yet. Mine is." Donald held up his keycard. "Looks like you are gonna have to join me—"

"I have no problem waiting here in the lobby," I asserted.

"… for dinner."

Two feelings went through me: relief I assumed incorrectly, and pain that I had another who-knows-how-long before I could be alone.

But I was hungry. "Fine." I turned to the receptionist. "How much longer until my room should be ready?"

"My apologies. Mr. Wilkie traded his deluxe suite for your standard room. Suites take longer to clean, but it should be ready within the hour. You can leave your bags with us if you want. There's a restaurant less than a block away."

Another emotion ran through me. Confusion. Maybe I misjudged Donald Wilkie.

"Um, sure." I wheeled my bag around the counter.

"I'll drop my bags off in my room and be right back," Donald said.

"You didn't have to give—"

He cut me off. "From the sound of it, you plan on spending a lot more time locked up in this place. I thought you should have the nicer room."

"Thank you. I don't know what to say."

"You can buy dessert."

"Don't we get food stipends?" I asked with dipped brows.

"I eat like a king on work trips. Sometimes I go over budget."

"Dessert's on me then." I laughed, wondering what else this trip would teach me about Donald.

"Excellent. Be right back." He disappeared into the hallway.

I decided then and there not to think of Donald in an ill light again unless his actions were atrocious. Perhaps I simply hadn't got to know him well enough to understand his quirks in our few interactions over the last few weeks at work.

The restaurant was more like a sports bar. I counted at least twelve televisions from my seat—vastly different from where I ate last night with Roman.

Easing into a better understanding with Donald became priority number one for this trip. Outside of the higher-ups' demoting eyes, along with the casualness of our location, a bit of courage to shoot straight with him climbed my spine.

"So, how did you make it so high in our company?" I asked in between bites.

"You mean other than my charming looks?"

"Pffft."

In the span of three seconds, I leaned back in my chair, crossed my arms over my chest, and analyzed my co-worker on a looks scale. As if he knew, he arched an eyebrow and gave a smolder. I'd give him a seven point seven. The rating might've gone higher had I not been so annoyed with his personality up until an hour ago. Donald always looked clean-cut and dressed in tailored suits. His sandy blonde hair helped him look younger than he was, though I didn't know his exact age. My best guess was we were at least five years apart. However, how he gelled his hair back always made me think of him as a bit of a schmuck.

"Yeah, other than that?" I clarified, shaking my head.

"I guess I'm simply a likable guy."

"Debatable."

"Whoa, Bubblegum. That hurt." He feigned pain as if I used my plastic knife to cut him.

"Yeah, yeah. Let's set some ground rules, shall we?" I quickly remembered why I used to be so annoyed by this guy as soon as he called me Bubblegum. "I thought I'd formed my opinion of you before, but it turns out I don't know you much at all."

Donald wagged his eyebrows as he leaned in.

"Scratch that thought now, buddy. I'm already seeing someone."

"Don't worry, I'm not interested in dating any of my co-workers currently." He raised his hand as if swearing-in at court.

While I tried to think of a comeback, he continued.

"I just have all this pent-up affection to give away because the woman I'm madly in love with is dating my best friend. Has been for years."

Now *that* hurt. However, Donald didn't show an ounce of pain on his face. Instantly, my heartstrings were tugged in his direction. Our stories might not be identical, but I knew all too well how it felt to want to be with someone you couldn't. For years, as well.

"Oh, Donald. Does she know?"

"Eh, probably." He shrugged as if it wasn't a major deal. Men were so different. "I'm hoping one of these days I'll meet someone who gets her out of my mind."

"I know what you mean." I frowned, about to touch his hand as a sympathetic friend but thought better of it. "Not me, though." I reiterated.

He laughed. "No worries, Tinker Bell. You aren't really my type."

So his type wasn't an introverted, reserved, book-worm? Shocker. Apparently, I wasn't most men's type past a couple of dates.

Then again, Donald probably referred to my looks since he barely knew me. My lips weren't exactly plump, and my eyes were the same coppery color as my hair. Both of which were rarely done up. A touch of mascara and blush and my hair pulled back in a low bun at the nape of my neck was how I looked Monday through Friday, 9:00 to 5:00.

I could learn how to improve my look some, for sure, but I didn't feel the need to. My model roommate begged to differ.

"What's with all the names?"

"You noticed that, huh?"

"How could I not?" I laughed.

"Truth is, I'm not the best with names." I recalled how he misused the secretary's name days ago and wondered if he even knew mine. "My Achilles heel, actually. I drill myself hard with clients' names, but I can't say I put in the effort with everyone. I'm working on it—" He looked at me with a question in his eyes.

"Londyn."

"Got it. Bridges."

"Bridges?" I furrowed my brow.

"The technique I'm learning. Associate the name with something else to help you remember it. London Bridge is falling down—"

"Right." His reference wasn't the first, and I seriously doubted the last time a person would mention the song.

"It's locked in now, Londyn. Bridges."

"Good to know. What should I expect on this 'workcation?'" I went back to eating.

"Each location is a toss-up, so it's hard to say one way or another. I have a feeling this place is going to be pretty cutting edge with the revenues I saw. Ralph had to write a big check for this one. I think he's hoping to absorb a few more companies in the area as well, this being the main reason he wanted to keep this office locally." Donald shrugged as if it was only his opinion, but seeing how he worked for Aspire several years, his assessment probably held weight.

"Sounds good. Maybe I'll even learn a thing or two myself on this trip."

"I hope so."

Was he suggesting I was uninitiated for the job? "How about that dessert I owe you?" I changed the subject, trying not to assume and be offended.

"Excellent idea."

I slept like a rock in the king-sized bed that was considerably plusher than my smaller, firmer one back home. Good thing too. Today would be a long one. On the day's agenda: review the last two years' worth of financials, get familiar with their software, and give a brief report back to Ralph. An enormous task for day one. I waited for the knock on my door, signaling me that our ride was here. A sense of pride pulled my shoulders back, knowing we'd be escorted around for two weeks. Alternately, I didn't love the fact I didn't have a mode of transportation other than my feet or someone else.

"Car's outside," Donald said after the morning greeting.

"I'm ready." The door swung closed behind me as I stepped out with as much energy and confidence as I could possess before my morning cup of joe.

Eight hours later, with no lunch break, I walked right back into my hotel room and fell face-first onto the bed, fully dressed. Numbers and I were besties, hung out all the time, but I needed alone time for the next several hours before everything repeated tomorrow.

Donald's assessment of this place wasn't just a little bit off; it was the complete opposite.

Crystal, the local accounting head, did a good enough job with the books. Problem was, she'd used the same computer program since 1992. Before I was alive. How that program still ran baffled me. The computer itself looked like a dinosaur. If we buried it, maybe it'd produce oil for us in a few years.

Still days away from teaching her the much more in-depth, new program, I dreaded every second of it. Crystal's eyes would probably tire with the much brighter, full-color screens. The numbers and letters on her small ancient screen were all a dull green hue.

My phone rang.

I slid off the bed like a slinky and dug in my leather bag.

Roman. I smiled.

"Hi."

"What're you doing?" His voice raised my mood.

"Trying to find enough energy to get back onto the bed." I chuckled, thankful no one could see me. Kicking off my heels, I fell back onto the mattress with a gust of air lifting in my wake. "You?"

"Realizing right about now how much it stinks for you to be away when I'm home."

So he was thinking about me. "Is that so?" I tucked a loose strand of hair behind my ear.

"Sure is. I'm gonna need for you to hurry back."

Aww! I bit my bottom lip as my eyes smiled. "I'll be happy if I'm actually able to accomplish everything I need to in nine more days. Might have to work through my weekend already."

"That bad, huh?"

"This place is one step ahead of the Dewey Decimal System."

"You mean that ancient method our ancestors used to keep track of library books?"

"Affirmative."

He laughed, the sound equal parts sympathy and humor. "Sounds dreadful."

"Can't disagree."

"Sorry, sunshine. If you were here, I'd take you out and give you a fun night of distractions."

Mmm. My heart swelled when he called me sunshine. It was the whole reason I came up with a name for him—although I wasn't sure he liked the pet name I chose.

"That'd be awesome, but seeing as how I barely have enough energy to use the phone, I think I'm gonna UberEats some dinner and try to read if my eyes will stay open."

"Oh, how the mighty have fallen."

"Happens to the best of us," I said without missing a beat.

"I'll let you go then. Eat and rest. I'll call you later this week."

"Thanks, beau."

"Goodnight." He chuckled. Yep. Not sure he liked it.

"Night."

My motivation to order food was fueled by an empty stomach save a stale granola bar from the office. Otherwise, I would've gone to sleep. After opening the food-ordering app, a red bar filled my screen, declaring UberEats didn't deliver to Belleville.

I mustered through changing into relaxing clothes, flipped the door guard over so I wouldn't get locked out, and knocked on Donald's door across the hall.

"I'm off the clock, Bridges."

I rolled my eyes, knowing I had more give with him than a day ago. "What did you do for dinner? UberEats doesn't service this little city."

"Haven't eaten yet. By the looks of it, your day was much more draining than mine."

"Ding, ding, ding. My backside's sore from sitting all day in a chair that's probably old enough to be an antique, but I'm too tired to walk to get food." I leaned fell onto the door jam.

"Want to split a pizza?"

I pointed in agreement. "Yes."

"What kind?" Donald asked.

"Meat lovers," I replied as I pushed to stand and walked away like a tortoise. "Ask for plates. I want to eat in my room. Alone," I said with my back to him.

He chuckled. "I remember. No dinners together."

Twenty-five minutes later, Donald brought over my half of the pizza. He could probably eat more than me on a regular day, but he hadn't skipped lunch.

"Day one in the books. Nine more to go," he said as he held the door open for me while I juggled the pizza on two plates.

"I can do this." The mantra wasn't so much a response to him as it was building myself up.

"Rookie." He let go of the door.

I'm not sure if he saw the mocking face I offered or not before the door closed.

3

Tuesday looked much like Monday, only I made sure to take a lunch break. Seymour, the company we absorbed, had a small staff of only a few people. Crystal, in accounting, Stan, who swapped sales tips and tools with Donald, Kevin, who oversaw the roughnecks (the oil field workers), and Blanche, the owner after her husband passed away three years ago—his passing the beginning of their slow decline.

Blanche was nice, but as firm as her name sounded. She probably had the money to be decked out in high-end clothes and jewelry, but she had more of a tomboy sense to her. The kind who'd most likely rather jump on the rig than attend a formal ball on her husband's arm. Even in her early seventies, more or less, Blanche was a spitfire. I was fairly confident after trying to run things for a couple of years, she figured it was time to let someone else have the stress while she collected the substantial cushion a buyout would provide her. Smart woman.

Lucky for Donald, Stan was really good at his job, which made total sense considering he was the *one* sales rep the company had all those years. We didn't see much of Kevin since he was typically out at the rigs, but when he did come in, he looked exactly like someone who worked in the oil field: sturdy boots, dingy jeans, rough hands with black lines around his nail beds. Oddly enough, Kevin was easily my favorite of the four-man staff, most likely because he was a hard worker and didn't look like your typical wealthy businessman. I wished he was around more.

By Wednesday, I mastered the Amiga program, the dino-software. Step one in getting all of the information over to the new system. When checking back in with my boss at the end of the day, I told him to ship three new MacBooks out here before next week.

Thursday was almost a waste. Crystal was sick. Technically, she had a migraine. Knowing my drilling of the new grueling data entry put her in such a mental state ailed me, but I equally desired a break of my own. However, I spent most of the day integrating the old data into the new system so she wouldn't have to do it all later. What took me one day would probably take her a week. Or month.

That night after working alone most of the day, I didn't feel so peopled out. On the ride back to the hotel, I overrode my no-dinner-policy and mentioned grabbing dinner to Donald. He pretended to accept the invitation with pity but agreed to join. After all, he didn't have anyone to eat with either.

"I feel like I need to hear more about this woman who has your heart in knots," I said after we ordered the exact same meal from four nights ago.

"I'd rather not, Bridges. Wisecracking with you is so much easier."

"But, I'd rather stick this fork in my thigh than endure your lame jokes all night."

"Sheesh. That bad, huh?"

I lifted my fork and slowly hovered a shaking hand over my leg. "No, not that bad. You're growing on me, as a matter of fact. It's much easier to ignore you or play along."

"Touché!" He lifted his glass of Dr Pepper. "How about your love life?" Apparently, the woman he pined for was off-limits of conversation.

"It definitely isn't a *love* life, more like dating life. Or life between dates. I don't know." I shrugged.

"How long have you been dating?"

"About two months."

Donald nodded. "He's still trying to decide if he's into you then. Test driving the car, if you know what I mean?"

"Roman is *not* putting *any* miles on this car."

"Gotcha. Has he called you his girlfriend?"

I sighed. That was precisely what I wanted to know. Donald was seconds away from rubbing whatever Roman and I weren't into my face. Or maybe, he could have great insight into the situation, being a guy and all.

"Not that I've heard." My upper lip curled a touch.

"Tell me what that's about." Donald pointed to my expression.

"It'd be nice to know where I stand with him, but I haven't asked. And it isn't because I'm afraid to. In fact, I'm afraid of what will happen when I *do* ask. I seem to run men off with my questions or assumptions. Roman hasn't made sure to clarify either. We have this rhythm we're in, but I don't know how to speed it up."

Donald sucked in a breath. "No man wants the pressure of labeling a relationship, Bridges. He's probably still figuring it out. But don't worry, if he's not ghosting you, I'd be willing to say he's simply taking it slow."

"Might be because we only see each other once a week, tops. More like once every ten days or so."

Donald pulled his lips back to one side.

"He travels for work," I clarified.

"Ah, gotcha. Agreed. Dating life is an accurate description."

"And you, any luck with the ladies here?" I took a sip of my Coke and almost spit it out at my own joke. His *only* option was Blanche.

"You hurt me." Donald shook his head, then laughed. "The company is *considerably* smaller than I anticipated—the whole city, for that matter. I think I've met most of the dating pool already. Not a single lady seems promising enough to make me stop thinking about Natalie."

"Sorry."

The statement was the most accurate thing I'd ever heard him say, but seeing as how I hadn't even told my roommate I still thought of an old love of my own, I wasn't about to fess up to my co-worker I barely started to not be annoyed by.

A couple of hours later, back in my room, my phone rang.

Roman. Second call this week.

"Hi." I hoped he could hear the smile the word escaped through.

"You've almost made it through the first week. Congratulations! How are you holding up?"

"Let's go with surviving, but not thriving. Maybe I'll turn the corner tomorrow or Monday."

"I applaud your optimism."

"Honestly, I have a whole new understanding of what work-life is like for you. This is exhausting."

"You get used to it. Not sure if that's a good or bad thing, though."

I curled my feet up closer to my chest and snuggled down into the bed. "Are you home?"

"No. Believe it or not, I'm in Louisville."

Scanning my brain for the lesser of my favorite subjects, I came up blank for why he said *believe it or not.*

"Kentucky," he continued in my silence.

I covered my eyes with my hand. Finally, I admitted, "Geography and I aren't well acquainted. You're going to have to fill me in on what you mean."

Roman snickered. "I'm three and a half hours away from you by car. Less than one by plane."

"How cool … and cruel."

"Not so cruel, actually. I had an idea."

"Do tell." My interest piqued.

"I haven't booked my return flight yet, just about to actually."

"Keep talking." His words caused me to sit up.

"I could make a pit stop in Belleville with a several-hour layover on Saturday."

"Yeah?"

"I'd like to, especially since you won't be home for another week. I'm pretty sure I'll be gone when you get back."

Wow! Roman altering his flight home helped me not worry about labeling our relationship, but equally had me questioning where he saw us. Apparently, it was more significant than I assumed.

"What an amazing idea!"

"Is there something we can do in town?" he asked.

"I'm sure there is. I'll check tomorrow at work."

"Great. Looks like I can get a five-hour layover, putting me in Belleville at 11:00 a.m. Do you think that'll work?"

"Yes."

"All right, booking it … now." A *click* was audible through the receiver. "I'll call you when I land."

"See you soon."

"Bye."

As soon as I hung up, I jumped up and did a jig on the bed. Falling back down into the cloud of blankets and pillows, my head filled with the same exhilaration as my heart.

A new fire was under me on Friday since not a single fiber of my being wanted to go to work on Saturday. My ~~boyfriend~~ guy was coming to see me. I continued inputting the financials into the new system while Crystal watched, took notes, and asked questions.

When we broke for lunch, I remembered to ask about something Roman and I could do around town.

"Finley's Orchard, hands down. I take the grandkids every year when they come to visit."

"An orchard?" I questioned.

"Yes. They have different crops throughout the seasons. Pretty sure it's apples right now. Pumpkin pickin' is fun, but we're several months too soon for that. If outdoor fun isn't what you're looking for, we have a historical theatre too. But they only play one movie all day. Not sure what's on the schedule for tomorrow," Crystal said.

"Thanks, I'll look them up."

"Either place is promising for romance if you ask me." She grinned like a mischievous teenager. Crystal was, however, plump with age and graying like a faded picture. The well-worn wedding ring occupying her finger almost looked like it was one with her finger. Her last first date had to be decades ago.

"See you after lunch. We still have all of November and December that I'd like to enter before the end of the day."

I didn't miss the groan she uttered.

―――――――――――

After the longest workweek of my life, I was thrilled to have something to do on Saturday other than working, sitting in the hotel room all day, or hanging out with Donald. Trying to pair together some of my work clothes with my casual clothes, I still couldn't come up with an outfit cute enough for a date. I even turned to the internet to look up "Ways to change your outfit from work to date," and still nothing. Ready to wear something full-on casual for the outdoor activities, there was a knock at my door.

Making sure my clothes were adequately fastened, I opened the door to find Donald.

"Hey, I was just going to let you know— You okay?"

"I didn't pack for a date." I motioned to my unappealing outfit.

"You look fine."

Seeing as how Donald rarely saw me in anything but my work clothes, I wasn't sure if it was a good thing to just look "fine."

I shrugged. "You were going to let me know what?"

"That I'm leaving for the day. Going a town over since I've already met every potential bachelorette here and still haven't met my *one true love*." Even his voice gave him away.

I seriously doubted he thought he'd actually meet the love of his life on a work trip and simply didn't want to be alone. Even if it was only for a few hours. *Same, friend, same.*

"I'll keep my fingers crossed for you."

"Thanks, something tells me I'll need it. Maybe cross both hands."

"Will do." I chuckled, lifting my hands into the air in proof.

"You know what? Hold on just a minute. I'll be right back." He pulled out his key card and disappeared into his room while I waited against my doorjamb. Seconds later, he reappeared with a white-collared button up. "Wear this, like kinda loose, and tie a knot in the front or something." He motioned his hand as he spoke. "I don't know, when Natalie does it, I can barely breathe around her."

Poor guy.

"This is your work shirt." I took the hanger from him.

"Yeah. I'll let you pay the laundry fee for me after you use it. Have fun."

"You too."

Even though I was hesitant to take fashion advice from a man, his shirt looked significantly better than anything else I tried on all day. Donald wasn't a big guy, and I wasn't a tiny girl, so it gave just the right type of loose fit. I left the back out and tucked in the front, rolled the sleeves up a couple of times, and left the top few buttons open. The outfit would've been one hundred percent date approved with my heels, but with a day full of walking ahead of us, my flats were the wiser choice.

Blanche let me use the company truck when word about me exploring Belleville traveled around the office. Having a colossal F-350 to drive around was a step above having to get an Uber or walk. I planned to drive to the airport where I'd gleefully surrender the keys to Roman, who probably wouldn't be as intimidated by the large vehicle as me.

Arriving a bit too early at the small airport I passed through less than a week ago, I pulled into a parking spot, which thankfully had no time limit or charge—one of the nice things about the smaller city tipping the scales at under fifty thousand people. There wasn't really a reason for me to wait in the bulky truck I needed a booster seat to drive, so I went in and scanned the two small screens for flight arrivals and departures.

Checking the time on my phone, his flight had arrived earlier than scheduled.

"Looking for me?"

His words startled me. The bright lights enhanced Roman's auburn hair, accentuating a fresh cut.

"As a matter of fact, yes, I am." I hugged his neck and greeted him with a kiss. His well-kept beard brushed against my face.

Honestly, all of our kisses could be considered a greeting or farewell kiss, barely above friendly.

"Do you need to get a bag or anything?"

"No, ma'am. This is it." He lifted his standard black suitcase on wheels that matched almost every other bag in the airport. "Looks like getting back in through security will be pretty easy too. Lucky for you, that means more time with me before I have to return for my flight."

"Sounds good to me." I lifted my hand, dangling the keys. In a natural reflex, Roman offered his palm and caught them.

"What's this?"

"The company vehicle. I'd much rather you drive if you don't mind."

It was almost comical, the two of us, driving around in an over-sized truck in Belleville, Illinois. Even though we were both Texans, neither of us owned a truck. Graciously, he had no problem driving the three-ton vehicle around, even with the massive racks for pumps and sucker rods and the company logo sprawled across both sides. As long as no one flagged us down to fix a rig, we would be just fine.

"You going to tell me where I'm headed?" Roman asked after lifting his luggage into the bed of the truck and opening the passenger door for me.

"Finley's." I smiled, knowing that wouldn't give him much clarity.

"Great. Just don't let us get lost."

We made small talk as I gave him turn by turn directions from my phone. It didn't take us long to arrive at the gorgeous apple orchard. Of course, it didn't take long to arrive at anything in Belleville.

As soon as we turned down the gravel drive, a totally new vibe filled the truck. Or maybe it was the excess oxygen floating around from the hundreds of plants. A little barn sat in the middle of a pristine throng of apple trees. Life-size painted wood cut-outs decorated the lawn—the kind with the blank slot to stick your face in.

"How cool is this place, sunshine?" Roman asked as he opened my door and lifted me out by my hips.

"Right?" I answered. "The pictures online don't do it any justice. Ready?" I asked with my hand held out for him.

"Take the lead, sunshine."

I checked us in, but Roman insisted on paying our entry fee. We grabbed a basket and chose an aisle out of the endless rows of thriving apple trees. I let him hold the lengthy stick to detach the apples. Much to my pleasure, he turned into a bit of a kid with an imaginary weapon. I'd never seen Roman so carefree. It was endearing.

Surprisingly, the trees weren't very large, some barely taller than Roman. But boy, were they *overflowing* with apples.

I repeatedly pulled out the color guide, which showed us which shades meant the ripest apples. Before I knew it, the basket was so heavy, the crook of my arm started to ache.

I shifted it to my other side.

"Oh, sorry. Let me." Roman relieved me of the task.

"What am I going to do with all of these apples?" I laughed.

"Very good question. It seems we got a bit carried away."

"Just a wee bit. Why don't we go find a place to sit and eat an apple or two. Or dozen." I suggested.

"Sounds good to me."

I snapped a selfie of Roman and me biting into our apples with the pleasing view of meticulous rows of trees behind us and posted it to my social media feed with cautiously well-thought-out hashtags. #hangingwiththebeau #daydate #justthetwoofus Before I put my phone back in my purse, a text popped up on the screen.

Camilla: Totes jealous, eat an apple for me. But OMG! Roman is there?

Before he could see her text, I shoved my phone into my back pocket to respond later.

"So when and where is your next trip?" I asked.

"I think it's one of the Carolinas or Tennessee. They're back to back trips, starting Wednesday."

Meaning he'd be gone again when I returned home.

Though the month on the calendar had changed twice since we met, his traveling schedule—and now mine—resulted in us only seeing each other a few days each month.

Processing our status by the number of actual dates we'd been on instead of the days gone by felt more accurate. Roman and I were still in the newness of figuring each other out.

"This trip has been enlightening about your life and also helped me not to hate Donald anymore. But I must admit, I'll be so glad to be back home to my normal schedule. I don't know how you do this regularly."

"What's this about Donald?" Apparently, Roman only heard one portion of my statement. I didn't miss the hint of jealousy in his tone. Interesting.

"It could've been I had next to no interaction with him back home in the office, but it turns out he isn't so bad after all." The annoyed arch of Roman's eyebrow was a new look to me. I'd be lying if I said his indignation didn't make me giddy and answer a few of my questions. "Don't worry, he's in love with his best friend's girl."

"Ouch."

"I know, but I think he liked her first, just never had the guts to say anything."

A crunch filled the air as Roman took a bite from his crisp gala apple. He pushed the bite to one side of his mouth. "You snooze, you lose."

"I guess so." I'd never seen Roman more relaxed. He often seemed stuck in work-mode around me, answering calls and lining up future connections everywhere we went. I took a bite of my apple as I pondered what his body language over the last two hours meant.

We left to grab some actual food before he had to be back at the airport—with far too many apples in tow. I planned on giving a few to Donald, leaving some in the office, and if they still looked fresh, taking a couple back to Camilla.

Through our late lunch, we enjoyed each other's company while laughing and sharing horror stories from work travels. Roman was a good guy, one I enjoyed being around. I didn't want to stay at this pace forever, but reminding myself again how our timeline ticked on a different-paced clock, I resolved not to meddle with what wasn't technically broken.

Our time together in Belleville went by in a hurry. I had a blast at the orchard, learning a whole new side of Roman, the powerful VP. And though the time was short, a part of me fell for him an inch deeper. After all, he rearranged his work flight to visit me in another state so he wouldn't have to go another twelve days without seeing me. His actions spoke for themselves, didn't they?

So when I walked him as far as I could in the airport without a ticket, I decided to let him know how thankful I was with some body language of my own.

"This is where I stop," I said.

"I can smuggle you in my carry-on if you have an exceptionally flexible spine."

"Bummer, my spine is only moderately flexible." I chuckled. Fidgeting with the necklace he gave me, I continued. "Thank you for coming to see me today. Best part of my week, hands down."

"You bet. I'm glad it worked out." Roman shrugged. "Made sense to me."

I leaned in and kissed him like he wasn't a friend, and like I wasn't saying bye with a juvenile peck. I *kissed* him. And taking full advantage, Roman *kissed* me back in the middle of the airport lobby as people hurried around us.

I pulled away before we gained an audience. "All right, you better go get checked in at the gate."

"Well, now I don't want to leave," he said with raised brows.

He pulled me in with an arm wrapped around my waist and gave me one more deep kiss. Perhaps simple greeting kisses were a thing of the past for us now.

"I'll see you soon, Roman." I smiled.

"Not soon enough, sunshine."

He turned to walk away. I did the same, feeling some kind of way. Before I made it to the exit, my phone went off in my back pocket.

Camilla: Hello? I need an update here.

As soon as I made it back to the gas guzzler, I called my roommate.

"What took you so long? I've been waiting for hours to get the scoop." Camilla spouted off instead of saying hello.

"So Roman came to see me." I matched her dramatics with some sarcasm.

"You don't say? Details, now!"

"He was close for work and booked his return flight with a layover to see me. Technically, I don't think I was on the *way* home, but he was in this part of the country and was able to swing by."

"Swing by? You make it sound like he picked up some ice cream for you before he got to our place. You don't really *swing by* in an airliner, Londyn."

"I know." A giant grin blossomed mini apples on my cheeks.

"I'm guessing this means you two are becoming official?"

My grin turned lopsided. "Nothing was communicated to that end, but I did give him quite the seeing off at the airport."

"You tramp! In the airport?"

"Cam, come on. You know me better than that. I kissed him like all of the characters in my books. He returned for seconds before he even left."

"Oh, of course. I forgot which friend I was talking to, nerd. Okay, backtrack. You went right to the seeing off at the airport."

"Right, sorry."

I told her about Crystal suggesting the best local spots and Blanche loaning me the company truck, to which she redirected our conversation back to Roman like a bossy GPS commander when I got off course. In my head, it was all part of the story, but apparently, Camilla was only interested in very specific details—the romantic ones her life currently lacked.

So I told her about the gorgeous orchard, the lighthearted and fun banter we kept while picking apples, the fruit picnic in the plush grass, the lunch at one of the few restaurants in town, and again about the toe-curling kiss, knowing that's what she most wanted to hear.

"Why do all the cool things happen to you? Can't I get one date that isn't completely boring?"

I didn't know how to respond to her, so I didn't.

The roaring engine died down as I parked in front of the hotel, leaving the cab of the truck the quietest it had been all day.

"Well, I'm back at the hotel and would love a shower. The light coat of sweat from the day is starting to make me itchy."

"Sounds good. Thanks for the scoop. Talk soon?"

"Yes, ma'am. Bye."

I grabbed two apples and climbed down from the tall truck, thankful I wouldn't have to maneuver it again. Donald could drive us to the office on Monday.

Navigating the lobby, elevator, and hallway, I arrived at his room and knocked on the door with my elbow.

When the door swung open, Donald's eyes widened.

"What?"

He looked away, choking on an answer.

I glanced down, wondering if my shirt had popped open. Instead, an apple filled each hand, directly in front of my chest.

"Oh, um." I was sure my face matched the splotchy red of the apples. "These are for you. We picked too many. I thought you might want some as a thank you for lending me your shirt."

"That's kind of you. Are you sure they're edible?"

"Please." I rolled my eyes and shoved the fruit into his hands. "I'll send your shirt to the front desk. You should have it back by Monday."

"Great, thanks. You look nice, but I must say, when Natalie wears stuff like that...." Donald sucked in a breath.

"You're a bully." I quickly turned to my doorway a couple feet over before I said something worse I'd regret.

"No, wait. Really, you look very nice. I was just messin'."

"Thanks." I straightened the shirt. And my attitude. "How was your expedition?"

"My search was a flop." Donald chuckled. "I hope you had a better time than me."

"I did."

"Thanks for these." He took a big bite out of one of the apples and pretended like he was poisoned.

"Bye, Donald."

4

Sunday was the only day of the week I had nothing to do, and I spent the entire day at the hotel reading. Monday came faster than I appreciated. The good news was, each day that passed was a day closer to home. Donald joked en route to work that I had an unrealized attraction for him, which was why I showed up at his door with the fruit. I paid him no mind but warned him that he'd find himself with an enemy if the apple story left Belleville. Plus, a tack or two in his desk chair. All I needed was the office back home, comprised of mostly men older than me, to think I was successful in my career based on anything but my brain.

By 9:00 a.m., I was back in work-mode. Crystal, on the other hand, looked at the screen like she was reading hieroglyphics.

"Do you need me to slow down?" I asked as I entered information into the latest system on the new laptop.

"Maybe a little. If you wouldn't mind, talking as you go would help me too. I know it's second nature to you, but I feel like I forgot everything over the weekend."

Oh, great. "Sure thing."

I coached aloud as I started at the top of the screen with the invoice number, then the date, parts or details, and the profit or loss, hitting tab between each set of data to get to the next blank.

"No wonder you never clicked on the mouse. I thought you had to click on each box. Where is the mouse anyway?" Crystal scratched her head.

I ran my finger in circles around the trackpad. "You'll get the hang of it, don't worry."

"I don't know. I'm only a handful of months from retiring. It's extremely tempting to start a little early and lose a few bucks a month. The saying about an old dog and new tricks is my life right now." She didn't laugh, so neither did I.

"I'm sorry, Crystal, I promise you can do this. Once we're all caught up, you won't have a stack higher than the computer screen. Keeping up will be easy, then. Why don't you grab a highlighter and go over the invoices getting familiar with where the information is located? Once your eyes are trained to quickly scan the documents, entering everything is pretty easy. While you do that, I'll keep hammering away at this stack. Then I'll help you enter the invoices you highlighted."

"That sounds like an amazing idea." Crystal leaned across the desk and pulled a pink highlighter out of a cup full of writing tools. I wasn't sure if she seriously struggled or if she simply milked the time. At least giving her a task gave her something to get paid for. Either way, I didn't really mind. Working with numbers relaxed me. It wouldn't surprise me at all if she took that early retirement.

Tuesday and Wednesday were much of the same. The week zoomed by since I worked, worked, worked, and didn't do much talking. I went ahead and did practically everything on Thursday as well. However, on Friday, I had to make sure Crystal knew what to do once I left. I didn't want her failure to look like a lack of successful training on my part.

At the end of the day, Blanche offered to take everyone to dinner. We left straight from the office and headed one town over to a nice steakhouse. The restaurant was a far cry from the upscale restaurant Roman took me to a couple weeks ago, but practically everything in these small Illinois cities failed in comparison to that over-the-top spot in downtown Dallas. The two hours at dinner were probably my favorite part of the trip— not including my orchard date, of course—filled with laughter and hilarious stories.

The best one was when Kevin challenged the rest of the office to a pipe pull—successfully unloading the stack of steel pipes from the truck's side brackets. Kevin had the advantage of doing the task day in and day out over the years as he slid long tubing down from the truck, but the other three had the advantage of moving the twenty-foot-plus sucker rods together. It ended with Stan, the sales guy, knocking out his front tooth. He even popped the false tooth out to prove it right there at the table. Talk about an interesting claim to workman's comp.

Back at the hotel, Donald said goodnight as I retreated to my room for the last time. Thirteen days sure went by fast. The whole lot of them better than I could've imagined. Perhaps traveling for work wasn't so bad.

As I turned the water on to wash my face before bed, there was a knock at the door. Looking out the peephole offered no help. All I saw was a blurry shade of tan. After I pulled the door open, Donald pursed his lips to hide his smile, holding two ice cream cones directly in front of his chest.

Even though he razzed me, the boisterous laugh I released was candid.

Donald extended one of the identical desserts to me. "Sorry, Bridges. Couldn't pass it up."

"Thanks for the ice cream. This trip was much better than I thought it would be. I actually like you now."

"Meaning you didn't like me before?"

"Let's just say you didn't make a great first impression."

"Fair." He shrugged. "I actually might like you less. But you'll do as a co-worker. Maybe even a friend."

"Deal." I offered the cone to cheers, which he returned, then drew it back to take a lick.

"I've already secured a taxi to the airport for our morning flight. Be ready at 8:45 to head downstairs."

"Will do. Goodnight, friend."

"Night, Bridges."

We made it to the airport with time to spare. I ordered Donald and myself a coffee at the coffee-shop past security since his food stipends were long gone. Only a few people were scattered out at our gate. Apparently, the early morning flight on Saturday wasn't popular.

As we boarded our plane, the number of passengers already seated communicated a connecting flight from somewhere else. Donald and I got situated in our assigned seats and half-listened to the flight attendant's spiel. After the how-to-fasten-your-seatbelt speech and the how-to-not-die speech concerning oxygen, exits, and seat cushion floatation devices, the captain came over the speaker.

"Welcome aboard those of you joining us on this flight from Rochester, New York to Dallas, Texas. We should touch down at DFW International in approximately one hour and fifty-two minutes on this last leg of the trip. Once we are at our maximum altitude, I'll turn off the seatbelt signs, and you'll be free to move about the cabin. Thanks for choosing us, and enjoy your flight."

The aircraft wasn't even close to full, barely over half. As soon as we had permission to move, Donald stirred.

"I didn't sleep so well last night. I'm going to find an empty row and sleep."

"Sure, I'll enjoy your seat then." As soon as he side-stepped out, I raised the armrest between the seats and made myself comfortable.

About ten minutes later, a gentleman a few rows up stood into the aisle, filling the space more than Donald. His broad-shouldered frame was covered in a bulky hoodie. Dark frames shielded his eyes, and the hood of his sweater was secured over his head on top of a ball cap. Perhaps he was famous. Why else would he be so covered up? He was going to sweat like a beast in Texas. His commanding presence intimidated me the closer he approached. I offered a polite, closed-mouth smile.

Much to my surprise, he stopped in front of Donald's empty aisle seat.

"Mind if I sit here?" he asked, causing my heart to thud with his words alone.

What's that about?

"Um, sure." I collected my things and moved back over to my seat, then pulled the armrest back down.

"Thanks. The guy next to me kept laying his head on my shoulder. Snored too."

I didn't know if I should laugh or not, let alone how to respond. It might've helped to look up at him, but shyness got the best of me. Any context clues on the man's face went unread.

"I'll try not to do the same then."

"It's okay if you do. You're more my type."

Oh!

My cheeks warmed like an oven, robbing my ability to think of a reply. A few minutes passed without either of us saying anything as I continued to read my book. I resisted the urge to look around and see if there was an empty row this man could've taken instead of sitting next to me but didn't want to seem annoyed. I stared at the pages without actually reading, trying to put my finger on why his presence had me so flustered.

"Are you heading home?" He finally spoke.

"I am. I was traveling for work." I glanced for a split-second, noticing a strong jawline—the only part of his face that was visible.

"I'm traveling for work as well; only New York is my home."

"That's nice." It wasn't a great comeback, but I hadn't planned on talking to a stranger today. Not to mention one who left me feeling so bizarre. My introverted self wasn't prepared.

"What kind of work do you do?" he prodded.

So this is going to continue, I see. I closed my book and placed it on my lap. "Accounting. Oil field precisely. You?"

"I do a bit of number crunching of my own. I'm an investment analyst. But the other job, the one I really like," he leaned in, his arm brushing mine, "I'm a fighter."

"I don't think I've ever met a real fighter before."

"Well, now you have." He didn't offer his name for a proper introduction, but since I'd never see him again, it didn't matter much. The lack of identifying himself lent to my someone-famous theory.

The conversation stalled for a minute or two. I opened my book again.

"I'm fighting tonight, actually."

"Oh, really?" His statement about traveling for work paired with his bulky sweats and concealed identity made more sense.

"Yes, ma'am. I weigh-in right after I land. Then I plan to find the best burger in town and eat for the first time in almost twenty-four hours."

"Whoa. I don't think I could go that long without eating."

He shrugged. "Just part of the job." The rhythm of his words was familiar. I closed the book with a *thud*.

My heart stalled. *Could it be?*

For as many times as I recalled his face, I equally wondered what he'd look like as an adult. I can't say the face looking at me was ever one that came to mind. It wasn't possible. I shook my head clear and tried to remember what we talked about.

"You should try Harley's. Best burger joint around. I recommend the blue-cheese bacon burger with homestyle fries. Their onion rings are award winning too, but I don't like onions, so I can't vouch for them."

"Thanks, maybe I'll check it out." He took off his shades. I finally got a better look at him, sure my assumptions were ludicrous. The eyes were too dark. Weren't they?

Talking about my favorite burger spot caused my stomach to come to life with a rumble. All I had to eat this morning was the cold cheese danish I grabbed as we exited the hotel.

"Sounds like you're hungry too."

"Shoot. You heard that?" I chuckled. "I'm surprised yours is quiet after so long."

"I practice intermittent fasting during training. Give it another hour or two, and it'll be roaring like a lion." After a pause, he asked, "Who was that guy sitting with you?"

"My co-worker. We were training at a new site for the last two weeks." I searched his face again, not feeling as crazy as moments ago. My heart rate seemed to agree.

"That's quite the stretch. My trip is quicker. I head back tomorrow. My other job resumes on Monday."

"That is quick. I hope you enjoy Dallas, and your fight goes well."

"Thanks," he offered his hand in a pause as if to ask for my name.

"Londyn."

"I'm Sebastian." The left side of his mouth curled into a smile. That grin wasn't only familiar; it was unmistakable.

"Sebastian!?"

I hadn't lost my mind after all. It *was* him.

"Hi, Londyn," he responded. "You haven't changed much."

Shock momentarily stole my voice. "You certainly have! I barely recognized you." He pulled off his hat and hoodie, revealing more of his profile and—hello—muscles. A few details of the face I memorized in high school shined back at me, one after the other—the one that filled my head over the years on nights when I couldn't sleep.

"Probably the nose. It's already been broken twice." He chuckled, situating his T-shirt.

If it wouldn't have been mega awkward, I would've turned and hugged him. But since we were in such a small space and we hadn't seen each other in close to a decade, I didn't reach out. Even though I *really* wanted to. Besides, just because I hadn't stopped thinking about him over the years didn't mean I'd occupied his mind at all.

"Did you know the whole time it was me?" I asked, still in shock.

"I saw you walk in and wondered. Then, when you were reading, I was pretty sure. But when we started talking, I had no doubt. Especially when you mentioned not liking onions. I was waiting to see how long it would take for you to recognize me."

My voice might not have changed, but his was much deeper than I remember.

"You punk!" I laughed, our familiar banter rushing back in an instant. "Can you blame me? You don't look much like you used to at all, you know?" Not that I minded his adult build one bit.

"In a good way, I hope."

I nodded a couple of times, slowly. How else was I supposed to respond to the guy I hadn't seen or even talked to since I was seventeen—the one who once made me feel alive. I could hardly even believe he was physically in front of me.

"So you live in New York?" Now that I knew who he was, I was going to be the one pressing the conversation. Suddenly, my two-hour flight that was already halfway over was entirely too short.

"Yes, in Rochester."

"I thought your family moved to Maryland when you left Texas?"

"We did. New York's where my job post-college landed me. Dallas for you, huh?"

"Came for college, stayed for my job." This was surreal. I shook my head in disbelief. "Wow, Sebastian." I hadn't uttered his name in years, especially his full name. After we started dating, he was Sebi—C-B—but calling him that now might be awkward for us both.

"What else?" he asked. "I want to know what I've missed. How's everybody? Have you kept up with any of the crew?"

"Uhh," I stretched out my response. "Not really. We still hung out at school, but you were kind of the glue, I guess. School sucked after you left." I laughed, but it wasn't funny back then. Not one bit. "But not hanging out with you led to extra time on my hands, which helped me secure more scholarships than I ended up needing. I haven't talked to any of them since graduation. You know more or less what you left behind. I, on the other hand, know nothing about what life was like for you." I waved my hands toward myself, prompting him to tell me about his life I repeatedly pondered over the years.

"Seriously, nothing?" Sebastian's brows furrowed, but he continued after I didn't respond. "I finished high school without making too many friends with only a few weeks left in the year. I was accepted to Johns Hopkins. Thankfully my scholarships transferred with me. My mom got a job in administration with financial aid services, so I was able to live on campus for free. Worked out pretty good, I guess. I had some independence, but my family was still close. Now more about you."

"No, hold on. How did you get into fighting?"

"I hurt my knee playing intramural basketball with my dorm mates. After wearing a brace for ten weeks, I had to do PT and some type of strength training. Sparring sounded like fun. Turns out, I seriously enjoyed it."

Sebastian played a few sports back in high school, but he wasn't the typical jock. In fact, he was more of a bench warmer. Perhaps that could've been due to the fact that his parents weren't on the boosters club, providing all the funding like the majority of the starters.

The facts he shared filled the gaps to my unanswered questions over the years. More blanks remained unfilled; there simply wasn't enough time to address them all. "Interesting. I never would've pegged you as aggressive."

"It's a sport, Londyn. I'm not aggressive outside of the cage."

"Good to know."

"Probably safe to say I'm not *that* different from the guy you used to know."

Really good to know. I nodded so slow I wondered if my head actually moved.

"Your turn," he insisted.

I wanted to discover more about him, but since I couldn't deny Sebastian, I acquiesced. "Like I said, school was lame after you left. We still hung out without you, but it wasn't the same." We being the lottery kids—the crew who won their tuition to the prestigious and expensive private school with our stellar academics. "I was accepted at UNT, moved onto campus, did the college thing, and got hired at a small oil company straight out of school. Then that company was bought out by who I now work for. They're still absorbing smaller companies, which is why I was in Illinois. Not a whole lot else."

What I didn't say: *With thoughts of you sprinkled all throughout.*

The moment was still too dreamlike. Like it wasn't happening at all. After all these years and states between us.

"Looks like life treated you well," he said, pulling me from my thoughts.

I wished I would've paid more attention to my looks this morning. I went for comfy over professional for the flight home. Not exactly what I would've chosen as my attire if I knew I'd run into a former boyfriend.

I ran a hand over my casual lounge pants. "I've done all right, I'd say. Looks like life has treated you well too." I pushed the attention back to him.

"Thanks. One day, I might quit my day job. I just have to wait and see if this part of my career takes off. I'm rather grateful for it at this particular moment, though."

His smile made me hope he insinuated it led to running into me. However, he could've meant ten other things. I noticed he wasn't wearing a ring, but he was about to fight, so maybe he still had one back home. I tried to figure out how to bring up his personal life when—

Ding!

The seatbelt light came back on.

"Flight attendants, please prepare for landing."

No! Not already.

"Do you watch any MMA?" Sebastian asked as stewardesses began their rounds.

"MM-what?"

"Mixed martial arts. That's the type of fighting I do."

"Oh, can't say I do. You know me, always more of the book-savvy kind of individual."

"Right. Well, if you want to come, I can add you to the guest list. I get four spots, and I don't have anyone to use them."

"Really?" The thought of attending a crowded, smelly sporting event was an easy no for me. Hard no. But having the chance to see Sebastian again made it a resounding yes. "Okay, yeah. Maybe I can convince my roommate to come."

"Excellent. I'll text my manager and get you on the list. Same last name?"

"Yup, still an Adams."

"Great." He smiled that mischievous grin.

Starting a new conversation as gears sounded and the wheels hit the runway seemed pointless, but I seriously wasn't ready for him to be gone. Again.

"I'm really glad we happened to be on the same flight," Sebastian said with warmth in his eyes.

"Me too." I think I smiled, but for some reason, I couldn't feel my body.

He gave me the information on where the fight would take place. I typed it all out on my phone along with the name I'd need to get me in if there were complications.

The clicks and clacks of everyone unbuckling seatbelts and opening the overhead bins to retrieve their belongings filled the cabin.

"I probably won't see you up close again, but I'll be cheering you on in the crowd," I said.

"Thanks, that means a lot."

We stood up and were finally able to give some sort of a hug that was awkward in the small space yet amazingly fabulous. Being in Sebi's arms had always been my favorite place to be. And of course, Donald interrupted.

"Hello, there." He rubbed the sleep from his eye.

"Donald, this is my friend from high school, Sebastian. Sebastian, my co-worker Donald." Friend wasn't an adequate word, but nothing else seemed appropriate in the setting.

"Pleasure," Donald said and offered his hand.

"Likewise." Sebastian returned the greeting.

"He's fighting tonight at Verizon," I added, utterly impressed.

"Awesome, good luck."

"Thanks. Nice to meet you, Donald. Good to see you again, Londyn." The sound of my name on his lips made my spine turn to jello. A solid, but barely. "I better go find my bag."

He walked away, which was no fun at all, but at least now, I had an idea of how his life had turned out. I wouldn't have to wonder anymore.

Sebastian. The one my thoughts traveled back to more times than I could count. Central Station.

The way he made me feel. The notes he used to pass me. The first, and later the last time he kissed me. It was as if the past was present again.

They say you never forget your first love, and though that statement proved true in my life, I felt lame admitting it. And perhaps love was a strong word. I was all of seventeen, but it felt real. Very real. Countless nights, Sebastian appeared in the subconscious thoughts that soothed me, filled me, taunted me. It had been eight years since his father accepted a job in another state, and just like that, he was gone with only two weeks' notice in the last semester of his senior—my junior—year.

He hardly resembled the teenager who called me stunning every time he saw me, causing me to wonder if any future dreams of him would possess his face now or the one solidified in my memories.

There were seasons the visions lessened over the years, typically when I started dating someone new and my dormant love-life jolted to life for a handful of short weeks. Still, the images always came back. I genuinely began to wonder if I'd ever stop dreaming about him.

Even though we started high school a decade into the twenty-first century, modern technology didn't help us. Neither of us had cell phones or cars before our sixteenth birthday, like all of our classmates. We were the lottery kids. Perhaps that's what helped us click.

Sebastian said he'd write to me, but he must've got too wrapped up in college life and forgot.

I pondered it many times, simply looking Sebastian up now that I did well for myself and had access to the internet on not only my MacBook but also my iPhone. But there was also something I wasn't ready to give up. What if I found out he was married or in jail or shipped away in the military? Even worse, what if he'd passed away? Keeping Sebastian as the best person in my life—though he hadn't officially been *in* my life for close to a decade—was how I chose to save it.

Until we met for the second time. Now I wanted more.

I should've asked for his number.

"Ready?" Donald shook me from my thought.

"Uh, yeah." I looked ahead. Sebastian offered a wave as he hunched over and stepped out of the aircraft.

5

"Get up and get dressed! You're coming with me tonight," I said as soon as I got back to the condo and barged into Camilla's room.

"My life wasn't lame without you, you know? Maybe I already have plans."

"You're sitting in bed with no pants on. It's two in the afternoon."

"All the good plans are eight hours away. I haven't even started swiping yet."

"No swiping tonight. *We* are on a guest list." Her eyebrows perked. "That's right, a guest list. As in V.I.P."

"Keep talking." Camilla sat up.

"It just so happens, I ran into someone I haven't seen in a long time, and he's fighting at Verizon Arena tonight."

"Fighting?" She lounged down again. "Not really my thing. Sounds more up your alley, Carnivore."

"Actually, I've never seen a single fight in my entire life, but I'm going. And you have to go with me."

"I'll think about it."

"Come on." I was prepared to beg when a better idea came to mind. "I bet eighty-five percent of people in attendance will be men."

"I'm in."

I knew that would do it.

A couple hours later, we headed to the indoor arena, dressed somewhere between date night and sporting event attire. While waiting in the paid-parking line, we watched an MMA video on Camilla's phone to get a grasp of what we were about to take part in. It didn't offer much help.

As we walked to the ticket booth along with thousands of other fans, I felt a tinge nervous the guest list thing wouldn't go smoothly.

"How many?" the attendant asked through the mic behind a glass partition. By his absentminded tone, he'd uttered the words too many times for his liking.

"I'm on the guest list. Londyn Adams."

He pulled out a clipboard and scanned down the page but didn't stop before running his finger back up.

"A guest of Sebastian Gomez," I nervously added.

"Yup. Found it." He passed us two fifth-row tickets.

Camilla and I navigated past the check-in barrier and metal detectors—my second screening of the day. Finally, we made it into the colossal arena.

The room was clammy and loud and rank. Men of all ages, ethnicities, social statuses, and degrees of manners were packed into the seats, most of them holding a beer or two. We were one hundred percent out of our element. Like dolphins in a desert. Nothing new to me, truthfully. Camilla, not so much. The disgust curling her upper lip was entertaining.

We were handed a flyer as we walked in, containing all the fighter's names and fights on the night's card. Scanning the list, I saw a total of five matches. Sebastian's was the third, smack in the middle.

Only fifteen minutes or so passed since we arrived before booming music filled the arena, announcing the first fighter. Everything was foreign to us; we simply spectated and stayed in our seats. I didn't see any trouble happening tonight. At least on my end, Camilla could be a live wire.

The announcer stood in the middle of the cage, calling off the fighters' names and stats. After a bell rang three times, the guys attacked each other. *Literally*, attacked each other.

"Oh my!" I gasped as the fighter in yellow shorts took a gnarly punch to the face, causing his legs to wobble. When the bell sounded again, I asked, "Is it over?" to no one in particular.

"No. That's the end of the first round. Each fight is three, five-minute rounds." The guy next to me in a shirt with 'Affliction' scrawling across the shoulders informed me above the noise. He taught me more in his short recap than the video we tried to crash-course with in the car.

"Great. Thanks for letting me know. I'm a rookie."

"No worries, I'm a veteran." He crossed his arms across his chest. I had no doubt he could snap me in half with one arm alone. The guy was Herculean. "If there isn't a knockout or a submission, the judges decide the winner after all three rounds."

"Got it. I hope to be properly informed by the third fight. I know one of the fighters. Came to support him." I yelled above the crowd.

"Lucky him," he said. "Don't hesitate if you have any questions," he added with a grin.

"Thanks."

"Camilla." My roommate screamed as she crossed her arm passed me to introduce herself.

"Rhett, pleasure to meet you." He looked back at me.

"Londyn."

"Welcome to the best sport in the world, ladies." His large arms lifted into the air, making me feel tinier than ever.

The bell rang again for round two. Before five minutes were up, the fighter in yellow shorts had the other guy pinned with his legs and pulled on the poor guy's arm like he wanted to yank it off. The guy about to lose his arm tapped the mat. A fraction of a second later, the ref slid in, waving his hands in the air to call the match.

"Yes. That armbar was deep," Rhett yelled, turning to face me. "He won."

Apparently, trying to pull someone's arm off was called an armbar. Noted.

One down, one to go before Sebastian. The good thing was, I wasn't bored. Even further surprising, I wasn't as into the fights as Camilla.

"Did you see that? Whoa, so intense. I thought his elbow bone was going to pop out."

By the end of the second fight, Camilla cheered for more bloodshed while I, on the other hand, wondered how the next fighters dealt with wrestling around on a mat covered in other people's blood.

The ring cleared out. Showtime. A new anthem spilled from the speakers.

"That your guy?" Rhett asked, a head taller than the crowd giving him an advantage.

I rose on my toes. "Nope. That's the guy I hope is about to lose," I admitted, feeling only a fraction remorseful about my statement.

As the next song started, I stood on my chair to get a better view of Sebastian's entrance. I could only see the top of his dark head above the sea of people until he circled the aisle and I gained a better view. He punched his gloved fists together, stretched his neck side to side, and bounced back and forth from one foot to the other. It was as if I'd never even seen him before in my life. I was utterly intrigued by this man. When he stopped outside of the cage, I stepped down from the seat.

Sebastian removed his shirt, revealing three tattoos, and underwent an evaluation by the referee. After pulling his lips wide to reveal a mouthguard, he climbed into the cage with his hands above his head. I leaned back and cupped my jaw, screaming as loud as I could.

"He's cute." Camilla leaned in and practically yelled in my ear. "How do you know him again?"

"Long story. I'll tell you later," I answered, matching her volume, but my eyes never left the ring.

As the announcer called out the fighters' stats, I found myself cheering so loudly, my voice cracked. The referee declared the rules and asked both fighters if they were ready. My heart began to race.

"Let's fight!" the ref roared.

The opponent came in with some kind of leaping punch that thankfully missed. Regardless, it still stole the breath out of my lungs. The two men sized each other up, landing a few punches here and there, but nothing rocked them from their strong stances.

My blood pumped through my body twice as fast as I dodged from side to side as if I could help Sebastian miss the blows coming toward him.

Sebi threw a punch that landed on his opponent's jaw, causing him to stumble. He rushed in to take the other guy down to the mat.

"That was good," Rhett, my seat neighbor, said.

"Good!"

I couldn't make out what happened as Sebastian and the other guy rolled around, fighting for a better position. Sebi ended up on top, but one of his arms was trapped against the other guy's chest. I was afraid he'd get his arm yanked off like the former fighter in the first fight and began to panic.

"Come on, Sebi!"

My fear was premature. Sebastian used his trapped arm to lift and slam the fighter back down into the mat.

The entire arena let out a resounding, "Oh!"

"That was good too, right?" I asked over the noise.

"Yeah," Rhett said while clapping.

"Oh man, I don't know if I can make it through much more with my pulse like this," I said to Camilla, unable to look away from the action.

She murmured a slew of, "Come on, get him. No, move the other … yeah, like that. Hit him again!"

Both fighters were barely back on their feet when the round ended. The crowd applauded their efforts.

"What do you think, did he get that round?" I asked Rhett, the professional—aka: the only person I knew who had a clue about MMA. Other than Sebastian, of course.

"Not sure. That was a pretty even round. Let's hope he can come in hot for round two."

I watched as Sebastian sat on a stool in the corner. A coach offered him water out of a bottle with a tiny curved straw, squeezing it right into his mouth. Another guy looked him over and made sure he didn't need any more vaseline or whatever it was they put on his face. I willed my own deep breaths into his lungs as his chest rose and fell in a gasping motion. If my pulse raged, I couldn't even imagine his.

Standing again, he shook out his arms and legs, stretched his neck from side to side, and punched his fist against each other. The ref called, "Fight!" and the second round began.

"All right, Sebi, you got this," I said more to myself.

He managed to do some kind of wildly impressive spinning kick, dropping his opponent. Half a second later, Sebastian was on top of the other fighter, dropping punches down on him like rain. The opponent bucked underneath Sebastian, trying to get free but ended up flailing his arms a bit too much. To his demise.

Sebastian was quick, wrapping his bicep around the guy's arm and neck like a cobra. As the crowd began to roar, I knew it was a good thing. My heart pounded in anticipation.

"He's got it. There's no getting out of that triangle," Rhett commented. Triangle. Noted.

A few seconds later, the referee waved his hands in the air. A scream I didn't know I possessed left my lips from the bottom of my gut. I cheered and hollered and jumped and clapped in pure adrenaline-induced excitement.

Sebastian stood and yelled his own quaking victory shout while flexing downward, revealing every muscle in his chest, arms, and abs in chiseled majesty. The man had more muscles than I knew existed. I tried hard not to stare, but he was a work of art.

After a few minutes, the announcer was back in the cage to declare the winner.

"And your winner, by submission via triangle choke, Sebastian, *The Basher*, Gomez!" The man held out the O and the E in his last name extra long as the ref raised Sebastian's hand in victory. The crowd erupted, namely me.

"He won! He won!" I screamed so much my throat felt like it ripped at the seams. Still, I didn't stop.

"It's pretty impressive he got that submission from the mount. Your guy knows what he is doing." Rhett turned to me for a high five.

Submission, mount. Terms to learn later.

Various people took pictures of Sebastian and his training team. A few minutes later, he exited the cage and left down the same aisle he entered. I was bummed it was already over.

I yelled, "Way to go, Basher," as he passed, but he didn't seem to hear or see me.

His emotions probably made mine look subtle. He had to be soaring. Before I sufficiently brought myself down to a healthy state of mind and wellbeing, music for the next fighter's entrance already blared. The rush of endorphins quickly evacuated my body.

For the first time since Sebastian's fight was the next on the card, I sat down, drained more than I could've anticipated.

"You all right?" Camilla leaned down and screamed over the noise.

"Yeah, that took a lot out of me," I answered, my throat sore.

"I bet. These are intense to watch without even knowing either of the dudes getting punched in the face," she said.

Wanting to rest for a few more minutes, I pulled out my phone and scrolled through my social media. The screen loaded slowly due to only two bars of service. When I heard the crowd crescendo with the beginning of the fight, I wasn't ready to stand up just yet. Camilla and Rhett were on their feet on either side of me, sometimes leaning across my legs to talk.

"Are you kidding me? That was a low blow, ref!" came from behind me a split second before an insane amount of liquid ran down the back of my shirt.

I jumped up in reaction and turned around.

"I'm so sorry, ma'am! The guy behind me pushed me forward. I lost my drink." At least he apologized. I expected a drunk guy, obliviously sloshing his plastic cup around in the air. The guy behind him, well, he fit my suspicion a bit more.

"It wasn't your fault." I tried to not sound upset. The frothy residue around the top of his now very empty cup let me know beer drenched my hair and shirt.

Camilla's large eyes bulged. A nervous giggle taunted her lips. "Sorry, Londyn."

"It's fine. I'm gonna go clean up in the restroom. I'll be back." I grabbed my purse from under the seat and inspected to see if it also took a beer shower. Thankfully it was safe. Sidestepping past the few people between us and the aisle, I left the loud arena and navigated the hallways, looking for a bathroom. Even past the closed main doors, the muffled hum of the crowd broke through.

When I finally saw the bathroom sign, I turned into the alcove only to walk right into a janitor's cart. Bypassing the cart to see if the cleaning crew was in the men's or women's room, a man stood in the ladies' room with a push broom, aggressively pushing the water that puddled around his feet toward the center drain in the floor.

My motion caught his attention. "Sorry, miss, this bathroom isn't going to be up and running for a while."

"I just need the sink, actually," I replied.

"Even then, I highly doubt you want to walk in here right now in your nice shoes." He pointed to my feet. "This isn't clean water if you catch my drift."

"Oh!" With each passing second, I grew stickier and stickier. If I couldn't clean up, we needed to make an early exit. Thankfully, the fight I came to see was already over. "I just had a whole beverage spilled down my back. Is there another bathroom?"

"Sorry to say, the other one's clear around the opposite side."

I knew why he apologized. The building was so vast, it would take me ten minutes to walk there. I'd be a walking sap tree by then. The last fight would probably be over before I navigated back. At that moment, I debated if it was better to text Camilla and leave or have to handle my situation here. My shoulders slumped. I was about to thank him for the info when he looked around and continued quieter.

"You didn't hear it from me, but there's an exit door across the hallway that leads down to the locker rooms. No ladies are fighting tonight, so that room should be empty. If someone finds you, tell them you got lost looking for the bathroom." He winked and pointed the direction I needed to go before looking back down to his dirty job.

"Thank you *so* much. I greatly appreciate it!"

Exactly as the janitor said, I found the exit and sign pointing to the women's locker room. For the first time all night, my ears were given a break, only to reveal a high-pitched ring resonating in my head.

Almost to the ladies' locker room, conversation spilled from an open door. Hoping they wouldn't notice me, I put my head down and walked a little faster.

"Londyn?"

Only one person in this building knew my name other than the people I left in our seats. Especially in an area I wasn't supposed to be. I stepped back and looked into the room. Sebastian sat in a chair as someone worked to take the tape off of his hands.

"Hey," I said from the doorway, flustered as soon as my eyes landed on him. At least I wouldn't get in trouble with *The Basher* to defend me.

"Get in here." He pulled his hand away from the guy cutting off the white bands. "You came."

"I did. And you killed it! I was screaming like crazy. Congrats," I uttered, my voice coming out strained as proof.

"Thank you. I'm hoping to get the submission of the night bonus. But seeing you is a bonus of its own. What are you doing down here?" He chuckled.

I pivoted so he could see my shirt merged with every bend and curve of my torso. My hair had to look awful too. "I was doused with beer. It feels nastier by the second."

"Oh, man. Here," Sebastian turned around, "take my shirt. I barely wore it before the fight."

"Are you sure?" I hesitated to take it.

"Yeah. I have to wear it for my sponsorships. I have a new one each fight. Got a drawer full."

"It isn't like a memento, then? If you keep them all."

He didn't answer my question. "I'd like you to have it."

"Thanks." I took the black t-shirt from his hand.

"I highly doubt you want to, but there's a shower in there." Sebastian pointed behind him.

"You're correct. I was headed to the ladies' locker room to clean up." His brow dipped in question. "Which I can not divulge who gave me the information about where it was located."

"Nice. You always were loyal like that." He grinned, causing my insides to flip over themselves. A smile filled my face. "Clean up in my room, I insist. Then you won't possibly run into anyone else who might question you."

"You got it." I went into the restroom and closed the door, listening for a minute to see if anything was said. Even though their voices were muffled, the conversation that followed was audible.

"Who's that?" a man asked.

"Someone I had the honor of dating a lifetime ago." Sebastian's words made my heart skip a beat.

"Ah, that explains your goofy grin," another voice said.

I licked my teeth in excitement as I smiled so big, my cheeks balled up.

Even though I wanted to keep listening, invading their conversation wasn't polite. I pulled—make that peeled—my shirt off and wet a paper towel to wipe my back down. Getting my whole back clean with my inflexible arms wasn't easy. I wished Camilla was with me. I did the best I could and placed my soiled shirt in my purse before putting Sebastian's shirt on. It smelled like him. Just like him. His face and body had changed, but he smelled precisely the same. Even after all those years, the scent was as familiar as recalling my parents' address. Some things you never forgot.

Trying to make my look a bit cuter, since Sebastian's biceps were the size of both of my arms—or bigger—I tucked the front of the shirt in. Thankfully it wasn't a cheap, stiff, cotton shirt. The fabric laid nicely against my skin.

I checked my hair in the mirror next. Unfortunately, the back middle was clumped together like two fat dreadlocks. Digging in my purse in search of a rubber band, I lifted my hair onto the top of my head in a messy bun. The stiff parts crunched under my hand. My look changed quite a bit since I arrived, but it would have to do.

Walking out of the bathroom, Sebastian was now alone, but I didn't think much of it.

"Thanks for the shirt. I really appreciate it."

"Looks way better on you than me."

"Debatable, I saw you in it too, remember. You filled it out more in this region." I motioned my hand around my petite arm. "I don't even think I have a bicep, especially compared to you. I have a negative bicep." The statement wasn't one I'd typically say to any other guy, but the familiarity we had—at one point in our lives, at least—allowed me to be more sanguine. Sebastian laughed at my statement.

It would've been good if he wore a shirt then because seeing Sebastian up close in only his fighting shorts distracted me. As if an art connoisseur in a museum, I admired his tattoos like his body was the frame and his ink the painting.

The seconds, or minutes, that passed since I last spoke were more than I intended. Surely he noticed.

"I'm thrilled you're here." Sebastian grabbed my wrist, pulling me in faster than my mind registered, and kissed me. The embrace took me back in an instant. However, the fresh encounter was entirely unique. I relished in his touch and didn't resist an ounce. I finally pulled away for a breath.

Never in my life had I been kissed like that. Especially not by—

"I'm seeing someone," I said, feeling conflicted when Roman came to mind. But as soon as the words left my damp lips, I wasn't sure why I spoke them. Sebastian lived in another state. It wasn't like I'd see him again. It also wasn't like Roman and I were exclusive. *Were we?* I wanted to take the statement back. Especially because I wouldn't have minded if Sebastian kissed me like that again. The embrace was *nothing* like the kisses I remembered between the sixteen-year-old and seventeen-year-old versions of ourselves.

Sebastian let go. Every place his skin touched me instantly missed his warmth. "I'm sorry. You didn't mention that on the flight, and you said you'd bring your roommate tonight, so I figured... Can we blame it on the fact I'm still hyped from my fight?" His left eye squinted, exactly how it always did when he was nervous.

The sentiment assured me I knew the man standing in front of me more than a stranger. Still, I knew there was so much more to learn.

"Absolutely." I smiled. "It was amazing running into you today and coming here tonight. I'm so glad I did. I hope your career takes off, Sebastian. You look like a natural out there."

"Thanks." He fidgeted with his hands, with no pockets to slide them into, drawing my attention to his washboard stomach. I forced my eyes to pan left.

"I better get back out there." I threw a hitchhikers' thumb. "Don't want my roommate worried about me."

"For sure. Take care. Uh, here. Take this pass so no one bothers you." He handed me a lanyard, seemingly insecure from our contact moments before.

"Thanks." I went in for a hug. A big, muscular, sweaty, extraordinary hug. My shirt was left damp again, only this time I didn't mind. One. Bit.

As I walked out, I turned around once more to take a mental picture of him. I waved before disappearing, much like Sebastian when he exited the plane hours before. Once I was out of his sight, I rushed back to our seats, flashing the silly pass relentlessly in excitement. My pulse had an all-new frantic rhythm, which had nothing to do with the fights this time.

Camilla stood in my place next to Rhett, screaming her head off and pumping her fist in the air. As I scooted past her to the open seat, she asked, "Did you visit the merch table?"

"Something like that. I'll explain later," I said as I bit my still-tingling bottom lip, recalling every fantastic second of what actually happened.

6

Five days passed as I mulled over the differences between my last and most passionate kiss with Roman and my last and most passionate kiss with Sebastian. And how one over the other left me feeling. They didn't even compare. I honestly couldn't remember much about Roman's embrace. Maybe it was since it happened a week earlier. That's what I tried to tell myself, at least. Because I couldn't stop thinking about Sebastian. However, every time I drifted off in thought, I reminded myself he was halfway across the country. Plus, I still didn't have a way to contact him. One magical gift of a night allowed me to stop wondering what became of Sebi.

Over the same amount of days, I also didn't tell Camilla how I ended up in the different shirt I'd yet to wash and stored in my bottom drawer the morning *after* I slept in it. She hadn't asked, and I tried hard enough not to build the whole night up in my head any more than I already had. At least I managed to get back into the swing of things at the office after being gone for two weeks.

Three tall piles greeted me from my desk. Steve could've helped out if he felt extra nice. They were my accounts, though, and had he messed anything up, the results wouldn't have been favorable for me.

Donald and I carried on our new teasing banter around the office, causing some heads to turn. He also asked about the fight night and only got, "It was cool," from me in response. The only people who knew what happened at the fight night were the two people who couldn't talk to each other about it now.

My phone rang on Thursday evening on my drive home from work. Roman. Guilt curled my stomach, but I didn't let it eat at me. We never talked about not seeing other people. For all I knew, he was kissing other people too. Had been the whole time even.

"Hi there," I answered.

"Hello, sunshine."

"You back home?"

"Just landed. Thought maybe I could pick you up for dinner."

"Sure. Did you already have something in mind?"

"I think somewhere kind of chill. I'm too worn out for anything that requires me to use my best manners."

"Got it. I'm actually driving right now. Let me know where to meet you."

"Barbecue or sushi. Which sounds better to you?"

"Those are pretty different choices there. Like opposite ends of the food spectrum." I chuckled.

"I know, but both sound good. So...?"

"Let's do sushi."

After we hung up, I readied myself to see Roman. The Roman who altered his flight plan to spend a few hours with me. The Roman I was interested in and didn't want to snub because of one kiss with a guy who had no potential to turn into anything. The Roman who treated me excellently and bought me gifts even though we didn't get to see each other all that often.

Thankfully, by the time I arrived and saw his smiling face, I was fine.

He greeted me with a kiss somewhere between how we always did and our deeper one, his arm wrapped around my waist. Our time together was typical: fun, lighthearted, pleasurable. We shared about our workweek and what came next on his schedule. And with each passing minute with him back in front of me, the fog filling my head since Saturday cleared. I didn't even mention the fight night as something I did while he was gone.

The day's worth of travel rimmed Roman's eyes, so when he mentioned going for coffee after dinner, I suggested heading home for bed was a better solution for his sleepiness. Besides, after slamming through my makeup work for the past two weeks, I was ready to call it a night myself. We said our goodbyes in the parking lot and headed home, unsure when his schedule would allow us to see each other again.

On Friday, I was almost entirely caught up when my boss walked in.

"Londyn, can you come to my office, please?" Ralph asked.

"Sure." I organized the forms I worked on, so I wouldn't be confused when I returned. Hopefully, not too long from now.

Ralph arrived at his office before me and left the door open. As I walked in, he dropped into the chair at his desk. The ordeal felt like getting called into the principal's office. Like I was in trouble, only I didn't know what for. I never got in trouble in school, or ever really, so my heart did an interesting panic dance in my chest. Suddenly, the banter I carried on with Donald that caught more than one set of eyes came to the forefront of my mind as I lowered into the seat facing my boss's desk.

"Have you been able to get caught up?" Ralph asked.

"Yes, sir. I'm currently tackling yesterday's invoices."

"Great. We missed you around here. Wasn't quite the same without our resident prodigy. I got my report back today from Blanche. She had nothing but amazing things to say about you."

"How nice of her. Thank you."

"I prefer to buy companies outright," he leaned back in his chair, causing squeaking and popping sounds to fill the air, "but there are times where keeping offices running on-site could be more beneficial. So—" He dropped his hand down onto his desk. I was still nervous, but it didn't sound like a scolding was coming. "I'd like for you to consider being our traveling trainer. Now before you say no," Ralph raised a hand, "like I said, this doesn't happen very often."

"I'm flattered by the offer, but does this mean all of those new accounts will become my responsibility?"

"Yes. If the scales start tipping too far on your side, we can give some of your old accounts to Steve."

Leftovers.

I already felt like I imposed when Steve gained me as an officemate. Personally, I enjoyed my own space—chalk it up to being an only child. Surely he wasn't thrilled to obtain a younger, *female* officemate. Our identical desks sat back to back, so at least he still had some sense of privacy behind the tall upper cabinets. However, if I got all the shiny new accounts, and Steve took over the smaller, less profitable ones, he might start to see a steep difference in our bonus checks. The checks *he* printed. If he didn't hate me before, he'd definitely despise me then.

"With all due respect, sir, Steve has been here longer than me. Shouldn't he be the one who gets this position?"

"The suggestion is very kind of you. Between us, I feel like you're more of a people person. The trainer kind. If it makes you feel any better, he'd be leaving his wife and kids for weeks at a time. That isn't ideal for a family."

It did make me feel a little better. "True."

"Great. Think about it. Let me know when you decide. Nothing is on the horizon currently, so no rush."

"Sounds good. I appreciate the offer." I rose from my seat and returned to the accounting department.

"You in trouble?" Steve asked as soon as I walked back in.

"No. Ralph basically told me since it went well in Illinois, he might send me again for other buyouts," I said, not wanting him to have more reasons to dislike me.

As I went back to work on the invoices in front of me, I pondered the offer. Part of me felt like I had to say yes since Ralph offered me the position. But the other half wondered how regularly I wanted to travel. There wasn't anything keeping me from saying no apart from I liked being home. I liked the day to day norm of waking up in my bed, going to work, coming home to my sometimes irritating, vegan—or vegetarian depending on her cheese cravings—outspoken roommate. Roots. In all reality, however, nothing kept me from saying no.

The thought of how often I would see Roman if I was also traveling floated in my head like a rhetorical question. Could we even make it work if we saw each other even less than we did now?

I planned on waiting a while and chewing on the proposition some more before giving my boss a definitive answer.

After such a busy three weeks, training in another state, then returning to the work that awaited me, not to mention the high that was Sebastian, my weekend evaporated like a pond in the desert. Not nearly long enough. The desire to call in and use a sick day on Monday was all too real, but if there was anything I knew how to do, it was work hard.

And it was a good thing I went in because, before lunchtime, Crystal called me from Illinois. Frustration was seconds away from bubbling out as tears in her voice.

"Londyn, I screwed up bad."

"Don't say that. I bet it isn't as dreadful as you think."

"Well, I was trying to save the invoices from July before I started on August," she spoke barely above a whisper, "but somehow, instead of saving, I deleted them. All of them."

First bad news: she hadn't started on August yet, and we were already in the second week of the month.

Second bad news: if she actually erased all of July, most of which I entered for her before I left, she might not catch up until September. Likely October.

"Okay. Take a deep breath." I coached us both. If I wasn't able to help her, I could picture Crystal walking right out of that office with her retirement portfolio in her hand before the end of the day. "Here's what we are going to do."

I explained how to navigate the computer and enable screen sharing. And perhaps I should've told Crystal precisely what I was about to do because when her home screen popped up on my laptop and I began to move the mouse to open a file, she screamed.

"My computer is moving by itself!"

"It's me, Crystal. Don't worry."

If she wasn't so terrified, I might've laughed.

As she sat next to me weeks ago like I taught her the whole spiel in Russian, I had a feeling something like this would occur. So lucky for her, I set up an automatic backup to the time machine every hour.

After a total of five clicks, invoice after invoice popped up on her screen like fireworks.

"Is that them?" I asked.

"Yes. How in the world did you do that?"

"They were saved in the cloud before you deleted them."

"What cloud?"

"Don't worry about it, Crystal. The good news is you didn't lose anything. Maybe a few invoices, if anything."

"You're a lifesaver. I have no idea how you just did all that, witchcraft, but thank you."

I finally laughed. "It's only technology, nothing more."

"I was two seconds from crying."

"While I have the connection here, why don't I walk you through entering the data one more time. You enter the next one while I watch."

"You mean I can still control the computer too?"

"Yes." It was probably mean of me, but when she started moving her mouse one direction, I moved it the other. "Just kidding," I said when she gasped.

I coached her through entering everything between watching where she moved the mouse and talking over the phone. Taking the call and helping Crystal left me feeling satisfied and leaning more towards saying yes to Ralph on the traveling trainer offer.

How ironic that I could help people who felt out of the loop be in the circle. Me, the girl who always felt like I was so far out of the circle I was a hexagon.

After an average workweek for the first time in what felt like forever, I didn't feel wholly spent before the weekend even began. It had been three days since I saw Roman—and fourteen since Sebastian. Not that I was trying to take note of how much time had passed since I was with *him* in particular. Trying *not* to actually. Fourteen days was exceedingly less than the two thousand nine hundred and twenty-one, which crawled by since the last, last time I saw him. Overall, I felt our encounter was nothing more than a deleted-scenes montage to answer some questions and not a full-on sequel. I managed not to dwell on it non-stop after a week.

Saturday night came with no plans. I lounged around most of the day in my condo, enjoying the downtime. I hadn't even brushed my hair.

Before lunchtime, I'd read half of the book I downloaded onto my tablet weeks ago, waiting for an opportune time to enjoy. When I finally left my room to eat, I ran into Camilla in the kitchen. Preparing a salad, of course.

"She emerges," Cam teased.

I saluted her like a military cadet. "I didn't realize how drained I was till I knew I didn't have to get out of bed today. A much needed chill morning for me."

"Good for you. Have you looked in the mirror, though?"

I raised my eyebrows and pursed my lips in a mocking response, not caring what I looked like.

"Any jobs today?" I asked. Camilla was mostly hired by makeup artists, online boutiques, and the like as a pretty face to further their brand.

"Nope. My day is free, but I do have a date tonight." She shimmied her shoulders.

"Let me guess. A dentist. No wait, a lawyer who's in town for a court case and needs someone to 'hang out' with for the night."

"Cold. Care to try again?"

"Um ... fireman?" She shook her head. "Another model? Librarian? Oceanographer? Single father of ten?"

"Such a quick decline. Still wrong, all of them."

"Let's hear it then?"

"Rhett." She smiled.

"The guy from the fight?"

"That's the one. We traded numbers while you went to clean up and have been texting a bit. He's pretty hunky. I think his thighs are bigger than my waist." She took a bite of her salad.

"Well, Cam, your waist isn't very big. Not really sure that's a compliment to him." I chuckled at my own joke before turning to open the fridge to find something to eat. I still hadn't gone to the store since I was back in town, and the stock showed it. Not wanting to get out of comfy mode and slightly bummed Camilla had plans and I didn't, I pulled out my phone and ordered a pizza. Meat-lovers. And I had no problem eating it in front of her, slowly if she commented on my food.

"Do you know where he's taking you?" I asked as I navigated the pizza app.

"Some sports bar. I might've led him on by meeting him at a sporting event, but what can a girl do? If he asks, I'll tell him I'm new to this world."

"Way better idea than faking it."

"Which is my second option."

"Go with plan A. If the buzzer rings and I don't hear it, please let me know. I'm gonna go back to my bed and read."

"No plans with Roman tonight?"

"Nope. He's gone again. Long trip this time. I think he gets back this upcoming Friday." I pouted, knowing there were long nights at the condo ahead of me for the next six days. Most likely alone, if Camilla and Rhett hit it off—or even if they didn't, she could get another date if she wanted. "Nothing new, though. This is how it's always been." I knew then, the main reason it bothered me that she had something promising with Rhett was that I still wasn't sure *what* I had.

"Sorry, friend," Camilla said.

I ate half of the pizza for lunch and the other half for dinner.

Camilla knocked on my open door to let me know she was leaving. "I'm out." She didn't even try to hide how wide her eyes opened when I tossed the last crust onto the empty box.

"Have fun. Say 'hi' for me. And you're welcome. I mean, you wouldn't know Rhett if it wasn't for me inviting you to the fight and then striking up a conversation with him. I'll take a dessert as thanks."

"Sure. I'll add you to my planner sometime this week. I don't think you need to eat any more today."

I stuck my tongue out at her.

She did have a planner, though, mostly to organize her jobs. Camilla also had more Instagram followers, dressed cuter, the whole shebang. But I could out-calculate her even if I had the flu, so I was okay with our rankings. I was used to the smart-but-not-a-ten role in social circles.

The tracker at the bottom of my tablet showed I only had twenty-seven minutes left until finishing the book when my phone went off. I smiled as I leaned to grab it off the nightstand, knowing Roman was checking in once he was off.

Only it wasn't Roman.

"Request for new message" from the messenger app was the notification on my screen. I swiped it to the right to open the message, and my heart about froze when I saw who the request was from.

Sebastian Gomez.

Sebastian: Hey Londyn. It's me!

He knew I'd read it because of the read timestamp, but I didn't know how to respond off the top of my head. Mostly because I still hadn't planned on looking him up. We had our night, and that was enough. Wasn't it?

Me: You found me.

Not the best conversation starter, but I'd already hit enter.

Me: How are you?

Sebastian: Great. Just finished practice. Now I'm lying in bed.

Me: You don't get a rest after the win?

Sebastian: I did. One whole day! Ate like a pig, too.

Because I knew him, well used to know him, I knew he chuckled at that. Or would've if we were in person.

Me: Nice! What else did you do today?

Sebastian: Nothing. I train longer on the weekends since I'm not coming from work.

Me: Which makes perfect sense.

Sebastian: How about you. What are you up to?

Me: Reading at my condo. Not a whole lot.

Sebastian: Sounds about right. That's what you always used to do if we weren't hanging out.

Me: I guess I haven't changed much. How lame is that?

Sebastian: Not lame, it's you. You have never been, nor will you ever be lame.

I blushed. Alone. In my condo. Me, blushing and feeling every bit sixteen again. I pulled my laptop out from my work bag so I could carry on a better conversation with a full-size keyboard.

As I hammered away on the computer, we laughed as we remembered scenes from our high school antics. In all honesty, Sebastian probably still knew me more than anyone else in the world, a fact that equally excited and saddened me. I should've opened up more to people, but I had my head so honed in on school and making sure I achieved the goals my parents and I had set for myself, I never really spent much time making new connections.

Even Camilla became a friend *after* she was my roommate. She knew my cousin. My cousin knew we were both looking for a roommate, so she paired us up. A connection that could have gone poorly turned out pretty good for both of us.

Sebastian and I settled into old times with ease, like only a couple of weeks had passed and not years since we were each other's favorite person in the world. Only it wasn't like old times because I was typing on a laptop in my condo, both of which I paid for myself. It actually would've been pretty amazing to pass handwritten notes back and forth between classes. Or work? Whatever the equivalent would be today.

A couple of hours quickly passed before Sebastian said he should get some sleep before his two-a-day practice started at 6:00 a.m.

Me: It was great catching up.

Sebastian: Agreed. We need to do it again soon.

Me: I'll be here.

Sebastian: And I'll be here. Later then.

Our "heres" were much too far apart. Had been for years.

7

He might've been able to fall asleep, needed to at least, but I was wide awake. So much so that I heard Camilla arrive home about an hour later. I sprung from bed to meet her before she could disappear into her bedroom.

"Ready for bed?" I asked.

She shrugged. "I could stay up for a bit if I had a reason."

I raised my eyebrows in alluring confidence. "Like how I ended up in a fighter's t-shirt after getting doused in beer, and what I just did for the last three hours, and how those two things go together?"

"Yup. Exactly like that. But by the sound of it, this conversation needs snacks." She tossed her purse onto the bar, kicked off her shoes, and retrieved our ice cream—well, hers was sherbet—pints from the freezer. "Start from the beginning," she added as she passed me the container with a spoon.

The beginning was the first time Sebastian spotted me at lunchtime the second week of my freshman year, his sophomore, ten years ago. I wasn't starting there; far too much to tell. I started at the new beginning.

"On my flight back from Illinois, I ran into Sebastian, the fighter. What I never told you was I dated him in high school."

"I love this story already," she said before scooping out some green sherbet.

"He recognized me and came to sit next to me, but we talked for a bit before I knew who he was. I grew suspicious, but it wasn't until he told me his name that I was certain. Sebastian looks like a different guy now."

"Was he as hot then?"

Her question caught me off guard. "I've never thought he *wasn't* hot." I grinned and hid it with a scoop of Bunny Tracks ice cream. Of course, there wasn't actually bunny in there. I wasn't that hardcore of a meat-eater.

"Oh." Her eyes grew wider, most likely because my cheeks were hot enough to melt my dessert.

"When he started doing some of his old quirks, I realized he didn't look different as much as," *what is the right way to explain*, "not what I would've pictured."

Camilla stuck her spoon down into her pint. "Two claps for gaining an adult body."

Clap, clap!

"Fast forward to me getting the beer spilled on me. I went to the restroom, but it was closed for maintenance. The custodian pitied me and told me where to find the ladies' locker room. Which I was headed to when I passed *Sebastian's* locker room."

Cam smirked, nodding in slow motion.

"When I told him why I was back there, he insisted I take his shirt."

"Like took it off and handed it to you?" Her already large eyes super-sized.

"No. Sebastian was still in his fighter gear. He handed me the one he wore before stepping into the cage." I blushed even more.

Camilla fanned herself as if securing her next big break hinged on that very reaction. I kept the part about him talking to his team about me to myself because even I felt like it hadn't been for anyone else's ears.

"He let me use the bathroom in his room, I changed, and before I left … he kissed me." I looked down and fished for a scoop I wasn't planning on eating.

"Shut up!" She slammed her hand against the back of the couch.

"He probably would've kept going too if I hadn't stopped him."

"Why on earth would you stop that man?"

"Because one thought led to another of Roman altering his flight home for me days before. Was that kiss wrong?" I balled a fist under my chin.

"I probably don't have the same opinion as you on the matter, but I feel like your question can be answered with two questions." She used her fingers to add extra dramatics. Nothing new. One slender, fully manicured finger came inches from my face. "Has Roman told you he wants to date you and no one else?"

"No."

On to the second finger. "Have you told him you aren't going to talk to any other guys or anything?"

"No," I repeated.

"You're single. You can kiss whoever you want, whenever you want to."

I felt a little bit better with her reassurance, although I didn't plan on kissing whoever I wanted without rhyme or reason.

"Take me to the part about the last three hours." She raised her eyebrows, letting me know she might not be as fascinated with the innocent version of what she suspected I was about to admit.

"Right. So I had no intentions of anything else coming from that night. I hadn't seen Sebastian in eight years, and he lives in New York. It was a nice night, now it's over, right? But he messaged me tonight. We talked, er, typed all night. He only got off because he has practice early tomorrow."

"Why hadn't you talked to him in eight years?"

I sighed. "Long or short version?"

"Mmm?" Camilla looked at the time. "Give me a medium version."

"All right. Each year, the most prestigious private school in my hometown chose a male and female student from the lottery of applicants to receive free tuition. The process wasn't exactly like the Powerball. It was basically on par with college acceptance ventures."

"Stop. Too far back. Where does your boy come in?" Camilla waved her hand, encouraging me to move the story along.

"Sebastian won the year before I did. He was a sophomore while I was a freshman. It didn't take the two of us long to hit it off with each other, and all of the other lottery students for that matter." Thanks to the lack of uniforms, we stood out by the fact we sported nothing higher-end than local superstore selections or old enough name brand to be found at the thrift store.

"We were inseparable until the end of his senior year when his father took a job in Maryland. Neither one of us had cell phones or social media. He told me he would write, but he never did. As the years passed, I never wanted to look him up in fear of what I'd find."

What I still hadn't admitted was how he was the one I thought of more than a dozen times over each of those eight years. Slipping back into thoughts of my adolescent life was never something I planned on doing. Every train of thought simply led back to Memory Central Station for check-in and took longer to depart than I sometimes could handle. Many nights, the train pulled in with him at the helm. Every detail of his face stamped into my ticket, marking the frequent visits. Sometimes it lasted two seconds, other times two hours.

"Londyn!"

"Huh?" My thoughts had taken me away from the couch. A few drops of melted ice cream dropped from my spoon and slid down my thigh.

"Now what?"

"Nothing. Not that I know of, at least. He's still in New York, but he made it sound like we'd keep talking. But that's what he said last time too." I shrugged. The gesture was weighty. What I wouldn't give to have more than digital conversations with Sebastian.

"Wow." She deflated, obviously unhappy with the ending. "At least you still have Roman."

"Yeah," came out breathy. "How was your date with Rhett?"

"Pretty good. I can confirm his thigh is bigger than my waist." She arched an eyebrow as she returned to her dessert carton.

"You're gross." I chuckled.

"It was purely PG." I gave her a *like I believe that* look. "Thirteen," she added.

"Are you going to see him again?"

"Most def. And to let him know that, I think I'll send him a selfie after I get into my pj's."

I shook my head. We had about as much in common with how we interacted with guys as how we interacted with food. "You done?" I motioned for her tub. She closed the lid and passed it to me. After putting them back in the freezer and dropping our spoons in the sink, it was almost 2:00 a.m. "I'm going to finish my book and go to bed. Behave yourself with those selfies."

"What's the fun in that?" She swiped her purse from the counter and sauntered to her room.

Imagine my surprise when Sebastian didn't even wait twenty-four hours to message me again. He shared about his training day—which made me tired only reading about it—and asked me what I had been up to. Sadly mine was nothing. Sitting around most of the morning, I escorted Camilla to a job in a part of town she didn't want to go alone in the later afternoon. We both had this fear one day she'd show up at an appointment, and it wouldn't end well. It had never occurred to Camilla yet, but unfortunately, it did happen to some other people she knew.

Sebastian joked I was her bodyguard. I returned his banter by suggesting he teach me some of his moves, secretly wishing he could—in person. We talked about anything and everything.

Monday was back to the real world. Both of us had our numbers jobs to return to. I didn't think I'd hear from him again until the weekend since he worked and went to practice after that, so the chime in my purse was even more shocking than the day before.

We recalled the time he asked me to the winter formal my sophomore—his junior—year. We spent the whole night laughing at all the people who looked like their outfits cost more than a full semester's tuition. Sebastian and I were always annoyed by how our classmates went through their parents' money like Skittles. He admitted he was nervous most of the night but thought it would be the perfect way to segue from friends to something more after knowing each other for a year and a half. I thought he'd never make a move, figured he wasn't into me if he hadn't already done so after an entire school year had already passed.

And *that* was the first time he kissed me. A memory I often replayed over the years. I wondered if he currently recalled that portion of the night or if I was alone in that sentiment.

As we waited in the parking lot for his dad to pick us up, Sebastian reached over and held my chin. I didn't resist. Not even a little. He took my secure body language as permission and closed the gap. The kiss itself could've been better, but after picturing myself doing so for months, I was elated the moment finally came. Chalk it up to me being extremely nervous and only kissing one other boy my whole life.

We didn't discuss our first kiss as we chatted. The conversation was more focused on the fun we had that night. He must have remembered the embrace, though, because he said:

Sebastian: Sorry I kissed you after the fight.

I was far from sorry about our moment, only the weird way I responded. Kissing two men days apart wasn't something I knew how to navigate.

Me: You don't have to apologize. You didn't do anything wrong.

Sebastian: Well, I shouldn't have gone from 0 to 60 without having more clarity.

Me: Don't worry about it. :)

No chimes came on Tuesday.

Wednesday's notification came as a sweet surprise.

By Thursday, I wasn't sure if I should consider an upcoming chat as part of my daily plans or not. But admittedly, it was my favorite part of the day if it came. I felt like I was in high school again when I talked to him—the carefree part, not the petty stuff —even though neither of us would've been able to do anything online other than send an email from the library computers.

Usually, if he reached out, it was by 9:45, which was 10:45 for him in New York. By that time, he'd finished training and was back home, showered, and ready for bed. I wondered how he functioned, keeping up with his schedule even before he added in our chats, but he reassured me he got plenty of sleep. Regardless, I wasn't going to blow up his phone since his schedule was so full. My phone chimed, and I smiled—every time.

The week flew by with the new activity added to my agenda.

At work on Friday, Donald came into my office to pester me, one of his favorite tasks when he was bored.

"Bridges, it's Friday. Whad'ya say you and I hit the town? Maybe find some *apple* pie."

"Oh darn. I heard all the apples within a fifty-mile radius have been deemed poisonous due to listeria, E coli, ringworm, *and* anthrax," I smarted back.

"That bad, huh? You sure it affected *all* of the apples?"

"Every. Single. One." I shrugged with mock pity.

Just then, a loud thud filled the air. Steve had rolled his daily apple—which he always ate at precisely 3:30—from his desk into the trash can. *Oops. Maybe I should tell him I was kidding when Donald leaves.*

"Besides, I have plans already." My plans consisting of sitting in bed, hoping to chat with Sebastian, who I ate up like poisonous apples, knowing the time spent "with" him would only leave me longing for what I couldn't have. I devoured the minutes anyway.

"Suit yourself. Steve, you like apple pie?"

"I'm married," he said, annoyed.

I busted in laughter, spraying my computer screen with a mist of spit.

"Well, you two enjoy your weekend then," Donald said as he tapped the doorjamb and turned to walk away. A Friday night with no plans would probably lead to another cut to his heart with Natalie's name as the source.

"You too," left Steve's and my mouth at the same time.

A few hours later, I was home and changed into comfy clothes for a night of messenger conversation. While waiting, full of hope, I surfed the web for some new books to add to my TBR (to be read) list. Like often happened, more time than I intended to spend on my computer had passed. My purse vibrated against the bed, letting me know it was already 9:45. I was thankful my bag was close because I forgot to take the device off silent mode after work and would've missed the message.

With a smile on my face, I dug out my phone and flipped the screen over in anticipation of how Sebastian started the conversation this time.

But the smile dropped into a straight line when the screen contained a text alert rather than a messenger one. And the time wasn't 9:45.

Roman: You ready to get cute so you can take me to dinner?

Right. Roman was back in town. I'd lost track of my days. Guilt pecked at my neck like a woodpecker. Roman hadn't crossed my mind all week after living in Messenger Land with Sebastian.

I shook my head in an attempt to recalibrate the facts and responded.

Me: I can be ready in 30.

For all I knew, Sebastian had plans for Friday night too. I didn't owe it to him to stay home *in case* he messaged me. Right? Even though that's exactly what I wanted to do. No matter how lame it sounded.

I got ready and waited in the living room for the buzzer. Camilla walked in before I left.

"You heading out?" she asked.

"Yeah. Roman's back in town."

"Don't sound so thrilled about it now."

"I know. I'm glad he wants to get together, but this whole talking to Sebastian thing has messed with my head."

"I already told you. You aren't committed to either of them, so don't feel bad about it."

"Which makes so much sense when you say it. I see other people do it all the time. It's just … not me."

She plopped down next to me on the couch, still wearing her glammed up face from the shoot of the day. Camilla's fake lashes were so long, I wondered how she could see. "Sebastian is a friend." I looked at her with squinted eyes, deeming her word glossed-over at best. "A friend who makes your heart pitter-patter. But not someone you can be with anyway. If you want to keep talking to him, then do so. And Roman's here and willing to take you out. He's never specified you can't talk to anyone else. There really isn't a problem, Londyn."

Words I needed to keep reminding myself.

The buzzer sounded.

I walked to the speaker panel and mashed the button. "Hello?"

"Hey, sunshine. You ready?"

"Be right down," I said, still trying to shake my funk.

"Have fun. Roman will probably have a gift for you, take you to eat, and kiss you goodnight like he always does. Don't make this something it isn't."

"Yeah, okay." I opened the door and walked away.

Roman's smile helped me jump into the moment as I stepped out of the glass door securing our building.

"How do you get so cute in only thirty minutes?"

My look was relatively simple, as usual, but his words made me feel pretty. "Natural beauty, I guess." I joked. When I would've typically leaned in to kiss him in greeting, I hesitated. And stopped altogether. Apparently, I wasn't entirely in the moment. Roman kissed me anyway. I wondered if he noticed anything different in my lips.

"You up for some cooking?" I turned to him in question, my forehead wrinkling. "Ever done Hot Pot?"

"Sounds like something you'd do at a frat party." Like I'd know. "Pretty sure it's illegal, though."

He chuckled. "Mongolian food isn't illegal. I don't think."

"Is there meat involved?"

"Yes, ma'am."

"I'm in. Let's go."

By the time we got to the restaurant, I was in a much better headspace. We simmered into our norm with ease, much like the strips of beef in the pot at the table.

That was until my phone chimed. At 9:45.

I never went more than a minute without responding to Sebastian, considering I waited for the conversation and all. If I ignored the message, he might keep prodding how he always used to when I was so focused on studying for a test I didn't give in to his flirtatious advances.

Pulling out the food before it was fully cooked so it wouldn't turn into jerky, I picked up my phone and started typing.

"Everything okay?" Roman asked.

"Uh, yeah."

Me: Can't chat now. Maybe later tonight or tomorrow....

I hated my response on a Friday night would likely communicate exactly why I couldn't message him. Just like that, I was torn between where I was and where I wanted to be. At least this path had the potential to be real. Roman, I could touch. If I couldn't get control over how chatting with Sebastian stirred old feelings for him, I needed to reevaluate the profit/loss margin of us talking.

8

I didn't message Sebastian when I got home last night. It was late, and he had an early morning. I tried to line up the emotions in my head with the wild ones in my heart. There was reality, and there was fantasy. Roman was real; Sebastian was fantasy. Although Roman wasn't *really* real. He was here in person, and I could actually touch him though he knew so little about me. While Sebastian, though I couldn't touch him, was one of the few people who knew almost everything about me—give or take the last couple of years, which didn't do much to change who I was beyond a few memories. So perhaps Sebastian was real, only unattainable across the country, and Roman was the fantasy as he strung me along on our few and far between dates with gifts and sweet talk, never planning to settle down with me. I was on a leash with them both, and I didn't care to be restrained. Neither guy felt one hundred percent right.

These were the thoughts majorly distracting me all night, and still today from the new book I started on my tablet. When I started chapter four and couldn't even name three of the characters in the book, let alone the setting or plot, I threw the tablet onto the comforter and slid down until my head became one with the pillow.

Thankfully, I sunk into a nap. A much-needed one. One hour melted into four. The knock on my door at 5:00 p.m. woke me up.

"Hello, sleepyhead. Rhett and I are going to another fight, smaller scale. Want to come?"

Still unsure of how to proceed with my trifecta dilemma, I knew for sure I didn't want to be out two nights in a row and miss another chance to talk with Sebastian. I needed to get a pulse on how he felt about me putting him off last night. If he seemed to think nothing of it, suggesting we were safely on the friend train, then I could also force my emotions into submission.

"I don't think I'm up for that. You two have fun, though."

"Your loss." Camilla flipped her hair as she started to walk away.

"What did I start in you?" I laughed. "You gonna start training yourself?"

"And mess up this money maker?" She motioned her hand around her face. "Not a chance. But the boys sure are nice to look at. I wouldn't pass up a ring girl position if it was offered to me, though, that's for sure."

"Does that mean Rhett has some competition?"

"We'll see. I'm not tied down to anyone. Later."

Tied down. Suddenly my nap didn't do me much good. I slammed my head back down onto the pillow, catching the edge of the headboard. Instant pain shot down my back as I squealed.

"You all right?" Camilla popped her head back in to check on me.

Rubbing my sore head, I responded, "I sure hope so."

———————————————

9:45 came and went with no word from Sebastian. That's when I knew I screwed things up. Only, it wasn't like there was anything *to* screw up. As I stood in front of the microwave, waiting on the popcorn to finish, I scanned through my laptop, trying to decide what to watch on Netflix, semi-wishing I would've gone out with Camilla and Rhett.

Unable to decide between two movies, I settled on a double-feature thanks to my nap that lasted half of the day. Ironically, one film was about a woman who dated a businessman above her social status. The other was about a girl and her high school sweetheart before they both set off for life after graduation. Maybe one of these movies would give me some perspective on my own life. Then again, those stories weren't real—wishful thinking on my part. I proceeded anyway.

With the bag of popcorn down to the last few kernels and the second movie, the high school one, not quite half-way in, a notification dropped into the top right corner of my screen.

Sebastian: Any chance you're awake?

It was just after midnight—when we usually closed out our conversation. Had he waited to message me because he figured I had plans again?

I paused the movie and minimized my screen to navigate to his message.

Me: I am, actually.

Sebastian: Up to chat? What are you doing if you aren't sleeping?

Me: Sure. Watching a movie.

Sebastian: Oh, I'll let you finish your movie.

Me: No, it's fine. I'm out of popcorn anyway.

Sebastian: And you can't watch a movie without popcorn. I know that about you. If that's still true.

Me: Still is.

All alone in my room, I smiled. He remembered. Not fantasy. Not reality. But I liked it, whatever it was.

He told me he had to go into work for a big project they missed the deadline on, bumping back his regular Saturday training. Most people probably would've skipped the practice after working their day job on their day off, but Sebastian wasn't like most people. We both knew the importance of hard work, one of the things that brought us together in the first place.

Sebastian: Did you get out tonight?

Me: My roommate invited me to another fight card, but I wasn't really in the mood to see guys get their faces smashed in.

Sebastian: I can't imagine why? ;)

Me: Eh, not as exciting when I don't have someone to cheer for.

We only talked for a few minutes since he'd had such a long day. I was simply thankful he still reached out since I worried our conversations were a thing of the past after last night. If I couldn't have Sebastian in my life physically, at least I could have him digitally. Something was better than nothing. He never questioned why I couldn't chat last night. But Sebastian was smart; I knew he knew. So when he didn't ask, I failed to gain any clarity on his opinion on the situation.

Sunday was off to a slow start but quickly picked up when my mother reminded me they were coming for a visit. "Home" was only two hours away, part of why I came to the metroplex for school—my parents couldn't handle me being too far. Our visit was great. I hadn't seen them in a few months. Before Roman. Before I started working for Aspire. Before I traveled for work. Before running into Sebastian. And how all of that jumbled in my mind now. My brain was like a game of Jenga, with gaps and different blocks getting attention at times. But move the wrong one, and it would all come crashing down. If only I could figure out which move was the wrong one before I made it.

I gave my parents a city-tour of my commute, office, and "exciting" life. Only for them, it was very exciting—their hopes for me to be more successful than them came to pass.

My parents had a plan, which I accomplished:

Study extremely hard.

Cross our fingers we win the school lottery.

Graduate with honors.

Get more free schooling based on scholarships.

Be successful.

Even though I was their only child, both of my parents worked low paying jobs, living from paycheck to paycheck, and wanted better for me. Honestly, I never thought our lives were that bad.

When the sun disappeared, they hit the road again. Neither of them had the luxury of missing work the next day. In all reality, my parents taught me something just as important as my education: the importance of hard work and commitment. I was beyond grateful for all they did to pave the path by example.

I returned to an empty condo, Camilla either on a job or out with Rhett—or a new lucky swiper. After a day of entertaining, I lavished the quiet.

I readied myself for bed by washing away the thin coat of sweat that clung to my body in the late summer humidity, unsure if I'd receive a message from Sebastian or not. I hoped so. Those couple of hours were usually the highlight of my day.

Until then, I read. An actual paperback I picked up while out and about with my parents. The smell of the aged pages in my hand took me back in an instant to the tiny blue chairs in our city's public library. As a kid, I walked to the library and read many summer days, simply so I wasn't home alone. A lifelong love for reading was the result.

The characters were my best friends. Siblings.

I especially loved the sound of my fingertips sliding across and flipping the page—something an ebook could never provide, simultaneously engaging multiple senses.

Lost in the story, my phone vibrated on the bed next to me.

Only it wasn't a message; it was a face chat request.

I stared at the screen, ninety-eight percent sure it was an accident, and waited for the request to vanish. However, it kept ringing until I accepted the call.

"Hello?" My reflection that popped up on the screen wasn't appealing. I almost hung up when Sebi didn't pop up, confirming the call was on accident. "Did you mean to call me, Sebastian?" I said before disconnecting.

The image on my screen went from dark to blurry to bright in a matter of two seconds and settled on his handsome face. Sporting a very black eye.

"Whoa. What a nice surprise. I wasn't expecting to hear your voice today, let alone see your face. What's going on?" He chuckled.

"You booty called me. Uh, butt-dialed. On accident. I think." *Great start.*

"Lucky me," Sebastian replied. "I didn't even know this was a feature on the chat."

"Not sure I did either."

"Gonna have to utilize this more often." Sebastian smirked, buckling his seatbelt and starting his engine.

At that moment, I couldn't care less about my appearance as long as I got to see him.

"I agree. Because you didn't mention, you had an impressive shiner. Are you okay?"

"Eh, part of the job, sweets."

Did he intentionally call me sweets? Sebastian hadn't called me the term of endearment in years, but it rolled from his lips like he'd said it yesterday. I tried my best to stay composed since he could see me.

"Someone throw a calculator at you again?"

He laughed. A good one, not just a chuckle. "Yeah, something like that."

When he went silent and appeared to be in observation mode, I got nervous and resituated myself. Sans makeup and in my sleep tank top wasn't an ideal getup for a face chat. Thank God for the lower half of my body being covered by the sheets.

"You look well."

Psh. "Healthy as a horse in my natural state."

Sebastian saw me without makeup hundreds of times. I rarely wore any freshman and sophomore year. But that was before my skin lost its youthful luster.

"Exactly like I remember. Still just as pretty, too."

As blush grew up from my neck and anchored onto my cheeks, I tried to decide what to do with my eyes. My face. My hands. My life.

"Samesies." Fail. The kind of answer I'd give Camilla, not a guy. With a nod, I clarified. "Same for you, still as pretty." Might as well own the awkward banter. He seemed to enjoy the perks of live chat more than me, proved by his gleaming face.

"You hanging at home?"

"Yup." I lifted the book into view, revealing the rose on the cover.

"Ah. Who're you hanging out with tonight? Extraterrestrials. Post-apocalyptic teens. Princesses in the eighteenth century. Wizards?"

"Nope." I laughed at his spectrum. "Regular people, like us."

"Like us, how?" he asked.

"A girl, a boy." *Please don't keep asking because I don't know how to describe "us."*

"Got it."

"What are you up to?" I changed the topic.

"Same as always. Finished practice and almost home, needing a shower. What did you do today?"

"My parents came to town, actually."

"Aww, good ol' Jim and Laura. How're they doing?"

"Great. Same, but great," I said with a smile. *He remembered my parents' names.*

He smiled at my smile.

"Uh, this is a bit awkward." I laughed.

"Why?" he asked, dipping his brows.

"Because I have to think about how I'm sitting, looking, what I'm saying before I say it. Kinda failing on all fronts. C minus at best."

"No way. I give you an A, but we can hang up if you want."

I shrugged because that wasn't what I wanted, either. After seeing his face, Sebastian seemed closer than six states away.

"So that's all you did today, hung out with your parents? No dates?"

I *seriously* wished he couldn't see my face then. Perhaps a timely drop of the phone or an accidental hangup could've helped. However, both options would've been weirder than simply addressing his question.

"Nope."

"Who's this guy you're seeing?"

"Eh, next question." I chuckled as I tucked some unruly hair behind my ear.

"Come on, who is he? Does he rock your world?" Sebastian unbuckled and rose from his car.

"His name is Roman, and he does *not* rock my world." I looked away from the screen for a heartbeat, trying to figure out my next move. "He's just a guy," I added before looking back at the screen and discovering my splotchy face. And his smirk.

I was terrified he was going to ask, "Am I just a guy?" How would I answer that? I wasn't even sure of the answer, let alone if I could admit it to him.

"You go on any dates?" I spoke up before he could continue prodding.

"No, don't really have time. You know, between work and training. Besides, most of my nights are spent with you." I heard his keys collide with some sort of hard surface.

I swear my heart started beating so hard my shirt had to be rippling like a flag in the wind.

"By all means, don't let me hold you back." *Why did I say that? Did I actually mean it?*

"Nah, I'm good." The left side of his mouth curled into his trademark smile.

"Okay then." I chuckled nervously but delighted in his response.

"Okay then," he repeated. "Read the book to me," he added after a pause of us looking at each other through the too small and too intangible screens.

"Are you serious?"

"Why not?

"Don't you need to shower?"

"Can you smell me or something?" He answered with a question.

Recalling his manly scent after his fight, I wished I could.

"No. But … won't it be boring for you?"

"Nah. It wouldn't be the first time."

Which was true. On occasion, when we didn't have any money to spend or anything to do, Sebastian came over to my house, where I usually ended up reading whatever book I currently enjoyed to him. He always said listening to me was better than reading himself. He liked the rhythm I put to it and how I changed my voice ever so slightly for the different characters. Sebi also enjoyed looking at me. A memory of his face looking up at me flashed to the front of my mind like it wasn't the same age as a fifth-grader.

"Recap first," he requested, visibly getting comfortable on some kind of chair.

After fulfilling this plea, I began to read from page sixty-four.

"If I was still teenage Maddison, every inch of paper on my desk would be covered in hearts…."

I didn't look up from the book but still caught his smirk with my peripheral vision.

Page after page, I continued in the story of a girl twitter-pated by a boy. Our encounter was redolent to a few of my senses. What I couldn't experience, however, was the sense of touch as my hand ran through his thick hair while he laid across my lap listening. The memory of it would have to do.

I wondered if he remembered that part as well. If he did, he didn't voice it.

9

I stayed up reading to Sebastian later than I should have, proven by how much I dragged at work the next day. What typically took me less than an hour to calculate and enter currently trickled into my third hour of the workday. But did I regret last night? Not one bit. Sebastian always had the ability to make me feel like nothing else mattered.

Only that mentality would be dangerous to slip back into. I had actual responsibilities now, dozens of accounts I couldn't let backup. There had to be some kind of limit set on how late we stayed up chatting when I had work the next morning. I wondered if he functioned any better than me, with an hour less sleep to boot.

So for the first time ever, I pulled out my phone and sent him a message instead of replying to his, fully expecting him not to respond until lunch break or even between work and practice. Or not at all until 9:45—his 10:45.

Me: Hope you aren't as tired as I am. I'm about to hook up a caffeine IV drip.

I put my phone back in the drawer and honed my brain onto the three-point-one million dollar account, which needed my full attention. That is, for all of twelve seconds until my phone buzzed against the metal drawer, causing more ruckus than if the ringer was on.

Sebastian: I might be on my third cup of coffee myself.

Me: I guess we can't pull all-nighters anymore like when we were youths.

Sebastian: It sure is fun to pretend tho, right?

I nodded my head and bit my lip, *and* caught Steve peeking over with not-so-pleased eyes. Never before had I felt like he looked at me as a typical young female until then. For all I knew, he'd been watching me since the clanging noise my phone made filled our office.

"Sorry." I slid the phone into my purse instead of the drawer in case Sebastian responded even though I hadn't replied to his last message after being "caught."

"Londyn," Sasha, the office manager, said as she walked in.

Relief my phone wasn't in my hand, or she hadn't come in one minute earlier, ran down through my legs and exited my pinky toes.

"Ma'am?"

"Ralph needs you. Head to his office as soon as you can."

"Sure." I stood and brushed my hands against my slacks, Sasha already halfway down the hall.

"Ooooh, they caught you," Steve said quietly. "Probably on one of the cameras."

"What?" I gasped and turned to face him. "I didn't know there were cameras."

"Kidding. Couldn't pass it up."

I was about to say, "I owe you one," but remembered how he didn't eat apples for a solid week even after I incessantly told him I was messing with Donald.

"Whatever" left my lips instead like a childish comeback, giving him further stereotypical ammo against me.

Navigating the halls made me want to bite my nails. As I turned the corner, I settled with myself it probably concerned the traveling training position. Or so I hoped.

The door wasn't entirely shut, so I knocked before walking in.

"Come in," Ralph called.

Upon entering, Donald occupied another seat, his face not so bright. A rush of fear for the previous scolding about co-worker conversations I seemed to escape hit me in the face like a burst of hot air.

"You wanted to see me, sir?"

"Sure did. Close the door, please." He took a stack of paper from his desk and slid them between his hands, tapping to line them up. Stapling the corner, he passed the pile to me. I noticed as I took the papers, Donald also held a copy. As I looked down at the cover sheet, I one hundred percent expected it to say "Office Code of Conduct" or something along those lines. It was blank.

"What's this?" I asked.

"A new buyout."

Every nerve ending in my body sighed in relief. Even my posture relaxed as I mollified into the chair. I lowered my head and turned to Donald to see the look on his face. He smirked. He played me. I squinted my eyes at him for the briefest of seconds before looking back up at my boss. If Ralph wouldn't have noticed, I might've stomped on Donald's foot with my heel.

"This time, however, we have a whole new venture. I need my dream team on it."

"He means us," Donald leaned over and whispered, but not like he didn't want Ralph to hear him.

"How so, new venture wise?" I asked.

"Natural gas. They have more of it up in the Northeast than they can handle. Seems like they need help from some Texans. Now I know I told you these traveling stints would be few and far between, and it's only been a month since the last one, but I need you. Whether you want to fully accept the position now or not is still up to you. This trip can be one more under your belt to help you decide."

"To clarify, by going on this trip, I'm not committing to the position yet?"

"Correct."

"Where is it?" I asked as I flipped open the packet he handed me.

"Pennsylvania. Bradford County. Monroe is the exact place you're headed."

"Monroe, Pennsylvania. That sounds far away," I stated.

"It's not too bad. About a five-hour flight. You actually fly into New York and drive about forty-five minutes south to the small town."

"New York?" I perked up. Again, I should've known which states touched and how our nation was sprawled out, but Geography was the subject I crammed for before an exam and forgot as soon as I aced it.

"Yes. However, this trip will be different from our last one." Donald spoke up. "Tell her that part," he said to Ralph.

I looked at Donald, then back to Ralph, waiting to learn what apparently they both already knew that I didn't.

"This trip might be a bit longer," Ralph said. Donald cleared his throat, apparently unhappy with the answer. "At least a month is the projection," my boss admitted.

"A month?" I asked. Double the time frame from Illinois.

"Yes. And...?" Donald urged Ralph.

"We rented a house for you both. *You* will stay for a month, Donald ... might stay longer."

I turned to my ~~co-worker~~ friend. "How long?"

He shrugged. "I won't get a return ticket yet."

"This is a lot of information all at once." I abandoned the papers in my lap and massaged my temples a fraction to reset.

"Agreed. Why don't you think about it and let me know by Wednesday? I need you, so I'm willing to make the compensation kindly worth your while." He motioned for me to flip a few more pages.

My eyes were a millimeter from physically popping out when I saw the figure almost quadruple my regular monthly paycheck—with a stipend budget on top of that.

"I'll do it!" If my interest hadn't already been piqued by being closer to Sebastian, seeing the amount of money I could make was really hard to pass up. And I knew exactly what I would do with the extra income: send my parents on a trip—a much-deserved vacation.

"Well, all right then, Bridges. It's you and me, round two." Donald raised his hand for a fist bump.

"So it is." I landed my closed hand on his fist.

"The dream team, he called us," Donald puffed his chest and tipped his head in Ralph's direction.

"You two can get back to work now. I have to make sure all my ducks are in a row. You leave one week from today, so do whatever you need to as well to get your things in order."

"Yes, sir," left my mouth as, "Sounds good," escaped Donald's.

He opened the door for me as we walked out of our boss's office.

I smacked Donald in the chest with my packet. "How long did you know about this?"

"The possibility? A couple of weeks. The details? Only this morning."

"And no return ticket for you? What's that all about?"

"I have the possibility to become the Northeast regional sales manager. This will be my trial run."

"How so?" I asked.

"I'm not so sure I want to stop doing sales myself and only oversee others. I committed to the interim position for three months."

Three months.

"Seriously?" I sighed a bit.

"You're gonna miss me, I know. It's going to be okay." He patted my shoulder.

"You and that big head of yours." I shrugged his hand off.

"Come on, admit it. You'll miss me when you leave and I stay," Donald prodded.

"Maybe two."

"Out of ten?"

"Percent," I said in a flat tone.

"Yes!" He pulled his elbow down into his side, his hand clenched in a fist. "I knew it."

"Two percent is almost nothing." I laughed at his false enthusiasm.

"But it isn't nothing." Donald lifted his pointer finger.

"Do you think you could actually make the move permanently?" I asked as we started toward our offices.

"There isn't a whole lot holding me here. Perhaps moving away will finally help me ... move forward." He rubbed the back of his neck.

Oh! That's why you're taking the opportunity. Natalie.

Or the lack of Natalie was more fitting. My heart held a beat for him.

"Three percent. I'll miss you at least three percent."

"Imagine how much higher it'll be after we live together."

"Or worse." I looked up and calculated in the air with a finger. "Yup, a greater chance of worse."

"*Or*, we could become besties." He shimmied his shoulders in a feminine manner. "A month is a long time."

"Not *that* long." I laughed. For a pause, I second-guessed if I should leave for so long. But like Donald, I didn't have anything keeping me here. Hopefully, a month away would solidify the relationships in my life with further clarity. "I have a ton to do. Better get to it."

"Sure. Oh, one thing Ralph forgot to mention. We get a rental car this go-round, seeing as how we have to drive an hour from the airport."

"How nice to have my own personal chauffeur." I touched my bun.

"Yeah, yeah." Donald kept walking past my open door as I turned into the accounting office.

"You were right, Steve. They caught me on camera. But they caught you too." I grimaced so deep, the tendons in my neck stood out. "Something about the printer/copy machine."

"Really?" His hands dropped from the desk to his husky thighs.

"Afraid so. Sasha said she'd come get you in a few. They had to cue the tape."

Steve's palm rubbed his forehead a little too aggressively.

"Whoa, Steve. I was only getting you back for earlier."

"What? Then how did you know about the copy machine?"

"Total guess. And I definitely *don't* want to know."

"I guarantee it's not what you're thinking," he said as he half stood to make sure no one occupied the hallway. "On occasion, I've used the copier for personal reasons—"

"Really!" I held up my hand. "Don't need to be in the know."

"For my kids. Art projects, homework, that kind of thing. We don't have a printer at home. I asked the first time, but after that, I went ahead and assumed the answer was always yes."

"So, you use the company equipment as your own personal Office Center?"

He pulled his fingers across his lips and threw away the fictional key.

Fine. I took his signal and changed the subject. "Looks like you're getting your office back to yourself for a bit."

"Oh?"

"I leave next week with Donald to Pennsylvania. For a *month*."

"Wow, that's quite the stretch."

"No joke." I huffed as I used my new found energy surge to get through the day and attempted to figure out the next portion of my life. Thank God I didn't cringe at the thought of being around Donald any longer. Had this been the proposal last go-around, I probably would've said no. And never would've run into Sebastian.

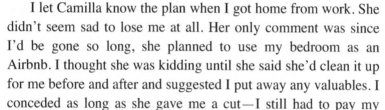

I let Camilla know the plan when I got home from work. She didn't seem sad to lose me at all. Her only comment was since I'd be gone so long, she planned to use my bedroom as an Airbnb. I thought she was kidding until she said she'd clean it up for me before and after and suggested I put away any valuables. I conceded as long as she gave me a cut—I still had to pay my portion of the rent even though I was gone. Which wouldn't be a problem with the extra pay and lack of any bills while in Pennsylvania. But still.

Typically, I didn't call Roman. He called me. I usually sent a text requesting, "Call me when you can," without insight into his schedule. That call came Wednesday night. He returned to town on Friday evening, so we planned on spending Saturday together before I left.

Oddly enough, after talking to Sebastian practically daily, I hadn't heard from him since our tiny conversation Monday while I was at work. The good thing about our lack of communication was I had more time to finish what I needed. And with all of the busywork, I hadn't counted exactly how many days passed since I talked to him. If I hadn't heard from him by Saturday night, I planned to reach out after I finished my to-do list.

At work on Thursday, I packed a box to ship to the office in Monroe. Some of my files and invoices couldn't be finished before I left. Not knowing how much time I'd have to devote to any of my other accounts left me a touch anxious.

Friday was spent collaborating with Steve on the accounts he inherited from me now that I gained such a huge one. As we worked together, I sensed he was a hair jealous I'd received the new big account. Steve didn't have the freedom to travel like I did. And frankly, being able to go without a reason to keep me home left me equally jealous of him. Neither one of us vocalized our insecurities.

9:45, Friday night, my phone rang the unique tone for the face chat in the messenger app. How he was so consistent in his timing was beyond me.

"It's about time," I said as soon as his picture filled my screen with a *swoop*.

"There you are." He ran a hand through his wet hair.

"Where have you been?" I asked, trying not to sound too insecure in my prodding.

"I got a last-minute offer for a fight in Arizona. They needed someone to fill in after a fighter tore his ACL. I used three vacation days to prepare, travel, and fight."

"Awesome. Did you win?"

"I did." As he smiled his iconic grin, the cut on his slightly-swollen bottom lip came into view.

"Why didn't you tell me sooner?"

"Believe it or not, I forgot my phone. I was so pumped, I left it at my apartment on Tuesday. Not that I had any missed messages from you anyway." His eyes kept on talking, morphing into a larger version of their typical size. "This thing works both ways, you know?" He shook the phone in his hand, tick-tocking his face around the screen.

"I know. My week was also a bit unusual."

"Do tell." He plopped onto a couch.

"I have another traveling job. I leave Monday."

"Nice. Where you headed?"

"A city called Monroe in Pennsylvania. I, uh ... actually fly into New York."

"What? Which part?" He sat up straight.

"Horseheads. And no, I didn't make that up, so don't laugh at me."

"Are you serious right now? You're coming up here?"

"I am." I nodded.

"For how long?"

"That's the kicker."

"Oh, not long enough to —"

"A month." I suppressed a smile, pursing my lips together with all of my might.

"No way!?" I shrugged and left my mouth shut. "Tell me everything." He pressed. "When do you get here? I need details."

"I haven't read the whole packet yet, all I know is I leave Monday, and they rented a house for us."

"Us? The same guy from last time?"

"Yeah, Donald."

He scratched his temple. "I wonder how far that is from Roche —"

"Two and a half hours," I interrupted, sincerely hoping it didn't seem extra that I'd already looked it up.

"I will see you while you're here. You hear me, sweets?"

I bit my bottom lip, forgetting for a second he could see every inch of my face.

"I'd like that," I said.

10

Before I could finish packing, before I could gleefully head to the airport with more than work plans on my mind, I had to see Roman. Feel out how my absence would affect him. After I told him about my travel plans, he planned a fun-filled day for us with a small commute to an outdoor festival at a massive lake. Activities happened in and out of the water, so I wore my swimsuit under a swing dress in case he wanted to get in the lake.

And it was a good thing I did because Roman informed me he planned on renting a jet ski. Two actually, but I told him I'd prefer to ride on his rather than trying to navigate one myself.

A decision I was very pleased with until the same youthful soul I saw in the orchard came back out to play. Had I been on my own jet ski, I might've maxed out at fifteen miles per hour. I wrapped my arms around Roman for dear life as we bounced on wave after wave created by the boats around us. He was nowhere near as fit as Sebastian, but calling him out of shape wasn't accurate either. Roman's build was very average. Not much fat, not much muscle. He hollered in excitement as we hit a big breaker, while I mostly sounded like a younger version of myself. The scared version.

"Roman." *Bump*.

"Slow." *Boom*.

"Down." *Thud*.

"What's that?" He turned his head.

"Please. Slow down. I'd rather not fly into the water if I don't have to."

He eased to a stop. "Sorry, sunshine. I didn't mean to scare you." Roman ran his hand down my leg in an affectionate apology that soothed my woes. "Now I know why you didn't want your own."

"Speed and I aren't like, the best of friends." I laughed, still a bit on edge.

"You know what, I saw an option you might like better. What do you say we head back and trade this puppy in for something a bit more leisure?"

"Perfect."

We returned to the dock and surrendered the keys and life vests.

"Can we reserve a catamaran?" Roman asked the lady behind the rental booth.

"Sure can." She grabbed a different clipboard and flipped the page. "One will be back in thirty minutes. Would you like that time slot?"

Roman looked over at me. Since I wasn't entirely sure what a catamaran was, I simply smiled.

"We'll take it. Thanks."

"I'm going to head back to our locker to get some more sunscreen out of my bag. My shoulders are feeling a little warm." I leaned in to say as he filled out the reservation slip.

"Sure. I bet it'll be here not long after you get back."

I walked down to the lockers, which had obviously been rented for this particular event. Rows of the stacked metal boxes sat smack in the middle of the grassy area of the park.

After locating our locker, using the code to retrieve my bag, and lathering up a full new layer of sunblock, I pulled out my phone to check the time. A notification bar decorated my screen.

Sebastian: I can't wait to see you.

I smiled. No, my soul smiled. Instantly, Sebastian's text centered me substantially more than moments before when Roman touched me. Interesting. But I didn't respond, not yet. I was here with Roman today and already had a hard enough time figuring out the happenings in my life regarding these men. Not to mention feeling guilty about the situation too.

It would be hard enough not to think about Sebastian when I returned to the lake.

As it turned out, a catamaran was a boat with a net-type thing in the back. Roman helped me onto the boat, and we sat on a bench seat until the captain got us to where we'd anchor.

The wind in my hair was refreshing and much gentler than how the jet ski caused the breeze to assault my skin. After heading out into the middle of the lake for about ten minutes, the captain pulled to a stop. The gentleness of the scene became more evident when the roar of the motor ceased.

"All right, folks. This is where we'll lay anchor. I'll head below deck to give you some privacy. We head back in about," he looked at his watch, "fifty minutes."

"Thank you, sir," Roman said before helping me stand.

I was a bit nervous about transitioning from the hard deck onto the netted lounge that ran almost the entire width of the boat like a giant water hammock.

"Let me go first so I can help you," Roman coached as he stepped ahead of me onto the netting with ease. As he helped me down, I was grateful crossing over went smoother than I feared.

"Thanks." I half crawled, half walked on my knees to get to the center of the net, hoping I didn't look ridiculous. Once I settled, Roman followed suit. A long pillow was attached to a portion of the netting, so I rested my head there and waited for Roman to get comfortable as well.

"This better?" he asked as he laid on his side, looking at me.

"Much better." I'd never been on a jet ski or a boat of any kind, so the day was quite eventful. Roman, per usual, had more experience with lavish affairs.

For a while, it was quiet. I laid on my back with my eyes closed, feeling the twitch of every pore as they absorbed vitamin D with pleasure.

"I can't believe you're leaving for a month."

Turning my head, Roman continued to look me over in my swimsuit. He reached out his hand and traced around my bare stomach. Unsettled with the more intimate touch, I grabbed his hand.

"I know. It's pretty crazy. I have a feeling it'll go by pretty fast. The last two-week trip did, at least." My eyes squinted in the bright sunlight. I wished I'd grabbed my sunglasses from the locker, but another situation stole my attention.

Roman brought his eyes to mine and tried a different approach, running his hand down my arm. "Maybe our trips will overlap regionally again. That would be fun."

"Yeah." *Would it?*

"Either way, we can still see each other when you get back." He leaned in and kissed me. I kissed him until he grabbed my hip and pulled me in. Prior to today, Roman hadn't been so forward in his physical advances. Was he assuming we dated long enough for him to earn something from me? Or was I reading into it? It could very well be because we were barely dressed, increasing his attraction. And temptation. But I wasn't up for that, especially if we weren't in a committed relationship.

At that moment, the necessity to ask Roman to clarify our status was greater than the fear of losing him. Plus, if he saw me as his girlfriend, that would drastically change my interactions with Sebastian from here on out.

"Roman?"

"Mmhmm?"

The words swirled in my head as I tried to pick the least clingy method of delivery.

"How do you—"

"Okay, you two. Head back up to your seats. It's time to go." The captain's interruption carried off my question like a seagull nabbing a meal.

Roman helped me up, never asking me to finish my question before taking me home.

What he didn't say: "I'll miss you."

What I didn't say: "I'll miss you."

However our relationship could be labeled, apparently it wasn't strong enough to warrant missing each other.

My time with Roman was nice as usual. Just nice. I found myself more excited to have the opportunity to see Sebastian here and there over the next month than I was sad to not see Roman in that same amount of time.

Though it was hard, I came to a decision that night as I stared at the textured ceiling. While away, I would only focus on Sebastian in an attempt to end one of these relationships whatever they were. If I was able to not worry about Roman's involvement in my life, wouldn't that speak for itself? Likewise, it could very well be a fantasy of the one who got away was greater than the actual connection I sensed with Sebi. Perhaps nothing would magically change in thirty days, but I hoped for clarity in my heart, at least.

———————⚓———————

My skin was a nice golden brown when I woke up Sunday morning, ready to finish packing and start the next thirty-one days.

I packed ten work outfits, a few of which could be swapped around to create new looks: both work and date attire.

"So you leave me tomorrow, huh?" Camilla walked up from behind me and wrapped her tiny arms around me in a hug.

"I do. First thing in the morning. Probably before you wake up."

"Very true." She squeezed one more time before releasing her hold but stayed right by my side.

"What will you do without me?"

"Enjoy the meat-free kitchen. Rake in the cash for leasing your bedroom. Hopefully, have a date or two. Dozen, whatever." Her voice wasn't the least bit saddened.

"If you let some creeper stay in my bed, so help me, Cam...."

"I'll wash the sheets. Don't worry."

"And I get *half* of whatever you make."

"Uh, I'm thinking more around a sixty-forty split."

"You're using *my* room!"

"But doing all the work of cleaning before and after and entertaining the guests."

"Fine, whatever. Make sure you know the guidelines in case something is damaged or stolen."

"Sure thing. I'm all over it." Only she wasn't because she pulled out her phone and started looking. "How was yesterday?" she asked as she read the fine print.

"Nice. Lots of lake activities."

"Not so sure about nice then. It's ridiculously too hot outside for me. I already declined a couple of outdoor photoshoots. I can't be getting this skin sunburned and wrinkled."

Camilla wasn't wrong. The heat index in Dallas, Texas, was still hot and humid at the end of August. Heading up north would provide a nice respite from the three-digit temperatures.

"Such a hard life you lead."

"Someone's gotta do it. Where are you at, up here?" She pointed to her head. I didn't have to ask for clarity to know she referred to my guy situation.

"Same. I almost asked Roman what we are, but got interrupted. He was rather handsy yesterday."

"Oh. Is my little Londyn rounding the corner from G rated to PG?"

"You are so extra." I chuckled. "Had I never run into Sebastian, this trip would have an entirely different tone. I'm kinda hoping to get some clarity on both fronts, actually."

She nodded. "And here?" She reached out and touched my chest, right above my heart.

Looking down, embarrassed at what my face might do, I admitted, "I'm excited to see Sebastian. And he is too."

"Ooooh. The love triangle intensifies." Camilla swirled her finger up into my hair, then rubbed her hands together at the juicy drama.

"Not so sure about that. It might be a triangle, but love is a whole other story. Feels more Bermuda-ish."

"Well, whatever's going on in that genius brain of yours, you better not mention Roman even *once* if Sebastian tries to kiss you again. Make that don't mention him regardless. You do you on this trip. As a single, uncommitted woman."

Was I truly single? "I'll try. Honestly, I don't know if I'll get to see Sebastian at all. Not to mention if it's a wise thing to do."

"But you want to."

I looked up, surrendering to let my face do what it will, and nodded.

———————

One minute late, at 9:46, I got a message from Sebastian.

Sebastian: All ready to head my way?

I internally swooned in an instant. I wanted to head his direction more than work—no doubt. Trying not to read into his level of excitement was hard.

Me: It isn't really your way, is it?

Sebastian: Sure it is. I

I what? Was that a typo? The screen froze for a second before the bouncing dots telling me he was typing appeared. Disappeared. Reappeared.

"What are you doing to me?" I said to myself, to him.

Sebastian: I thought maybe I could meet you at the airport before you're even farther away.

Me: That would be nice, but I'm not really sure how long I'll be at the airport. And I have my co-worker with me too.

Sebastian: I don't mind if it isn't a long time. What if I came, and we got something to eat before you head to PA?

Me: In the middle of the day? Don't you have work?

Sebastian: I can take up to three half-days a month. This is the last week of August, and I haven't used any.

Did I want to take him up on that offer? One hundred percent.

Did I want to face the razzing from Donald? Not even one percent. However, I'd get the end result of seeing Sebastian.

Hoping I wasn't making him nervous by delaying my response, I looked up how far he had to drive for these plans. An hour and thirty-six minutes. Surely he hadn't looked it up.

Me: It isn't a short drive. Are you sure you want to make that commute just to have lunch with me?

Once again, the little dots forced me to hold my breath in anticipation of his response. I looked away, hoping the answer would come faster. You know, like the whole, "A watched pot never boils" thing.

Sebastian: It isn't a bad drive at all. I'll gladly make the commute to see you.

Lord, have mercy. If my heart didn't melt down into my stomach and morph into butterflies, fluttering back up into my chest cavity with energetic pulses. How was he able to make me feel like this after so many years? With words on a tiny little screen at that.

Me: Let's do it!

Sebastian: Awesome. Send me your flight info, please. You, miss, will be seeing me tomorrow.

"Ahhh!" I threw my phone down onto the bed, and victory danced like a professional running back after a touchdown, going back from one foot to the other like I stood on lava.

My door flung open before I finished my move. Camilla instantly pulled off her house shoe. "Is it a spider?"

"Yeah, a huge one. Crawled under the door and went straight down the hall to your room." When I changed my dance to another move with my subpar dance skills, the gig was up.

"You're annoying," she said before throwing her shoe at me. I wish I could say I dodged it, but book worms don't move very fast.

I woke up more excited than I ~~had in years~~ could even remember. Today, I'd board a plane and fly to New York. Yeah, it was for work, but I could see Sebastian. Him. The one I never stopped thinking about—the facts registered in my head but didn't fully compute in my brain.

After thinking all night about what to say to Donald, I finally fell asleep, more concerned about looking refreshed in the morning. Bags under my eyes wouldn't be a good accessory to my look.

We planned to meet at the office, and Sammy, the receptionist, would take us to the airport. I arrived a few minutes early and went into my office to make sure I didn't forget anything and left the file cabinet key for Steve.

"Have fun," Steve said as I gathered my bags and walked toward the door.

"Thanks. Don't miss me too much."

"Oh, I'll try." He wouldn't have to try.

In the main lobby, Donald waited for me. I should've known he'd mess with me today.

"Ready to head to the Big Apple with me?" he asked, holding a pair of apples a few inches under his chin.

"I don't know whether to hit you or laugh."

"We *are* on company property. You might get in trouble for hitting a fellow employee, so I suggest laughing. Or eating." He tossed one of the apples to me. I stuck it in my bag while he took a bite so big out of his, half the apple disappeared.

"You guys ready?" Sammy asked.

"Sure are. Let's get going," Donald answered, still chewing, full of excitement.

As soon as we checked in and settled in at our gate with an hour to spare, I turned to Donald in the seat next to me.

"Um, personal space, please."

"Oh geez," I quipped.

"What's that weird look in your eyes?"

"You know how you shared the situation you're in with Natalie?"

"I recall spilling my soul to you, yes."

"Well," I paused, hesitant to share personal details. "I have a situation of my own not too far off from that." I sighed, preparing myself for his kickback but prayed he wouldn't. "So, the fighter I ran into on the plane..."

"Yeah?"

"We weren't just friends. He was my boyfriend."

"Nice." Donald extended his hand for a high-five.

I lowered his arm. "It was nice. Until he moved away, and that was the end of us. I hadn't talked to him in eight years before that flight home."

"Wow. Tragic."

"Tell me about it. And like you, I might not have fully moved on, like … ever. Didn't stop thinking about him for sure."

"I see. And you're telling me this now because?"

"Because he and I have been talking for the last couple of weeks, and he wants to come see me."

"Oh."

Here we go.

"Today. When we land in New York."

"*Oh,*" he stressed his reply.

"This is the part where you get to be the super cool friend and wait to start our drive until after I can grab lunch with Sebastian."

"Ah. It's all making sense now. Does he live in the area?"

"Not quite. He's in Rochester, but he's going to make the ninety-six-minute drive."

"Wow!"

"What?" I asked.

"This guy is going to drive for over an hour to take you to lunch."

I pressed my lips together to hide my girlish grin and nodded.

"You must have left an impression on him."

I sure hope so. He left one on me.

Lifting one shoulder, I replied, "I guess I did."

"And I'm assuming you don't want me to be the third wheel at your lunch?"

"Ideally speaking, no, I don't."

"Understandable." Donald ran his hand along his jaw from his chin to his ear and back, scratching his faint beard. "I'll tell you what. I've wanted to see the new superhero movie, so why don't I find a theater that serves meals, and we can both get 'lunch' before we hit the road to Pennsylvania."

His calm and strategic response surprised me. "Are you serious right now?"

"Of course."

Somehow I had a feeling Donald would pull a "you owe me one" in the future, but it'd be worth it. I hoped.

"Thank you." I sat forward and grinned.

"Now boarding group A for flight four-sixteen to Elmira/ Corning Regional New York," left the overhead speakers.

11

My heart pounded in my chest as we walked down the terminal. I messaged Sebastian before takeoff, letting him know I was headed his direction, and again as soon as we landed—even though I didn't get the all-clear to take my phone off of airplane mode. God forgive me if I caused something to go haywire with the landing gear.

Donald suggested I still go with him to get the rental car so we could leave our stuff in the trunk before he went off to the movies, and I left with Sebastian. *Left with Sebastian, are you kidding me?* My palms turned clammy.

Sebastian called me through the messaging app to let me know he just parked in short-term parking and was about to walk in. My stomach twisted in anticipation as we waited out front after dropping off our luggage in the silver Nissan Altima—our car for the next month.

"Hey," Donald interrupted my scanning the crowd for Sebastian. "Send me your number so we can meet back up."

"Oh, right. That would've been a disaster," I nervously chuckled.

"And," he paused. *Here comes the teasing.* "Have fun."

"Thanks. This is very cool of you to do for me, Donald."

"Don't mention it." He mock-punched my shoulder. "Is that him?"

I turned. It was *him*. "Yeah." I waved and walked forward, every step a resounding yes. Yes. Yes. Feelings I somehow managed to hold at bay as we chatted the last couple of weeks were front and center. Present for class.

"Hi," was all I could say when we got close enough. Much to my delight, Sebastian opened his arms for a hug.

"Hey, Londyn. Welcome to my state."

"Thanks." I giggled.

"Same to you, sir." It wasn't until Sebastian addressed him that I knew Donald had walked up behind me. The men exchanged a firm handshake.

"Thank you. So you're taking Bridges to eat, and then?" Donald asked Sebastian as if investigating his intentions. Instead, I answered.

"Can he drop me off at the theater you're going to?"

"That works. I'll let you know when I get my ticket so you'll have a better idea of what time you need to be back."

"Sounds good." I looked from Donald to Sebastian and smiled.

"I don't think we have to check-in at the office today, but we might not want to push it too late to head to Pennsylvania."

"For sure," I said.

"Please take care of her. I'm responsible for keeping that brain in working order for our company," Donald requested, but his tone wasn't entirely joking. In fact, it was kind of a big brother thing I never experienced in life.

"Of course. I'll return Londyn to you safe and sound." Sebastian snickered.

"You ready then?" I asked.

"Let's get out of here," he said, his left-sided grin quickening my pulse. Sebastian was familiar but foreign. I spent less than two hours with him in eight years. The familiarity he pulled from me made me want to reach out and grab his hand, but the foreign was so … foreign—unwelcomingly foreign. I honestly didn't know how to act or what to do.

My heart knew him. My head knew him. My eyes were learning him all over again.

"You don't have any bags?" Sebastian asked as we walked away.

"Of course I do. I'm out here for a month." *A whole month, close to you.* "We put them in the rental already."

"Darn. How am I supposed to kidnap you if you don't have your bags? So much for that plan."

"Oh, please." *Please!* Escaping with Sebastian wouldn't be so bad.

His flirtatious ways swayed me once again on the pendulum from the guy who once knew everything about me to the man I was barely getting to know. We made it to his car, a black Mazda Miata. Sebastian was right behind me to open my door.

"You drive a Batmobile?" I flirted, testing how it felt coming out and what type of response I'd get in return.

And God help me because my choice caught his attention rather well.

He leaned in, his jaw almost grazing my neck, and whispered, "Shhhh. Don't give away my secret identity."

Yup, I still had much to learn about this man who had me weak in the knees within minutes.

As Sebastian closed the door and walked around to get in, I uttered, "Oh. My. Gosh," to myself in the silence before praying time would go slowly for the next couple of hours.

"I looked up a couple places we can go. I wish we were closer to my home so I could show you my favorite place. You'd love it." How he said, 'you'd love it' with such confidence made me bite the inside of my cheek not to smile. I was young again around him. And I was more than okay with that.

"Wherever you want is fine with me."

"Let's *do this* then." Sebastian rolled the windows of his sports car down and navigated the airport's departures, arrivals, and long term parking jumble of lanes to the exit. The air was already much cooler than we experienced in Texas a few days until September. The breeze sweeping through my loose hair only further enticed a carefree state of mind.

I looked over at Sebastian as he drove, still in total shock this was actually happening. He turned and caught me in the act, then smiled.

"This is pretty surreal," I admitted.

"Sure is," he agreed.

What I wouldn't give to eat him up along with my lunch. Hold his hand, kiss his lips. But what would be the point? Our few hours would be up, and I'd be headed to a different state from him once again.

"Can't say I pegged you as the sports-car type." I started a conversation in an attempt to not waste away our time in negative thought.

"Well, that's because I was the no-car type back in the day." Sebastian chuckled as he ran his hand around the steering wheel.

"True." I laughed.

"I know it's more car than I need, but I figured I'd earned it. And it isn't like I went out and got a Ferrari or anything."

"You for sure earned it." If his work ethic remained the same, I knew it to be true.

As soon as Sebastian pulled into the parking lot, I began to laugh. Even after all these years, he remembered I preferred a simple place over something ritzy. My heart did a flipity-flop at the sentiment. *He knows me.*

Our go-to spot in high school was a mom and pop diner that made breakfast twenty-four/seven. The restaurant we parked in front of looked about as old and not-so-well-maintained.

"This is the closest thing I could find to Franky's."

Franky's was close enough to my house for me to walk and on his bus route. Thankfully, the food was good because I don't think we could've met up anywhere else anyway.

His statement communicated he looked up the area and tried to find a special place to take me. Which shouldn't have come as a surprise. Sebastian had always invested in me. Into us. Into the time we spent together. We, of all people, knew you didn't have to spend a lot of money to have a good time together, outlasting all of the couples at our school by several months. Until he moved.

The last thought pulled me back into the present.

"Shall we find out if their biscuits and gravy can compare?" I asked.

"I'm sure they won't, but let's try them anyway."

We opened our doors at the same time and headed for the entrance. A bell clanged against the inside of the glass door as Sebastian opened it for me.

The booths looked like they were made in the seventies. However, they didn't show five decades of wear. The lighting was low, mostly lit by a dated hanging pendant light above each table. The whole place probably only sat forty people, tops. Perfect.

"Table for two?" the waitress dressed to match the old decor asked.

"Yes, please," Sebastian answered.

Being referred to as two, paired with Sebi, was exactly right.

She led us to a booth and waited for us to slide in before placing menus onto the table.

As I looked over the menu, my phone sounded in my purse. Donald sent a text to let me know his movie started in ten minutes and was two and a half hours long. Even though it wasn't long enough, I was thankful the span was longer than a typical lunch break.

"Everything all right?" he asked.

"Mmhmm. You have me until 5:15-ish."

Sebastian looked down at his watch. "Good."

Besides our online conversations, this would be the longest stretch of time we had together since high school. Our flight weeks ago was right under two hours, and he didn't sit with me for the duration of it. At the fight night—when he kissed me, though I tried not to think about that—we had all of ten minutes. Ten, fantastic minutes. It helped that Sebastian sat across from me, wearing a shirt. Though the tight fit around his arms and looseness around his waist helped my mind recall how well maintained *he* was.

We ordered our own entrees and a plate of biscuits and gravy —like we always use to do. The biscuits and gravy went in the middle of the table for us to share. I liked to eat the salty portion of my meal first and save the sweet bits for last. Sebastian, on the other hand, ate a bite of this and a bite of that until it was gone. He out ate me then, probably still would now.

"How's this fitting into your diet plan?" I asked, looking at the large spread.

"It doesn't. I should be okay if I keep my next few meals low. Probably do a protein shake for dinner. Either way, I don't have a fight coming up soon, so I should be fine."

"Good, because these biscuits and gravy give Franky's a run for their money." It was also fair to say since I hadn't had the local comfort food from our home town in close to six years, perhaps my memory simply remembered how it tasted to eat a meal with Sebastian looking back at me. It tasted amazing.

We settled into a conversation about work, what our jobs had in common, and what traits were nothing alike. He made predictions based on previous numbers, whereas all I did was enter numbers and make sure more came in than went out.

It was fairly obvious he hadn't eaten some good calories in a while as he wiped every bit of the gravy from the plate with a piece of toast. I chuckled.

"What? Might as well enjoy it if I'm going to bust my butt for it later."

The waitress brought the ticket, which he paid for when I tried to split it.

"Can you tell me what that is?" Sebastian asked when she brought back his change from a fifty dollar bill. He pointed to the wall behind me, one I hadn't noticed. With his question, I turned to look myself.

"The dollar wall?" The waitress shoved a pen in her hair. "People who eat here can sign a bill and tack it up there. I honestly think it's the owner's method of creating a savings account for when they have to pass it on to someone else."

"Smart." Sebastian laughed. "Do you have a tack?"

"Sure thing, hun. Be right back."

He pulled a pen from his pocket and grabbed one of the bills from his change.

"Care to give me your autograph, miss?"

"I guess I can spare it this once."

I scrawled my name on the top left corner and passed the bill and pen to him. After taking a minute to write more than his name, Sebastian passed it back to the middle so I could see what he added as he put the pen back in his pocket.

Londyn & Sebastian
Reunited, and it feels so good.

Sebi solidified our reunion by etching the lyrics from the song that played on the oldies station during our meal. Tangible proof of our encounter.

I couldn't bring myself to look up and expose the blush on my cheeks but watched how his arms flexed when he pinned our memory marker onto the wall as high as he could reach.

With the food long gone and another hour and a half before he had to drop me off, we headed back to his car and drove around until we found a place to stop. A small park in memory of a fallen state trooper was the perfect place to sit and talk as we looked over the large pond. After reading the monument detailing the tragic loss of the officer and offering a moment of silence, we sat at a bench. A feeling of loss loomed over me for a moment. Loss also happened to us.

"What do you miss most about Texas?" I asked.

"Uh?" He looked off in the distance.

I wanted to believe his hesitation held my name on his lips, but that was most likely a pipe dream.

"The people. New Yorkers aren't as friendly."

Maybe I was included in "the people." I pretended like I was even though the thought would leave me feeling even sadder when he left. Again.

"Hopefully, I encounter some nice people at this new job. If not, it'll be one long month."

"I hear that," Sebastian replied. "Want to walk the path?"

"Sure."

"Good. Those extra calories are hitting me hard."

Not a single preconceived notion was in my head. Okay. That was a lie. I pictured us like we were still dating. Like eight years hadn't passed. Like we could only stay out until the sun went down, but we'd see each other the next day. And the next.

Two emotions warred within me as we rose to walk: the remnants of love for him that never fully faded and frustration for most likely leading myself on. I didn't know if I should soak up the moments or not make them something they weren't. Because in thirty minutes, Sebastian would drop me off, and that could be the end.

Before I could decide how much sentiment my heart could encapsulate, his fingers brushed the inside of my wrist, down my palm, and intertwined with mine.

When I didn't pull away, he gave a squeeze.

"So, numbers chick, can you please explain to me how almost a decade can go by, but it can feel like no time has passed all at once?"

I looked up the few inches he had on me and replied. "That's the kind of numbers you do. I only count and factor." My head dropped. The sight of my hand in his was one I'd seen more times than I could recall, but none felt as special as this moment. One I never thought we'd get. "But I agree."

With only about an hour left before the sun surrendered to the horizon, we walked a couple laps around the park. I locked every moment into my memory, so when I thought of Sebastian in the future, which I no doubt would, I'd have fresh things to recall. But when I was on the verge of tears that our time was almost over, I suggested we go ahead and head back—no need to draw out the inevitable.

Sebastian opened the door for me once again. I wasn't as talkative on the last drive, a characteristic I shared with my younger self. One he hopefully didn't remember.

"Don't shut down on me, Londyn." Make that definitely remembered.

"Sorry. This has been so nice, we just—"

"Still live in different states. I know."

I pointed at him in agreement and bit my bottom lip, forcing myself to hold back the craziness bubbling inside of me.

We pulled into the movie theater parking lot with time to spare, but I couldn't emotionally manage to draw out the last few minutes.

"I'm going to head inside. Thank you so much for coming so far to see me. I had a great time."

"Don't mention it. Me, too. Glad I made the drive." Sebastian's voice was warm, genuine. His honey-brown eyes kept communicating after his words ceased.

I leaned in to hug him across the front seat.

"Oh no, I need a real hug. Get your behind out of my Batmobile."

Another thing he apparently remembered about me: I needed to laugh when I was about to cry.

"Yes, sir." I walked to the back of his car, where he leaned against the trunk.

"Bring it in, Londyn." He opened his stupendous arms and pulled me in. Never in my life had I been hugged like that. Not even by him. His eighteen-year-old arms and chest couldn't compare. Total comfort surrounded me. If only it wasn't fleeting.

"I should go," I said against his chest right over where I knew one of his tattoos was hidden. I shouldn't have allowed myself to remember the image because it caused me to picture him how he looked after his fight. When he kissed me—too good for my sanity.

"You don't have to go yet. Wait another minute." He leaned against his car.

I should've known better. Should've walked away right then. Said my goodbyes and see-you-on-the-flip-sides and gone on with my work trip. But I didn't. Instead, I fell into him and buried my face against his chest, inhaling deep. And because I didn't let go, he pressed his lips to the top of my head and held his position. I was afraid to move because I doubted I could handle a kiss from him. One wouldn't be sufficient.

"Okay." I pushed back a fraction and held my position, allowing a split-second for a kiss before I moved further, unsure whether he'd try or not. He didn't. "I'm gonna go now. Thanks again."

"No, ma'am." Sebastian's strong hands weaved into my hair as his lips sealed our time together with a sweet kiss on my cheek. Was he waiting to see if I'd offer my lips? Should I? "You aren't getting rid of me, Londyn. You'll hear from me again. See me again, too, if I have a say in the matter."

"Okay," I repeated, unsure how else to respond but thrilled at his desire for more. I clasped my hands together in front of me so I wouldn't touch him again. Mustering the strength to make myself walk away proved difficult. But our time was up.

"Talk to you soon, sweets." He waited until I headed inside to refer to me as such. Maybe he hadn't even put much thought into it. Perhaps it rolled off his lips as the distance between us grew.

I turned around once I knew I was far enough that I wouldn't go back for him. He stood in the exact same spot and offered a small wave. I wondered how it felt for him to be the one watching me walk away.

As soon as I got into the theater, I headed to the bathroom to let my emotions function as they willed. Closing myself in a stall and dropping the toilet seat shut, I sat there, heartbeat racing. My heart was evidently clear, it only took one day to reveal, but it didn't solve our distance. A few silent tears dropped from my cheeks.

Today, though it was amazing, only left me wanting more. More I couldn't have beyond the next month.

Why did I do this to myself? How would I get over Sebastian this time?

I stayed there until I needed to meet up with Donald.

"I hope your time was better than mine. That movie was *sad*. Great, but sad," Donald said as he approached me from behind.

I turned. "That's the perfect way to describe my time too."

"Sorry, Bridges. I'll help you feel better with my wit and charm."

"Thanks." I tried to chuckle, but it fell back into my throat.

"You don't look very 'safe and sound.' Do I need to have a talk with that boy?"

"No. I'm fine. Or will be." *I hope*.

"Me too."

I wondered if I had said my last thought out loud or he knew the emotions on my face after experiencing them himself with Natalie.

As we passed the road sign declaring we left New York and entered Pennsylvania, I wished it was as simple for my mind to leave the former state.

12

Sebastian didn't even wait until our drive was over to message me, leaving me to wonder if he was as wrapped up in me as I was in him. Being the passenger in the car, I was fine to type on my phone, but I told him I didn't really like him texting and driving. Sebastian assured me his Batmobile was equipped to keep him safe and did all the messaging and reading for him.

Interacting with Sebastian was two-fold: intrinsic and detrimental.

It brought me life and joy and left me feeling every mile between us. Far. Too. Many. Miles. And I wasn't even back in Texas yet.

Donald pulled into the driveway of the house we'd call home for the next month.

"Do you want to go in first and pick your room?" he asked.

"I don't see a need in that. You're going to be here long term. You should get the master."

"That's kind of you, but the master also most likely has its own bathroom. Which is why *you* should have it."

"Ah. I didn't think about that."

"Yeah. I don't need to see you walking around in your face masks and curlers, giving me nightmares."

"Good news for you, I don't mess with those things. But yes, I'd prefer the bedroom with an attached bathroom if you're offering." Walking around in my nightclothes in front of Donald didn't sound appealing. And perhaps that was also what he was trying to avoid, only didn't want to voice it.

"I am."

"Okay then. I'll clean it before I leave so you can move on over if you want."

"No need. We get cleaning services once a week as part of the deal."

"Nice," I cheered.

"Right?" Donald responded like we were best gal-pals, making me laugh. "Now, that's a better look on your face than what you wore the last hour." I stuck my tongue out at him. "That one too. I'll take anything over the sadness you had going on in this region." He circled his fingers around my face and rushed out his door before I could land the fist I cocked back on his arm.

After popping the trunk to retrieve our bags, Donald called out the digital combination to unlock the front door. I hoped no one around us heard, but it wasn't like this place was booming with people. I walked up the front steps and opened the door, then turned to get my luggage. Instead, I got a *shoo* wave from Donald, so I went inside.

The space was nice. Extremely nice, actually. I wondered how a fully furnished home in such a small town was available for rent. Either that, or our company also had to lease all of the furniture, kitchenware, and linens. I knew this trip cost our company quite a bit, which led me to wonder how much money this account would bring in. For Ralph's sake, it better be a profitable venture.

Peeking into a few rooms, I found the master suite. I fell face-first onto the giant bed dressed with neutral blankets. The mattress was so comfortable, and my heart still so sunken, I could've fallen asleep right then and there.

And I almost did until: "Maybe I take my offer back. This bed is substantially bigger." I lifted my head. "Kidding. Here's your bags, madam. No need to tip."

I dropped my face back into the blanket. "Thanks," came out muffled.

Two-point-four seconds later, I bounced around like a jelly bean in a plastic egg.

Donald jumped on the bed as if it were a trampoline.

"What the heck, man?"

"I'm not letting you get mopey again." He huffed between jumps.

"Get your shoes off my bed! They're full of airport juices."

That made him laugh louder than I'd ever heard. With one more bounce, he pulled his legs out in front of him and collided into the bed on his butt. At least one of us was laughing.

"Airport juices? What are you talking about?"

Even I didn't know why I said juices instead of germs. It was rather funny.

"Germs. I meant to say germs, all right?" I hopped up and hurried away.

"Where are you going?"

"Payback!" I ran into his room and jumped all over his bed. Shoes on and full of airport juices.

Day one was a whole lot of meeting people, learning the differences between crude oil and natural gas, and trying to get my head in the game. Every few minutes, *What's Sebastian doing right now?* popped into my mind. In all reality, our situation wasn't much different from when I was in Texas. We were still hours apart on our own journeys. But how I wished they had the ability to intertwine.

I felt particularly awful for Donald, who tossed me the keys to drive and rubbed his temples. He hunched over the whole drive home.

"You okay, bud?"

"This is not what I expected. I feel like a fish out of water. If I had to decide today, I'd tell Ralph to book my flight back home and find a new person for this position."

"Hey, don't do that. It's day one. I'm sure it'll come to you."

Donald turned to face me but didn't move his hands, peeking through his fingers. "I'm glad they sent you with me. You're growing on me, Bridges."

"Thanks. I'm discovering you aren't a total meathead yourself."

"What are you making me for dinner?" he asked as he dropped his head again.

Instead of awarding his sarcasm with words, I flung my hand in his direction, connecting with his shoulder. Unfortunately, that only encouraged him.

"I saw an apron in the kitchen last night. You can make something from scratch while I enjoy a cigar in my recliner."

"Sure." I decided to play along. "Don't get out of your chair for a single thing. I know you've had a long day and worked so hard. You deserve this."

"Wow! It worked."

"Fat chance, friend." I chuckled.

We ordered a pizza when we got home and watched a show called *Naked and Afraid* on TV. Two strangers, one male, one female, were left in a deserted area to live off the land for three weeks with only the one item they were allowed to bring and each other. Oh, and they are naked. Censored, of course.

"Do you think you'd survive?" Donald asked.

"Um, I'm going to go with a no on that one. Maybe a week, but for sure, not three. What about you?"

"I'd like to think I could. I'm very competent, you know?"

"Are you? Prove it."

"All right. Why don't I show you right now that I could start a fire on my own."

"Have at it, Eagle Scout."

Donald jumped from his seat, went into the backyard, and came back in with a few sticks and dried grass. I tried hard to swallow my laugh.

"Don't burn the house down."

Grabbing a bowl from the cabinet, he assorted the grass into a little bird's nest type thing as we'd seen on the show and began to rub the sticks together. For a second, I thought he actually knew what he was doing.

That was, until he took the stick, held it over the stovetop, and lit it on fire with the gas burner.

"And ... fire! Told you I could do it."

I laughed so hard, a little bit of my pizza crept back up my throat.

When the flame on the grass engulfed, Donald panicked and threw the tinder in the sink to douse it with water. My laughter continued at the shock on his face.

"I guess the one item you'd need to take is a stove then, huh?"

"Sure. A camping one."

My phone vibrated against the coffee table. 9:45.

"See you in the morning. I'm calling it a day."

"Night. I'll let you know if they make it the whole twenty-one days."

I didn't respond because I wanted to hurry into my room to answer the face-chat call. As soon as I accepted, Sebastian's face bloomed onto the screen.

"Hello," escaped my lips through a grin.

"Hey, sweets. How was your first day?"

"Not too bad. Being on the number side of this job means not much changes for me. However, Donald has a ton to learn if he's going to be the regional sales manager out here. We watched a dozen videos on the similarities and differences in mining oil and natural gas."

"Sounds like an eventful day."

"More like a boring day. How was yours?" I asked as I settled into the bed.

"Same as always. Work, train, you. That's a good day in my books."

A smile crept onto my face, but I couldn't hide it.

I saw Sebastian last night and deeply inhaled his scent, hoping it would linger in my nostrils. However, I still wanted him now, closer than the cell phone provided.

———————

Tuesday, Wednesday, and Thursday were so taxing with continued training, I craved the weekend before I even clocked in on Friday morning. And if I was worn out, Donald had been through the wringer. I don't think either one of us fully knew what to expect when we came out here to Pennsylvania. Especially considering our last traveling trip was a breeze. All I could think was *Week one is almost over, but I have to do this three more times.*

When I finally got my hands on the accounting files before lunch, it took all of my strength not to let my eyes bulge out of my skull. *No wonder they can afford to pay me so much. My check isn't even a drop in the bucket.* I'd be lying if I said I didn't feel any pressure whatsoever to keep this account in order, but the challenge was equally invigorating. The situation was empowering, starting out as the poor lottery kid in high school, to now managing accounts that would make even the rich kids drool. A part of me wondered if any of them actually earned a job all these years later or if they simply continued to live off of family money.

Donald and I went to lunch together, and I asked if he had any idea what the monthly—let alone annual—revenue was for this location. He played it cool with a slight tip of his head and a raise of his brows, but I wondered if his insides bounced around like a pinball machine.

"You sure you're up to this big of a responsibility?" I questioned.

"Bridges, I was *made* for this." His comeback was fast and full of pride. Or was it just confidence? I still couldn't accurately decipher the two.

When the clock read 5:00 p.m., relief spilled out of every nerve from my spine. Trying to recall a workweek that had been this grueling was impossible.

"This calls for a celebration. You're taking me to a restaurant tonight, so pick a good one," I said to Donald as I rescued him from his desk.

"What happened to your no dinner rule on trips?" He asked as he put his laptop into his bag.

"Oh, hush. I mostly said that because I thought you were annoying back then. Come on."

Barely able to shut my brain off, I swear it was as if the Matrix faintly ran in my vision, number after number. The only thoughts able to break through the code were about Sebastian.

One thing that hadn't happened all week was a text from Roman. Another thing that didn't happen all week, Roman coming to my mind.

My weekend would be filled with a whole lot of nothing requiring me to use brain activity. A big part of me hoped Sebastian would suggest meeting up. Only I knew I set myself up for disappointment because, on Saturdays and Sundays, he had two-a-day practices.

At the restaurant, I recalled how Donald was all jokes on our last work trip, only to find the dating pool rather stagnant. "You got any dates lined up for this weekend?" I asked before taking a swig of my Coke.

"Yeah, with the couch. I have plenty of time to search for eligible bachelorettes later. What I don't really have time for right now is having my head half in my work and half on my social life."

Ouch. Did he mean that toward me?

"I'll keep my ears open for you as to which ladies around the office might be available."

"Thanks, Bridges." He shoveled some food into his mouth, visibly still not in relax-mode yet.

Dinner wasn't as lively as other times we ate out together. When we got home, much to my surprise, Donald excused himself to his room for the night. He claimed he had a few ideas he wanted to hammer out so he wouldn't forget them before going to bed early.

All of which was fine with me. I looked forward to a call that would come shortly. Only it didn't.

I felt stupid, waiting up for Sebastian's call, but time quickly passed with reading—I hadn't been able to look at my book all week.

Three minutes until eleven, my phone went off.

Sebastian: You awake?

Me: Now I am.

Me: Just kidding. Yes.

Sebastian: Sorry it's so late.

My heart worried he had a reason—more like someone of the female species—for being late. Practice never ran *this* late. He could tell me if he wanted to, but I wasn't going to ask.

Me: It's fine. Did you have a good day?

Sebastian: Eh, more like a long one. But I'm good now.

Me: That sounds better.

Sebastian: Honestly, I can't chat for long, two-a-day tomorrow and all, but

Here we go. My heart raced. Why did he always break up his thoughts between messages, making me crazy? *Punk*. I chuckled.

Sebastian: What does your Sunday look like?

If I was sure I wouldn't terrify Donald, I would've squealed.

Me: It looks like a whole lot of hanging with you, actually.

Sebastian: Exactly what I wanted to hear. You good to meet in the middle?

Me: Wherever I need to. You know the area better than me.

Sebastian: All right then, I'll figure it out tomorrow night and let you know.

Me: Perfect. Now go to bed so you aren't dragging in the morning.

Sebastian: Hey, you aren't supposed to remember my flaws.

Saturday was a sloth. How could a whole week go by in a speeding blur, but with only one day between Sebastian's and my reunion, each minute stretched into twenty? I let Donald know about my plans, which required the car. Thankfully he didn't seem to mind even after learning Sebastian and I would meet somewhere in the middle—about an eighty-mile drive. The commute wasn't short, but it was the closest I'd lived to Sebastian since high school.

When he messaged me that night, Sebastian gave me the coordinates for a small town almost precisely in the middle of our two cities. It looked like a leisurely trip up two major highways. He suggested we start the drive early in the morning so we'd have the majority of the day together. Which meant even more. Sebastian was never a natural morning person.

I fell asleep with a smile on my face.

13

The high was only predicted to be a cool seventy-one degrees on the second day of September. I wanted to wear shorts and feel cute. However, I didn't want to be cold all day, so I went with some tattered jeans and a gray shirt knotted in the front, peeking my stomach. I wondered if the look was too much, but Camilla did it all the time, and she looked fabulous. But she was Cam.

When I walked out of my room, Donald stood in the kitchen in his lounge clothes, making breakfast. And by making, I mean heating up a Jimmy Dean sandwich in the microwave.

"Don't you look nice today," he said, drawing his hand through his hair, fixing his tousled morning look.

"Is it too much? Should I not tie my top?" I asked. Not that he was a fashionista, but Donald helped me in the past on date wear—aka: lending me *his* shirt. Plus, he was the only one here.

"Not at all. Cute and still modest. If that's what you meant."

"Yeah, thanks. Are there any of those left?" I pointed to the breakfast sandwich.

"Yes, ma'am. I'll make you one if you do the coffee like you've done all week. I have no clue how to operate that thing."

"Deal."

Once the coffee pot spurted out the last few drops of liquid-awake, I poured myself a portion in my to-go tumbler. Donald handed me the warm sandwich on a plate seconds later.

"Do me a favor, please?"

"What's that?" I asked, expecting him to say something along the lines of, "Be careful," or, "Have fun," or, "Make him drive here next time," but none of that left his mouth.

"Will you let me know when you get there safe and again when you leave, so I'm not worried if you're stuck in the middle of nowhere?"

"Sure." I smiled at his request, thankful we'd far surpassed our awkward co-worker phase. Donald and I had secured our supportive friendship. "I'm out."

"Have a good day."

"You too."

The drive wasn't bad at all. With the temperatures already lower than I expected, I looked forward to seeing some autumn colors in the trees. However, it seemed I was two weeks too early to experience that particular scenery. I hoped if today went well and another drive was in my future, I would catch the "fire" in the trees comprised of russet, amber, and carmine—something I could never experience in Texas.

Last night before I fell asleep, I picked an audiobook to listen to on the drive. Between letting myself engage in the story and excitement to see Sebastian, the time passed quickly.

As I made the last turn the GPS directed, Sebastian came into view, leaning against his car in the parking lot. Better accustomed to the New York weather, he wore a tank top that enhanced his muscular physique. As soon as my eyes took him in, it didn't matter that we lived hundreds of miles and a lifetime apart. He was here, and I was here.

I waved, then parked and got out of the car. Before I made it to him, Sebastian rushed over and picked me up in a spinning hug.

"Good morning, sweets."

"Why, hello," I offered through light laughter.

"Was your drive okay?"

"Wasn't bad at all. What about yours?"

"Simple and worth it."

I smiled. "So, what are we going to do today?"

He shrugged. "I found a few things online, but I figured we can drive around. See what this area has to offer."

"Sounds good to me. Are we taking the Batmobile?"

"Sure." He laughed and opened the passenger door for me.

I mashed the button more times than needed to make sure the rental car was locked since it would sit there all day, unattended.

As he walked around the car, I sent a text to Donald to let him know I arrived safe and sound. He replied with, "Thanks. Have fun."

As a Texan, when I thought of New York in the past, the only thing I pictured was New York City. Much to my surprise, the region we navigated was full of small mountains and thousands of trees. We drove another forty-five minutes, but I didn't care how much of our day was spent in a car if we were together.

When Sebastian came to a stop, I asked him where we were.

"It's a state park. Easy walk, some caverns, a few waterfalls. Nothing fancy."

"Nothing fancy." I chuckled. "Good thing I wore decent shoes."

"Come on." He lifted his crooked smile and bounded out of the car.

His hand grabbed mine like it had never let go over the years. As if my hand and his were each other's home.

I was thankful for my choice in pants when the air dropped even cooler as we descended into the cavern. Much to my delight, Sebastian noticed the chill that shook through me and pulled me in closer.

"Sorry. I should've told you to bring a jacket."

"I'm okay. You're the one with no sleeves."

"Yeah, but all these muscles keep me warm."

I laughed. "For sure. Good thing you don't look like the seventeen-year-old you."

"What's that supposed to mean?"

Oh, he wasn't joking. I needed to clarify. "I liked how you looked then, and I like the way you look now. Just saying."

My words appeared to bring him some reassurance.

"Same." He winked.

As we followed the path, the rock walls appeared to come alive. Layer on top of layer of sheet-like rocks were stacked in jagged piles. The hues of gray, white, and a hint of green filled my vision in every direction. This place was a mountaineer's dream. As the trees grew sparse and the rocks consumed the view, we rounded a corner. I heard it before I saw it.

A rushing waterfall dropped from a cliff and collided into a small river a few stories below. The cascade caused a drifting rainbow to fill the air in front of me. So obviously there, but one hundred percent intangible. The sight was absolutely breathtaking.

Mist tickled my skin as we drew closer. "Wow," escaped my lips. I barely heard my own voice under the roar of the water that jutted out over the path we walked on. My reality dropped to only two things: the pulse of water in front of me and the rush of electricity that shot through me as Sebastian turned and cupped my face.

As he kissed me, hidden behind the water curtain, nothing else mattered. Not our distance, not our lost time. The embrace was nothing like his endorphin-high kiss after his fight over a month ago. Kissing Sebastian was like hearing a song I hadn't sung in ten years. It took a split second to recall, but then I knew every. Single. Word. My mind never forgot the feel of him.

We stayed there longer than we probably should have, considering there were other people on the trail. But I possessed zero-point-two strength to pull away this time. It appeared the same for him.

"Okay?" Sebastian asked as he pulled back an inch.

"More than okay."

He kissed me one more time before lacing his fingers through mine. Our entire bodies were covered in minuscule droplets that collected during our moment as we continued down the path.

Everything inside of me begged time to slow down, to pause, to allow us to stay here longer than reality permitted. However, minutes continued to slip from my grasp. I couldn't hold on to the day any more than I could grab hold of the rainbow we walked away from. Not one part of me, even a fraction of a piece, wanted to leave, wanted to get back in his car, knowing our time together was almost over. I found myself in the exact same frame of mind I was last week when we saw each other. Was it even worth putting myself through this every time just to see him? Seeing Sebastian was living again. Leaving him invoked a giant void I knew all too well. Only each time, it seemed to grow larger.

I began to drag my feet as his car came back into view. Our day wasn't over, but leaving the majesty of this place hurt in a manner I neither liked nor desired. The need to know what went on in his head was immense. But asking could run him off, which I wasn't willing to risk. Plus, knowing could possibly taint my experience.

We found a dive and ate a late lunch. Sebastian sat next to me in our booth this time. After our meal was eaten, I rested my head on his shoulder. As he rubbed my knee, a callus on his hand caught in the tattered white strands of my jeans, scratching my skin underneath. My slight jump caused him to laugh.

"Sorry. My hands are beat up from training and weight lifting." Turning his hand, Sebastian revealed a few callouses.

"I don't mind your rough hands." He could touch me with his hard-worked, strong hands any day. "What now?"

With still a few hours left in the day before needing to drive back, we ended up going to a bowling alley. Never the athletic type, I was simply thrilled to have time together. I didn't care what we did. However, Sebastian's very competitive side emerged when I was up by three pins in the seventh frame.

"How are you beating me right now? This doesn't make any sense."

"I'm using the arrows and trying to aim. You aren't *really* upset, are you?"

"Nah, nah." But his face said otherwise. Not wanting his mood to sour, I stopped using the arrows. He beat me by nine pins.

When our game ended, we stayed put and let the "Bowl to start a new game" sign bounce around the screen. It wasn't like this place was surging with people waiting to use our alley.

I didn't want to drive back too late, especially since I had work in the morning, but a little before dinner time, I was in no hurry to say goodbye.

Looking down at my ugly bowling shoes, I swung one underneath and placed it between his feet. "Your shoes make mine look like a kids' size." Something I didn't remember from our dating days.

"I grew another two inches after I moved away. My dad said the same thing happened to him."

"Hmm. I guess I didn't notice the height difference when your whole physique is totally different."

"Totally?" he questioned.

"In appearance, yes. But you're still very familiar to me in other ways."

"I like what I hear." His eyes brightened with flirtation.

"Eh, don't read too much into it." I tried to hold a straight face, but laughter erupted before I could play it off completely.

Sebastian retaliated by tickling me from my ribs up into my armpits. The high pitched squeal that left my mouth was more than a little embarrassing. Unfortunately, it only encouraged him all the more.

"Mercy, mercy," I pleaded as a man a couple of lanes down looked at us in pure annoyance.

"Feed me dinner, woman," Sebastian teased, introducing a new, more seasoned side to me. His banter did dangerous things to my insides.

"Oh, is someone cranky now? Speaking of familiar, I happen to remember you don't do well on an empty stomach."

"I'm a growing boy."

"That you are." I chuckled. "How does that work with your fasting eating schedule thing?"

"I'm not the best to be around. Let's just say The Basher nickname was created when I was starving."

We drove back the direction of where my car was and found a pizza place along the route, situated next to a park. Ten minutes later, we sat on a bench and ate right out of the box.

The encounter was simple. And perfect.

One of the things I enjoyed most about my time with Sebastian was it was never forced. I didn't feel out of my element with him. We could do absolutely *nothing* together, and it was terrific. No fluff, no pretense. I wasn't filling up his time with something to do, or vice versa. I wanted every moment with Sebastian. His presence was a gift all in itself.

"I'm so happy you're here. Even if it's just for a little while."

"Me too." I smiled but took a bite to hide how wide it tried to grow on my face.

"One week down. Three to go, huh?" he asked.

"Yep."

"It's going by pretty fast."

"Last week felt extremely long during those training videos, but yes, today feels like it's going by too fast."

"I haven't seen you in years, and here I got to see you twice in one week. What a treat," Sebastian said before taking the last bite of his crust and dusting the crumbs from his hands.

Two pieces of pizza rested at the bottom of the box. The sun wasn't setting quite yet, but it was closer to the ground than the clouds. I sighed.

"Does that mean it's time to go?"

"I don't want to, but I also don't want to be driving back in the *dark*, dark," I said.

"I hear you. I don't want you doing that either. Thankfully, we still have a few minutes together on the drive to your car."

"I know." And I honestly attempted to not shut down, but it came in like a hornet on a mission. I already felt the sting.

On the drive back, I held his hand as if it meant we wouldn't have to let go. We didn't talk as much as we had the rest of the day. I hated how I always did this. I swore to myself that if I couldn't end our time together without turning into an emo teenager, then I wasn't going to see him again while I was out here for work. And *that*—not seeing him at all—was surely worse than seeing him leave, I decided.

"I'm thinking the same thing next Sunday?" Sebastian said, making our final few minutes not as painful. "At a different location, I mean."

"Perfect." Although repeating today's events would be wonderful too.

He pulled into the parking lot where we met up. My car was the only one left. Much to my delight, Sebastian turned off the car and got out to give me a proper goodbye. *At least this makes goodbye a little easier,* I lied to myself. Because walking away from him hadn't gotten any easier. The third time was just as hard.

Coaching my face to smile, I waited in front of my driver's door after setting my purse on the roof. His strong arms wrapped around me, navigating every curve like a sled down a snowy slope. Before my brain could warn me otherwise, I inhaled deep and let my fingers grip his back.

"Thanks for coming to see me today," he said.

"More like, thanks for coming to see *me* today. You're the one who had to change up your routine," I countered.

"With pleasure." Sebastian held my face with both hands and kissed my lips. I longed to stay there for hours. "I'll see you soon."

"Okay."

He stood in the fading light to make sure I drove off safely before getting into his car.

Not many thoughts filled my head on the drive back. However, one was clear. Our day together hadn't been long enough. Next time, I'd suggest we wake up and meet even earlier.

14

The only thing that made the workweek tolerable was knowing I got to see Sebastian on Sunday. Work kept my mind semi-occupied, and Donald kept my nights entertaining. Trying to think back to when I only looked at my co-worker as a total arrogant buffoon seemed like an eternity ago. Thankfully, seven days went by faster than I feared it wouldn't. My second Sunday with Sebastian was even better than the first. We met up in the same small town and drove another hour to a lake. He rented a boat. We spent our day sightseeing and cuddling under a blanket. I always thought Sebastian was handsome, but seeing him steer a boat, oh my. Bonus points were earned for the picnic lunch he brought too.

New York was more beautiful than I ever expected or gave it credit for. After a full day on the water, he suggested heading back so I wouldn't have a pitch-black drive home. But, watching the sunset over the lake with Sebi was worth driving in the dark, in my opinion. Thankfully, he gave into my desire. I'd make that decision ten out of ten times. And because I wanted to see him again and had made a pact with myself, I didn't turn melancholy when our day came to an end back at our cars. He kissed me like he was burying his passion in my soul—I didn't stop him. Finally, Sebastian ended the night with his routine, "I'll see you again soon."

The drive was actually a bit scary, but replaying the day in my head made it like a drive-in movie. I only needed some popcorn. Not to mention how vastly different it was from my only other time on a boat. The man on *that* vessel didn't pull at my heartstrings even close to as much. Not even a small fraction. Interesting.

Two weeks down, two to go.

One night, while I was in the shower, I got a text from *that* guy on *that* other boat.

Roman: I hope your time away is going well. I'm in town and wish you were here to take me to dinner.

By the time I saw the message, it was too late to respond. Besides, I didn't wish I was there. So how would I even reply?

I felt a tinge guilty for basically agreeing to this trip in order to have the opportunity to see Sebastian, but I gave my all at work. Even after the slight learning curve to the accounting software they used, I already zoomed past their on-site accounting department.

Donald was much more himself after acclimating to the new role and protocol. We often had lunch together during the day, even though we already knew we'd share dinner at home. For whatever reason, I didn't get to know the people here like I did in Illinois. Ultimately, it probably involved the fact I barreled through the week to get to Sunday—Sebastian.

Our third weekend together was as fantastic as the other two. I soaked up every minute of the day like a parched desert. The first guy I ever truly loved, whether he knew that or not, still knew me better than I perceived. Sebastian found one of the oldest libraries in the region—a hundred and twenty-five years old—and drove me there, with no other plans made for the entire day. It was possibly even better than the lake or the cavern. We searched through every aisle, taking in the variety of texts. I read, sometimes out loud, sometimes to myself, while he watched me and stayed close. How was a quiet, do-nothing day with Sebastian so much better than any other day with anyone else?

Donald acted like he wasn't bothered that I took the car every Sunday, but I feared otherwise. I resolved the joy on my face was hard for him to deny. Surely he wouldn't rob me of something I craved so badly. However, he did mention that I needed to fill the gas tank with my personal account, so Ralph didn't question the numbers of charges on the company card. "They won't check mileage with the rental company, but they'll wonder why we have so many gas receipts," he'd said. That hadn't even crossed my mind. I probably should've paid for the gas longer than this last visit.

Knowing it was the last time I'd see him almost made me not go. Almost. Because I was now fully convinced, the pure bliss of seeing Sebastian was worth suffering the pain of walking away. The high I experienced in his presence was still vaster than the low I felt leaving. It was almost unfair how fast my month in the Northeast went. Before traveling, the time seemed ungraspable. Here I was, less than a week left, the brevity of it mind-boggling.

The worst part about my last several days out here was I'd see Sebastian on our weekend get together, then had a full week of work ahead with no reward at the end. I flew home on Friday evening. *It isn't Friday yet,* was on repeat in my head. I wished it helped me.

Sebastian and I talked almost every night over messenger or face chat, even though we had our dates each Sunday, much like we did when I was home in Texas. I knew it wasn't the same. My permanent home was almost ten times further away from him than my temporary home in Pennsylvania. Although it was true, it was hard to admit: I was his, or at least wanted to be. All the things. I wanted to do all the things with him in my life. In his ~~heart~~ mind, I had no idea how I was labeled or what we were considered. I wasn't sure I possessed the courage to even ask. I allowed this to happen and had no one to blame but myself. Besides, what would it matter in one week?

Sebastian did so much research and planning for our last four ~~dates~~ meet-ups, I wanted to reciprocate and plan our last day together. I'd be lying if I said I wasn't nervous about his response.

My alarm went off at 5:00 a.m. I was in the shower by 5:05. My work bun was the easiest hairstyle to maneuver, thus its frequency, but I never did my dull work look around Sebastian. In fact, I spent more time getting ready these past few weekends to see him than I had in ages. I washed my hair and left it down, knowing it'd be dry by the time the drive to him was over. My outfit wouldn't matter much today, but I still wanted to look cute, so I threw something together that boosted my confidence.

Throughout the morning, I experienced the beginning of the void but tried to pull the chasm shut before it could suck me in.

Donald wasn't awake just shy of 6:00, so I left him a note on the countertop, letting him know the coffee pot was ready to go if he turned it on.

Before leaving town, I went by a drive-thru for some coffee and breakfast. Sebastian swore he didn't mind meeting up *extra* early for our last day together, but I wondered if his non-morning-person grog would linger for the first hour or so.

I beat him this time, which wasn't much of a surprise. I simply hoped he wouldn't leave me waiting too much longer. Leaning my head back against the headrest, I said a silent prayer today would go well, and I wouldn't shut down at all. Or at least until I drove home out of his view.

Unintentionally, my silent prayer led to a cat nap. I jumped and accidentally honked the horn when the *knock, knock* on the window woke me up. Sebastian doubled over in laughter as I opened the door. I placed my hand over my chest, attempting to regulate my speeding pulse.

"The only reason I'm letting you laugh is because that was kind of funny," I said as passively as possible. Sebastian continued to laugh. I crossed my arms and leaned against the car, waiting for him to embrace me. I might've looked like the spoiled kids we avoided in school. I didn't care.

When he noticed my posture, Sebastian placed both arms on the roof of the car on either side of me. His weight pinned me down. I still didn't know much about fighting, but I knew I wouldn't tap. He could stay there for as long as he pleased.

"I wasn't laughing *at* you." He kissed my forehead.

"Sure, sure. Call it whatever you want." I looked away like I was annoyed. In all actuality, I still tried to get my heart rate down. Even more so with his closeness.

His hand secured the back of my head before I registered his movement. The kiss he gave me sure didn't help my pulse either.

Still not tapping.

"I'm sorry," Sebastian said as our lips brushed.

"Forgiven." I smiled, pulling our kiss into a new position.

He returned his hand to the car and proceeded to do pushups toward and away from me, kissing me briefly each time. If this was what training and working out looked like, someone sign me up to be his sparring partner. Sebastian spoke between pecks as he drew close and far away. "So. What. Are. We. Doing. Today?" Masterfully, he held himself a few inches from me, his arms in mid pushup. My arms would be a wobbling mess if I tried. His: steady and secure.

"If today were a novel, it'd be called *Blast from the Past*."

"Sounds good. Tell me more."

"First stop is a skating rink."

"Oh, I think I'm on to you here. What else?" Sebastian prodded.

"Let's just start there."

"Does this mean you're driving?"

"If you turn over the keys to your Batmobile, I'll gladly drive." Being in the rental, not truly my car, made our time together seem all the more temporary.

"I like this Londyn. Where did she come from?"

He wasn't wrong in his assessment. I attempted to be more of the master today. In all reality, it was a coping mechanism.

"She comes out from time to time." I winked.

"Seems like the name 'sweets' doesn't fit so well anymore. Hottie might be a more appropriate title."

"Sweets is still fine with me." The moniker took me back to the best season of my life.

"What about sweet-thang?" He flavored his question with copious slang.

"Just give me the keys, Sebi!" I held out my hand.

"Wow. I haven't heard that name in a really long time." A crooked smile took over his face.

Had I not called him Sebi to his face all this time?

"Keys," I demanded, unsure how to respond.

"Yes, ma'am." With one hand, he dug into his pocket, then returned with a one-handed pushup and kissed my cheek while shoving the keys in my back pocket.

When we arrived at the skating rink only ten miles away, it wasn't open yet. Staying in theme with my plan for the day, I recalled something else we used to do. As a pair, we knew plenty of methods to entertain ourselves without spending money.

I turned to face Sebastian, which was weird since I was accustomed to being on the passenger side, and asked, "Would you rather eat vegan for a week or have to eat meat in every single meal for a month?"

"Is that even a real question? Meat. You know me better than that."

Which was true, but I couldn't think of anything better on the fly. His turn.

"Would you rather," he pondered, "have one of our old schoolmates as a boss or work at McDonald's?"

"Ooh, good one. Um, seeing as how I already know how to put up with their annoying antics, I'm gonna say, schoolmate boss. Because then at least I could work my way up and prove to them we were on the same playing field now."

"This spicy woman again, she's *muy caliente*." Sebastian didn't speak Spanish fluently, much to his grandmother's disdain. However, he was around it enough to know some. Even though his last name was Gomez, his mother was whiter than me in complexion. Being mixed gave him the perfect tan year-round.

I rolled my eyes. "Would you rather have to dye your hair pink for a month or shave it bald?"

Now I stepped on toes. Sebastian had terrific hair. He knew it, and I knew it.

"I'd dye it pink in October for breast cancer awareness. That would really get the crowd on my side at fights."

"Okay then, Mr. Sneaky. Your turn."

"Um. Why didn't you—Nah. Wrong type of question. Uh? Would you rather date me long-distance or be single?" He asked as if the question wasn't too serious for this game.

What? His query gave me pause. Maybe he didn't mean it as deep of a question as I let it take root in my head. Could I handle a long-term, long-distance relationship? How would that even work?

"Raincheck."

"Huh?"

"They're open now. Let's go in." Talk about gracious timing. As we walked toward the doors, I tossed his keys back.

"Do you think you'll be any better than you were nine years ago?" Sebastian asked.

He remembered.

"I hope so." I lacked confidence, though.

One of the first times we hung out outside of the school was at another one of our friend's birthday party when I was crushing on him hard. Skating rinks weren't technically cool, but it was something cheap to do. Thus, the lottery kids frequented the place. The upside to that, we didn't have any of the snobby kids around to annoy us. Most of them wouldn't be caught dead in a place so dated, sticky, and musty.

That day, I fell so hard on my third lap around, I thought I broke my wrist. Sebastian spun around to help me up. I was mortified but elated he was who stopped as everyone else whizzed around me. Having a naturally non-athletic body was no fun at times. Even though I wanted to give up and sit the rest of it out, Sebastian encouraged me with a few pointers. More time with him was worth it, and I did get better by the time we left. Barely.

Part of me was shocked Sebi remembered, but then again, not too shocked at all. Over the last several weeks, he'd remembered his fair share of our remarkable past.

We grabbed our tan and orange skates and headed over to a table to put them on, leaving our shoes on top as a reserved sign. Not that it truly mattered, no one else here yet.

Sebastian had his skates on faster than me, no surprise there, and held out a hand to help me stand when I finished. Good thing, too, because my right foot slipped forward. I would've fallen for sure had he not been my sturdy pillar.

"Oh no. Doesn't look like much improvement." He teased.

"Let's say I'm rusty. Give me a few minutes to work it out."

He chuckled. "Like ring-rust?" I tipped my head in question. "Supposedly fighters get that if they haven't had a fight in a long period of time. It takes them longer to get in the groove. Sometimes the rhythm never returns during the first fight back."

"I hope that isn't the case for me, or this will be atrocious." I laughed as I started to inch my feet forward one at a time. At least I didn't have to worry about breaking an arm or ankle like he did. My job only required my brain. One of his livelihoods required his whole body.

Thankfully, after a few laps, I was confident I wouldn't cause myself bodily harm. Sebastian let go and got fancy with his moves. He lapped me twice as I ~~leisurely~~ slothfully made it around once. Watching him showboat was almost as fun as having his fingers laced with mine.

Thirty minutes in, still not another soul had shown up. It was also when the deejay played the first slow song. Sebastian slowed back down to join me. He kissed me on the temple before asking if I'd be his partner for the couple-skate. When I said yes —like I would say anything else—he found my hand without even looking and pulled me, daring me to pick up the pace. Speed wasn't as scary with him at my side.

I swear, as he held my hand and flowed to the beat, no time had been lost between us. How my stomach quaked with anticipation when we were teenagers topped the Richter scale all these years later.

"I like you," Sebastian whispered into my ear.

Biting my bottom lip so I wouldn't cheese myself into embarrassment, I replied, "I like you too." After a pause, I added, "Are you only saying so because that's what all the boys say during the couple-skate? You know, hoping it leads to a make-out sesh behind the claw machine before their mom picks them up?"

He laughed. "I wouldn't be mad about spending some time making out with you. But no, that isn't why." As soon as he ended his statement, he pulled me directly to the center of the rink, no hiding to it, directly under the rickety disco ball missing more than a few mirrored squares. He kissed me with significantly more skill than the younger versions of ourselves. I tried not to be jealous of whoever it was that he perfected his abilities with.

"Allllll right," the deejay boomed over the microphone. "Couple-skate is over. Let's be safe as we pick the pace back up. And remember, this is a G-rated facility."

I laughed at his words, thankful no one else was there to hear the scolding and spied around Sebastian's arm to discover the deejay pointing to a sign on the wall listing the rules.

Before my legs turned into absolute noodles and we traded our skates for shoes, a handful of people finally showed up. By then, it was time for lunch. Something about greasy, cheap food was comforting. I'd put money on the fact it was who I ate with, not solely the food alone.

Some young girls treated the rink like it was made of ice, and they competed for the Olympics qualifier. I was glad I wasn't next to them, rocking my tortoise speed. Sebastian and I laughed our heads off as we pretended to create the voices for the people as they rounded our table time and time again. As usual, he was funnier and had me rolling harder than when I had wheels on my feet.

Hours passed as we sat there and talked—and laughed some more. Our time together was effortless and always left me wanting more. More than unfortunately, this time was our last before I headed to Texas in a few days.

"Are you ready for phase two?" I asked, not letting myself dwell on the end of our time together before it actually arrived.

"Bring it on, sweets."

15

"Our story would be amiss if we didn't recreate one of my favorite moments," I admitted, hoping my cheeks weren't decorated red.

"Are you going to make me guess which moment that was?"

"While I like that idea," *and would love to see us through your eyes now more than ever*, "you don't have to guess anything."

"Could be fun, though."

"Have at it then."

After thinking for a minute while rubbing his chin, Sebastian confessed, "Okay, maybe I need a clue."

I laughed but did as he asked. "First," I gave a dramatic pause, "kiss."

"Oh, man. If I get this wrong, I'm going to look like a total jerk."

Maybe he had several more first kisses in Texas before me. I hoped he was joking about his memory accuracy.

"It was … at the school. Yeah! Winter formal."

I was thrilled he remembered. Granted, we had talked about the night over messenger barely over a month ago. Even though we had such a vast gap of not talking to each other, I couldn't believe it had been two months since we ran into each other on the flight to Dallas. Time currently lacked proper framing in my life.

"Ding, ding! You win."

"What's my prize?"

"More like a challenge." I lifted my eyebrows a few times. "We're headed to Goodwill to find a nice outfit for tonight. Twenty dollar limit." I didn't have to explain how this type of store tied into our former lives.

"I love it. Let's do this."

Although I enjoyed driving his car, once was enough for me. The gas pedal was so sensitive it gave me the jitters. After all, not everyone could drive a superhero's car. I entered the destination into my map app and let it coach him in the directions while I relaxed in the passenger seat, faintly running my fingers over his giant arm.

In high school, I tried hard *not* to look like my clothes came from a thrift store. I felt—at least when I wasn't standing right next to an "it girl"—I accomplished that task. Sebastian always told me I looked good too. But as we pulled up in front of the old shanty of a building, I wondered how good of an outfit I'd find in this small town secondhand shop.

"Yes," Sebastian said at the sight of the store. "I bet there's some vintage stuff in there."

"Glad you're excited." Because I was a little scared, honestly. "So the rules are: you have thirty minutes to find your best 'winter formal' attire, *and* it has to be under twenty dollars."

"Shoes and everything?"

"Shoes and everything." I smiled.

"Are you trying to look goofy or good?"

"Good, of course." I chuckled.

"Is that part of the rules?"

"I guess not."

"Cool. Time to shop." Sebastian leaned across the front seat and planted a quick kiss on my lips.

He raced to the door and winked before heading inside in full competitor-mode.

"Thirty minutes," I yelled out, earning the attention of the three other patrons in the store—old enough to be our grandparents based on their looks.

If I knew Sebastian as well as I thought I did, he'd try to look as cool as possible while teetering the line of goofy. As soon as I scanned through the first rack, I wondered if I needed to do the same. Was anything in this building made after 1994?

Referring back to my old thrift shopping checklist, I knew I had to scan every piece to make sure I didn't miss anything hidden on the rack. After about ten minutes, I pulled the best options available—not that I loved them—and headed to the fitting room. And by fitting room, I meant a tiny square enclosed by a thick blue curtain.

The first gown was full of glittery rhinestones glued onto the top of sheer fabric. The fit wasn't awful, but the gown was for someone three generations older. The second piece was better, but not by much. The dress was somewhere in the teal spectrum, v-neck, and came with a shawl. The fabric reminded me of a thick, elegant tablecloth.

Dress number three was some type of iridescent pink and orange. Once I got it on, a massive stain was visible in the front, so it was an easy no. The thought of not washing what I bought before wearing it made me cringe and hope whatever I purchased was clean. Over the years, I learned only some people washed clothes before donating.

And back out to the racks I went.

As I walked down the next aisle over, Sebastian snuck up behind me. "Find anything good yet?"

His closeness caused me to jump.

"Not yet, you?"

"Maybe." He smiled as he hurried away.

After going through every single dress in the store, whether my size or not, I figured I had to go with the teal gown. However, one more idea came to mind. Camilla once did an ad for slip dresses. Not knowing what that was, I played along and looked it up later. A few of the examples I found looked precisely like a slip you'd wear *under* a dress. Maybe, just maybe, there'd be something in the slip and pajama section I could pull off as a gown.

There it was. My slip dress. It didn't look like much on the hanger, but I crossed my fingers and beelined it to the fitting room.

As I slid the smooth, cool satin over my head, I instantly felt glamorous, slightly afraid to turn around and discover the whole thing was a fail in the mirror. I took it in by merely looking down at my body, too nervous to look at my reflection. The champagne color was elegant all on its own. I think the neckline was called a cowl or something, the type where more fabric than necessary was draped across the front, creating a small fold.

One second before I was about to turn and look in the mirror, the curtain pulled open quicker than I could yell, "Occupied!" Thankfully the face that took me in wasn't a bad one.

"Wow! Um … sorry. I thought this room was empty. You forgot to put the sign out." From Sebi's reaction, I had a feeling the outfit would work just fine.

"Oops. Try the next one over." I pushed Sebastian back out, discovering his stomach was firm even when he wasn't flexing. Closing the curtain, I flipped the rope over with the "In Use" sign on it. My heart pumped faster than usual.

Finally, I turned around and saw what wowed Sebastian. This would work. I felt beautiful and elegant and confident and nothing like the fifteen-year-old girl nervous about going to the dance with her crush. The gown hit me a couple inches above my knees, which I wasn't sure was an ideal spot to land for my body type or not. I didn't particularly care. The fit was loose, in a flattering not-too-far-away-from-the-body style, enhancing my natural shape.

The only other thing I needed was shoes. And with the slip only costing four dollars, I was confident with a large surplus in the budget.

The shoe selection was as dated as the rest of the stock, but I managed to find plain nude pumps. Pumps hadn't changed much over the decades. Since I was still under budget, I looked at the jewelry to see if anything would complement my look. However, the selection of costume jewelry was too gaudy for me. Hopefully, the gown did all the decorating I needed to look fabulous. Equally, I hoped I wouldn't be too cold.

I went to the checkout and paid my nine dollars and thirteen cents. Not bad. Not bad at all. A couple minutes later, while I waited in the front, Sebastian came to the register with a smirk on his face.

"Is it okay if we change into these clothes now that we've paid?" he asked the middle-aged woman as she handed him his coin.

"Sure. Thanks for shopping here today," she replied. I didn't miss how she appreciated his appearance.

I followed as he headed to the fitting area. "What was your total?"

"Sixteen dollars and eighty-four cents." Sebastian was proud of his under-budget total, but his smile fell a centimeter when he heard I was more than fifty percent under budget.

My go-to work bun would perfectly show off the gorgeous exposed back of my dress. And of course, I always had a spare rubber band—or three—in my purse. I fixed my hair and made sure my face didn't need any primping.

"Are you ready?" I asked before opening the curtain.

"Not yet. Give me, like, two more minutes."

I folded my clothes, put them in the store bag, and got everything ready to leave.

"Okay, on the count of three," he said before counting down.

When we emerged at the same time, both our faces lit up.

Sebastian wore gray tweed pants with a slight black check pattern sewn throughout, paired with a white button-up long-sleeved shirt—another thing that hadn't changed over the decades. His pants, however, hit him above the ankles. High-waters was what they were called back in school. Nowadays, I think the correct term was hipster or skinny or something. The look, sans socks, with some classic loafers—tassels and everything—didn't look bad on him at all. He even had a sleek black belt, bringing the look to perfection.

"Nice," I said with a slight giggle. I wasn't sure if those were the type of dress pants he wore these days or this was part of the goofiness he was excited about. His fighter-legs filled out the pants so much, they almost looked a size too small. However, they fit him perfectly in the waist—the belt was merely for looks.

"Me? You. I have no words."

I shimmied the smooth, shiny satin up and down my thighs as I gave a little dance. "I can see your ankles," I chuckled.

He did his own little twist of his foot to show off his exposed skin. "Saved money not buying socks. I've seen guys wear their dress pants like this and vowed to never do it. I guess it isn't that bad."

I shook my head in agreement. *Not bad at all.* "I think you win in style, and I win on budget."

"Not so sure about that, sweets. You look—" Sebastian effortlessly pulled me in with one arm around my waist and kissed me like we weren't in the middle of Goodwill. "Hold on. If I won, what's my prize?"

"A date with me, obviously."

He chuckled. "Perfect."

"You ready?"

"Oh yeah. Where to now?"

"Well, there's only one dance hall in this town, so let's hope it isn't awful." I laughed to hide my insecure worry.

"You and I both know we'll make it fun no matter what."

Back outside, his car appeared even classier, simply because of how we were dressed.

The dance hall turned out to be an event center with two rooms: one for public use and one for party reservations.

The music wasn't terrible, and the room wasn't as dated as I thought it would be. But like everywhere else we went today, there weren't many people there. And everyone knew, when you wanted to have a blast dancing, you didn't want to be alone on the floor.

Sebastian wasn't talking much as he stared out the exit. I feared the date I planned was the lamest of all our weekends.

"So, I have an idea," he said above the music.

"Oh yeah?"

"Do you trust me?"

"Absolutely," I declared so loudly I'd be yelling if the song didn't fill the air.

Sebastian took me by the hand and led me out of the dance hall. Once in the lobby, he faced me in the quieter space even though sounds from both rooms spilled out into the entrance area.

"We're going to *that* party." He pointed to the noticeably fuller and livelier hall. "It's a quinceañera, which means more extended family members and friends fill that room than anyone will actually recognize. I've attended so many of these parties over the years with all of the cousins I have. We'll blend right in."

A few girls back in school had quinceañeras sophomore year. Naturally, I was never invited. "You really think no one will notice?" I asked as I looked at the huge picture on an easel, honoring the young lady. I was never brave enough to do something so daring on my own.

"One hundred percent. People arrive late to these things all the time."

Sebastian walked in like he owned the place, even signed us into the guestbook, filled an envelope with a twenty, and dropped it into the gift card box.

My trust in him wasn't unmerited. We were welcomed and offered food and drinks, all with joyous faces and kind greetings. At some point, I spotted the birthday girl dressed in a poofy white gown. The lengths this party traveled easily paralleled a wedding. Sebi was right; this room was much better.

After we ate and he asked me to dance with him, *I* felt fifteen again. Serene and full of life in Sebastian's presence. No part of me, not even the logical adult side, wanted to leave this room. Leave this city. Leave his arms. When the songs slowed in tempo, he pulled me closer and tighter.

"Thank you for doing this with me tonight and for giving up all your weekends to come see me," I said, looking up into his amber eyes.

"Are you kidding me? This has been the best month I've had in a long time." He lowered his head, bringing his lips a breath away from mine. "You know, I can't help but wonder where we'd be now if I never moved away."

How did the unspoken words that lived in my head for years just come out of his mouth? When I didn't know how to verbalize what went on in my mind, he added, "Ya know?" like maybe it was only a passing thought.

"For sure," was all I managed to utter. Quite the opposite, my insides fired off like a sparkler, sending embers haphazardly in every direction.

He kissed me in the middle of all the strangers as we swayed to the music. To me, Sebastian was a known stranger, someone I once knew so well but enjoyed learning all over again. In a room of dozens of people, we only had each other. Much like in our earlier years, our duo was more than adequate.

I was afraid to look at the clock, feeling every bit like Cinderella. I knew time wouldn't be kind to me.

10:15 p.m. with an hour and a half drive home ahead of me. What I wouldn't give to miss it all, skip work, and not have to say goodbye again.

"Hey, we should probably—"

"I know. One more song," Sebastian protested.

I rested my head on his shoulder and demanded my tears to stay inside, relishing every second.

We eased out of the party precisely like we came in. I walked to his sleek car. One. Last. Time. Sebi opened the door for me but grabbed my wrist before I could sit.

"I think we won the lottery twice. Once back in school, and once being on the same plane. Both times I won you." As he kissed me, one stupid tear disobeyed and fell onto his cheek. "No, no. Don't cry."

Here we were, kissing outside of the dance again. Only this time, I already knew he was leaving.

"What are we, Sebi?" I couldn't take it anymore. I had to know what he thought and hoped my question wasn't going to push him away. He had my heart for years. I don't even think I got it back before he moved away.

"Two people with history. And sometimes, history repeats itself."

Like us getting separated.

I couldn't say that felt like an answer. I wanted him to say something like, "You are mine, and I have always been yours. We will be together forever." But of course, that was only in my books. This was reality.

Reality. I still hadn't figured out what mine actually was.

Confidence to demand a clearer answer vanished with the breeze. What would the point be in defining a relationship with someone who lived across the country anyway?

I sat in the car and held myself together for the last bit of our time together, possibly ever. He sensed my quietness and didn't push. Sebastian simply ran his calloused hand over my satin-clad knee.

The rental car came into sight far too soon, but it was inevitable. What you wanted and what you received weren't always the same thing. A life lesson I knew all too well.

He parked the car and got out to see me off. My strength wore down to the center strands of a fraying rope.

"I'm *so thankful* I had this time with you. You've always had a grip on me, Londyn."

"Same." If I said anything longer, I'd crumble. And crumble fast.

Our embrace only lasted a few minutes. Any longer seemed like self-induced trauma.

"I'll talk to you soon, sweets."

"Take care, Sebi." I kissed him once more before popping off my shoes and getting into the car, wondering if he felt the quiver in my lips.

What he didn't mention: The six states between us.

What I didn't mention: The six states between us.

Perhaps in today's world, working and living across the country from each other wouldn't hinder a relationship as much when we had camera phones and money to pay for flights. Time would tell. I hoped another eight years wouldn't pass before I saw him again. Still, I left with no more guarantee than we would "talk soon." Asking for more before I walked away required a backbone I didn't possess.

One block away, as our tires pulled us in opposite directions, I cried. I cried every mile back. On that drive, in those particular moments, I was no longer convinced the pain of leaving was worth the short time we had together after all.

A few miles past halfway, my phone rang. I figured it was Donald since I forgot to tell him when I left, but Sebastian's face chat request lit up my dark ride. I didn't want to answer. Didn't want him to see the mascara melting to my chin. I also couldn't *not* answer. Hopefully, the night would conceal the whole truth.

"You making it okay? You're not falling asleep, are you?" he asked as soon as our call connected.

"I'm awake." *Painfully so*. I casually rubbed the back of my hand under my eye, more like scratching an itch rather than wiping a tear so maybe he wouldn't notice. It was pretty dark; only the lights from my dash and phone illuminated my face.

"Good." He leaned closer to his phone. With my phone on the air vent mount, I wasn't close to the screen either.

But I knew: he knew I was not okay. That's why he called to check on me. He probably also remembered when I wasn't okay, I needed time to reflect.

"Sounds good. Message me when you get home, please, so I know you made it safely."

"Will do." I forced a smile and thanked God for the dark that veiled my heartbreak.

I hoped this trip would clarify my guy situation, and though it had, it only disclosed a new issue. The person I wanted was just as unattainable as the one I hadn't even missed. Only now, I was invested in an account I couldn't withdraw from.

16

There wasn't another word in the English language to describe my last workweek in Pennsylvania other than atrocious. Well, that wasn't entirely true. It was also awful, depressing, too-long, painful, awkward, gut-wrenching, void, and lame. Allowing myself to get lost in the numbers seemed to be the only thing to dull the ache even marginally. There was only one upside to my last few days in Pennsylvania: Donald. He went out of his way to make sure I belly-laughed at least once a day.

On Wednesday, with only two more workdays before leaving, I went to lunch with some of the team. They were actually really cool. I was pretty disappointed that I allowed myself to be so distracted by Sebastian that I didn't take the opportunity to get to know my co-workers. One of the females, Tamika, was seriously one of the most rad ladies I'd ever met. She was like a blend of Cam and me rolled into one person—the best of us both. I knew I'd still be working with her, even if it was solely over phone calls and emails, so my last few days, we were practically glued at the laptop screens.

And perhaps that's how my mood perked up a bit. Enough for Donald to investigate at dinner. As we ate out of our square, tri-compartment, white styrofoam boxes from the Korean BBQ joint—one of our go-to places over the last month—he started with question one of many.

"Can you believe how fast this month has gone?" He asked from across the kitchen table.

"Not at all. *Ridiculously* fast." My thoughts weren't solely work-related, however.

"Are you going to miss me?"

"Actually, I am." Donald did a dance in his chair. "But not much. It's only like a four."

"Out of ten?"

"Percent." I laughed.

"Four, huh? If I recall correctly, you said three last time. I'm growing on you, Bridges." He bumped his hand into my arm.

"Barely." I dug for a bit of my food.

"So did that fool break your heart?"

I looked up and made eye contact as I pulled the fork from my mouth. "Say what?" came out muffled.

"I saw you come in all brokenhearted Sunday night." Donald's eyes were troubled, but I saw the concern before he dropped his head and picked at his dinner.

"Oh. It was just, I knew I wouldn't see him again. *That* was heartbreaking." My dinner was groomed by my fork, leaving the tracks of the tines in the white rice.

"I see. So I don't need to hunt the guy down and beat him up?"

I huffed in laughter. "While that sounds pretty awesome of you as a friend, A- he didn't technically hurt me, and B- he'd *seriously* hurt you. Sebastian's an MMA fighter, remember?"

"Eh, I could take him. No one messes with my Bridges' emotions and gets away with it." Donald flexed his much smaller arms, still covered in a long-sleeved dress shirt. His face would not be left so pretty-boy after an altercation with Sebastian, *The Basher*, Gomez. Not to mention the havoc on his gelled hair.

"I saw him five times in less than a month. Five times he went out of his way, quite literally, to come see me. That isn't *nothing*, right?"

He shrugged. "Not in my opinion. Did y'all make any plans or talk about what comes next?"

I shook my head low and slow. "He just said, 'Talk to you soon.'"

"Okay. That isn't goodbye. But whatever you do, don't get all wrapped up in him, you hear me? You call the shots. He doesn't get to have a say any more than you do."

"You're probably right." I smiled.

"Of course I am. You have, uh, some pepper in your teeth."

"I do?" I smiled even broader and dorkier. The sentiment was better than thinking about whatever Sebi and I were labeled.

He chuckled. "Yeah. Right ... there." He pointed and passed me a napkin to clean my teeth, much like a big brother would do to his little sister.

"Thanks." I took a drink of water to erase the dryness the napkin left. "Seven." Pushing away from the table, I put my box in the trash. His head tilted in question like a curious puppy. Before I disappeared down the hallway, I turned and clarified, "I'll miss you seven."

He didn't reply, so I didn't know if he heard me.

Thursday and Friday basically felt like one excruciatingly long day. So much was left undone. I had to work through lunch both days to finish everything. A part of me wondered if I was actually all-in during the workweeks seeing how much I had to do the last few days before leaving for good.

Sebastian and I talked on face chat Thursday night one last time while our cell signal only had to travel a couple of hours. In all reality, my time at the house talking with Sebi was the only reason I knew it had been two workdays and not only one. When he asked me what time I'd get back to Texas, I figured it was so he'd know if and when he should message me.

Donald drove me to the airport almost two hours before we would've typically headed back to the rental house on Friday.

The ride was quiet at first; my brain was fried. Not only that, but my heart was also as heavy as a storm cloud. The latter probably contributed to my silence more than I cared to admit. Surprisingly, Donald was equally as quiet. Typically, he joked, so I wasn't sure if he didn't know how to handle my staring daze, or he had a long day too.

My stomach grumbled when we were almost there, reminding me of the lunch I missed. Fingers crossed, I'd have time to eat something before getting on the plane.

"Hungry, are we?" Donald finally spoke up.

"I guess so. You haven't eaten either, have you?"

"Don't worry. After I drop you off, I'm going to trade this sedan in for something a little more single bachelor. Then I'll swing by somewhere in my new wheels."

Even though I wanted to, I didn't ask if it was because we—*I* —had put more miles on the car than we were supposed to and simply allowed myself to believe he wanted a hotter ride now that he got to drive it all alone.

"Lucky you. Do you feel like you've made any roots out here yet?" I asked.

"Um, I don't know. Going back does sound a little tempting right now, with you leaving and all."

"Sure, sure." I looked over at him, waiting for the next part of his sentence that countered his compliment, but I only found a polite candidness in his eyes. Turning to face forward again, I added, "You'll be fine. You should ask Tamika out. She seems like a great catch."

"We'll see." He shrugged. Natalie was probably still his top choice as much as Sebi was mine. Both people physically unattainable.

"Okay," I said with a sigh as he pulled up to the curb drop-off in front of the airport. "I guess I'll see ya when I see ya?"

He nodded with a closed mouth smile and got out to help me pull my luggage out. "Hey!"

"Yeah?"

"Let me know when you get home, please," he requested.

"Sure thing." I grinned at our new norm of a brother/sister relationship.

"Cool." He shut the trunk and gave me a hug as I held my luggage before getting back in the car and navigating to the rental car section. I was thankful to have a friend in Donald, but there I was again, close with someone who lived across the country. Thank God for Cam—the only other person I had in Texas.

Except for Roman. He barely crossed my mind over the last month, the one time he texted me. It wasn't uncommon for me *not* to hear from him while he was on his trips, so perhaps since he knew I was gone, the exchange was pointless. I had no clue what our encounters would look like from here on out. Or if I even wanted them.

The airport wasn't huge, with only two entrance doors and two exit doors—all four less than a hundred yards apart. Three terminals were all the backside of the airport possessed. I hurried to check my bags so I could eat dinner empty-handed. One restaurant filled the small airport, but one was all I needed. After skipping lunch, my standards for quality weren't too high.

After dropping off my bags and rounding the corner, a shiny heart balloon caught my eye. One second later, the person who held it grabbed my attention.

Sebastian.

"What are you doing here?" I asked through an awkward chuckle as I hurried to his side.

"Hi, Londyn." He wrapped his giant fighter arms around me and hugged me so tightly a few of my vertebrae popped. After letting go, he handed me the balloon—which I doubted I could take on the plane—with a white rose tied to the string.

"Hi." My eyes had to be popping out of my head between shock and the lubrication my happy tears provided. "I wasn't expecting to see you again."

"I know." His crooked smile graced his face, noticeably proud of himself. "I wanted to surprise you and see you one more time before you left."

The sentiment was stupendous but would also make getting on the plane ten times harder. I tried to smile genuinely, but my heart was equally troubled as much as it was excited to see him.

"Getting to know you has been even better the second time around." Sebastian's words caught me off guard. My brain tried to tune back into our conversation after the pounding of my chest became evident.

"I feel the—"

"What if you moved here? Put in a transfer request." He said it excitedly like it'd be fun. And easy.

For whatever reason, moving here had never crossed my mind. Perhaps because for close to a decade, I was *here*, and he was *there*, and that's just the way it was. Being with Sebi was otherworldly, simple, natural, a piece of home no matter where we were on the globe, but could I uproot and move across the country to start a new life with him so soon? Plus, even if I did move, we'd still find ourselves two and a half hours apart—a much closer *here* and *there*, but apart nonetheless.

"What?" was more of a breath than a question.

A full sentence to convey all that cycloned in my head failed to form. Did I want to be with Sebastian? Yes. Was I ready to displace my entire life for a weekend boyfriend? I couldn't say. And with him right in front of me, looking directly into my soul, making such a strong proposition made it all so much more difficult.

"I...."

Before I could say anything else, his hands cupped my face, and his lips collided into mine with a strong yet gentle force that quaked through me. Perhaps he hoped his kiss would bring me clarity, leave a longing in me stronger than any uncertainty, but when he pulled away and saw the trepidation in my gaze, his hands lowered to his sides.

Apparently, my eyes said what my heart couldn't: *I don't know.*

At least not now. I already knew what it was like to only get to see someone on occasion with Roman. It was no relationship at all. Maybe it wouldn't be like that with us, though? Wasn't Sebastian here now, asking for more? Only for me to put him in a triangle hold—him, me, and distance? What was happening? What was I supposed to do? I didn't have enough time to decide.

"Pre-boarding for flight seven-twenty-three to Dallas Love Field is now open," a female voice declared over the intercom, stealing our last few minutes within touching distance.

"Please don't hate me," was all I could say as my insides shook so vastly I wasn't sure how I stood still.

"Hate you? I could *never* hate you, even if I wanted to," he chuckled. "I just don't want to leave you again."

"Sebi, I don't—" His positive demeanor slipped. My brain couldn't factor the new information quick enough. Fear I could draw a line in the sand for us caused me to second-guess anything I said. Was I screwing everything up? Was I an idiot for not saying yes and worrying about the logistics later? Instead, in my uncertainties, I teetered on the brink of a breakup with the one guy who never moved out of my mind. Was it even a breakup? Or possibly a final—and finite—goodbye?

"It's just an idea." Sebastian lifted a shoulder in the weakest shrug of all time. His left eye twitched into that nervous squint. "Think about it, okay?"

"Okay." I owed us that much. The anxiety dancing up and down my spine in erratic pulses caused me to lunge forward on my tiptoes and kiss him again—possibly for the last time ever. I didn't want to believe it was, but it surely could be.

"Now boarding all passengers for flight seven-twenty-three to Dallas Love Field."

"I gotta go," I said with my forehead pressed to his.

"I feel you slipping through my fingers. I wish I could hold on tighter."

Unfortunately, even Sebastian wasn't strong enough for that.

Allowing myself to embrace him one more time, I felt every throb of his heart beating wildly in his chest.

"Talk to you soon." Perhaps that was easier for him than saying goodbye. He pulled away enough to kiss my forehead and quickly walked away with one hand deep in his pocket and the other pulling through his hair. I wondered if he occupied his hands so he wouldn't grab ahold of me—a feeling I fully grasped.

As I watched him leave, I knew a sliver of my life would always reside in New York. The memories we'd made here would stay with me forever, much like the old memories from a decade ago still did.

I hurried to my terminal only to remember I still had the balloon in my hand. Not sure what to do with it, I untied the rose and secured the shiny red heart balloon to the arm of a chair in the gate seating, hoping not to draw any attention to myself. Thankfully, most of the passengers had already boarded. Once I secured a decent seat onboard and collapsed into the chair, everything from the last several minutes played in my mind again. Then again. And God help me when I looked out the window and saw the balloon swaying inside all alone. I was literally leaving my heart in New York.

When my eyes couldn't bear the sight any longer, I returned my line of vision to my lap—his white rose. The new view didn't help me either.

Did I just make a huge mistake? Should I have said yes and let my heart do more of the thinking than my brain for once?

What was I thinking? It had always been Sebi for me. Perhaps my responsible, adult mind knew his suggestion wasn't simple. Saying yes would create hundreds of new questions.

It was too late now; we already angled into the sky.

Part of me wanted to sleep so I could stop thinking. However, I knew my troubled mind would spill into my subconscious. I didn't know if I could handle seeing Sebastian's honey-brown eyes again. Especially filled with uncertainty.

My stomach surpassed growling and roared. I hadn't eaten in over twelve hours. When the flight attendant passed, I asked for an extra bag of almonds.

After giving myself a tiny bit of nutrition, I stared out the window.

I was too troubled to sleep.

Too confused to cry.

Too afraid to face any decisions.

Here I was, in love with someone across the country from me. Again.

The reason we didn't last eight years ago was the very reason we couldn't now. Distance. Only this time, apparently, the choice of the distance was mine.

17

Thank God it was Saturday. My eyelids looked like fully fattened caterpillars ready for a cocoon. When I arrived home last night at almost 11:00, the weight of it all—walking away from Sebastian, him suggesting I move, the vast distance—body-slammed me onto the bed. I didn't change my clothes. Didn't even take off my shoes. An Uber picked me up from the airport and drove me home. Cam wasn't there to talk, so I went to bed. And cried buckets. Because I didn't like the cards I played with, but I didn't know if switching them out was worth the risk of ending up with a worse hand.

As I lay in bed, two things became clear: I loved Sebastian, and we'd never work unless we lived in the same town. Because at this point in my life, I wanted roots. Like we had before. Even though we were young, we were together every day. I didn't want a weekend, holiday, special occasion boyfriend. Even if I transferred to Pennsylvania, we'd still be long distance.

I still hadn't figured out how to deal with A- all of my emotions, and B- the nature of Sebastian and my relationship moving forward. Would he quit talking to me if I told him I couldn't move?

The blender let me know Camilla was up. I didn't even change my clothes before walking into the kitchen.

"You have to work today?" she asked at my appearance, shoes and all. But when I turned and revealed my face, she rushed over. "Oh my goodness, are you okay? What happened?"

"Stupid life responsibilities, that's what," I answered. The blender still wailed from the kitchen bar. "Finish that, then I'll explain." Finally, after twenty-six hours, I let my feet breathe. They ached from being confined by shoes for so long.

Camilla retrieved her liquid meal and joined me on the couch a minute later. Her eyes digging into me with concern was endearing, but I knew if I didn't want *my* eyes to be sealed shut for days, I couldn't go into detail. Not yet.

"Well?" she asked as she drew the green ooze into her straw.

I dropped my head back against the top of the couch. "Basically, I spent every Sunday with Sebastian. He said I should move there, and I didn't answer him. What did you do for the last month?"

"Whoa, whoa, whoa. You did what? And he *what*? And you gloss over it and ask me about my month?"

"Yeah. I'm not sure if he was legitimately asking me to move there and be *with him*, with him, or it was simply an enchanted, wishful thought. So, I'd like to talk about something else. Anything else, honestly."

"You should probably find out, don't you think?"

"Yeah. Your turn to talk."

"As long as you agree to discuss this later. I'm not letting you off the hook that easily."

"Fine."

"You look like you were homeless for the last month, not in New York. And here I hoped you'd come back more fashionable."

I turned my head, still against the couch, and attempted to roll my eyes at her. Lucky for her, they were too swollen to maneuver. "Pennsylvania mostly."

"Whatever. You ready for this?"

"For what?"

"I met a guy. Well, not just a guy. The love of my life." She sat her glass on the table and clasped her hands together.

Camilla could lean toward the dramatic side. More like cannonball and moon-bounce on the dramatic side. I took her statement with a grain of salt.

"Did you now?" I sat up a fraction and willed myself to be involved in the conversation. The momentary distraction would be nice.

"Mmm, yes. Branch is absolutely perfect. Like ... my soulmate. It was the best two nights of my life."

"Two nights?" That didn't seem long enough to fall in love.

"Yeah, but we already have plans for our future."

"How did you meet him?" I asked.

When she laughed, I feared her answer.

"He stayed here with the Airbnb."

In all of my own mess, I forgot my bedroom was rented out. After we talked, I planned to go inspect my belongings to make sure nothing was missing. "I hope you hung out in your room. Please, Cam, tell me my bed is untarnished?"

She shrugged; I punched her thigh.

"Ow!" She chuckled.

"Why did he need a place to stay?" I asked.

"He came for a football game."

Came. Meaning Branch didn't live here. Meaning he lived somewhere else. Meaning Camilla was in love with someone who lived somewhere else. I couldn't do this now.

"I need to go wash my sheets. We'll talk later."

A significant part of me wanted to disinfect my entire room as I did an inventory sweep of my possessions. The deep cleansing I did could've been considered "spring cleaning" if it wasn't two days away from October. Allowing myself to get lost in the task, however, was good for my brain. And my heart.

In the desired distraction, I ended up moving around some of the furniture in my room to make the place feel different. Only when I was done, everything was unintentionally set up like my room in Pennsylvania. Memories of my last month came flooding in faster than I could stack up sandbags. That wasn't going to work. I moved everything a second time but didn't like the layout and ultimately put everything back where it started. I was successful, at least, in using up my day.

Jitters ran through me in a cold shiver as the thought of what would happen at 9:45 crossed my mind. For the first time, I wasn't confident I'd hear from Sebi.

And I didn't.

Not at 9:45, not at 10:30, not even by 11:15, when I decided to stop waiting and went to bed.

What had I done?

I managed to distract myself with my room yesterday, but Sunday stared me down like a bully. The first Sunday I wouldn't get to spend with Sebastian in over a month.

I decided if he hadn't reached out to me by 10:30 tonight, I would message him. And I had an answer to his proposition—whether he was one hundred percent serious or not—for me to move. *Not yet.*

It wasn't a no or a yes, more like a maybe—kind of. The idea of being with Sebi had me packing all of my belongings into cardboard boxes, getting rid of whatever wouldn't fit in my car, and driving for twenty-plus hours to be with him. But the thought of possibly flinging myself across the country, fueled by only the sparks in my gut, left me to believe I might end up stranded in the middle of nowhere all alone. Maybe not on day one, but eventually. Because what if, like the last time we were separated, he said he would keep in touch—write—and didn't?

So not yet felt exactly right. We'd only been back in contact for two months, and though my heart screamed, *"Go!"* my analytical brain said, *"Wait."* What was the rush?

Well, the rush was I missed him already. And with no timetable for when I'd see him again, the missing seemed endless. I could put in a transfer later as easily as I could put one in now. Time would tell how things settled between us. There was no easy solution to my situation. Waiting felt like the only wise and logical answer.

The book I read to pass the day wasn't doing a good enough job engaging my mind. I closed it on my lap and bounced my head against the couch cushion a few times. The condo was quiet. Too quiet. I forgot how often Camilla was gone, leaving me alone. While I was in Pennsylvania, I was never home alone. Donald was, however, every Sunday when I left him without a car. For the first time, I felt terrible about how seeing Sebi meant leaving Donald all alone.

Walking back into my room to grab my phone off the charger, I dialed as I crashed onto my bed.

"Hello!"

"Hey, friend," I said, excited he answered.

"What's going on?" Donald asked.

"Not a whole lot. Finding myself a bit disoriented after returning home. What about you? You miss me?"

"For sure. I don't have anyone to make the coffee anymore. I'm two days clean."

Laughing, I said, "You can FaceTime me if you want, and I can teach you. Sorry I didn't think about it sooner." Apparently, there was a lot I hadn't thoroughly thought about concerning Donald.

"Cool."

"So, what have you been up to? Partying it up?"

"Eh, not too much partying. More like working it up."

"Donald, it's the weekend," I scolded. "I better hear something from Tamika the next time we correspond. What kind of car did you trade for?"

"I got a Benz," he answered nonchalantly.

"Oh, just a Benz, huh?"

"Yeah." He didn't seem too into talking at the moment. I wondered if he was preoccupied—mentally or otherwise. I kept my end of the conversation flowing, hoping he'd perk up.

"Going back to work here tomorrow is going to be so weird. I bet Steve isn't looking forward to it either."

"I'm sure he missed you at least a tiny bit."

"Not so sure on that one. I'm the invader, remember? Took over his job, then his office, and now the big accounts. Not to mention, I'm almost young enough to be his daughter."

"Everyone misses you at least a little bit, Bridges."

God, I hope so. Only I thought of solely one person.

"Right, because of my number skills, coffee-making skills...."

"To say the least," he responded. "What about me?"

"What about you?"

"Is that seven really real?" *So he had heard me.* "You miss me too?"

"I'm calling you, aren't I?"

"I knew it. We are besties."

"Apparently so," I laughed again, happy for his lift in attitude. Our relationship was easy. Uncomplicated. He was there, and I was here, but I felt no distance or awkwardness. Of course, we didn't have a history together, including adventures and kisses.

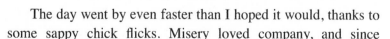

The day went by even faster than I hoped it would, thanks to some sappy chick flicks. Misery loved company, and since

Camilla was still out and about, I had to have other voices in the condo. Two bags of microwaveable popcorn were devoured by 9:15 p.m. as the second movie ended. I tried to decide if I wanted to pop a third bag and start a new film or stop. After a day full of binging, I was actually pretty tired and would probably go to bed soon. Unless Sebastian reached out to me. His contact would be an upper that could keep me awake for hours.

Taking a few minutes to clean up the kitchen and living room, I retired to my room fifteen minutes later, hoping and praying I'd hear from Sebi before twenty minutes had passed. Trying to read when my mind anxiously awaited something wasn't easy. I reread the same page twice, hoping to engage in the story. Reading was a part of me, had been for two decades, but something about how things settled with Sebastian and I left my book friends and siblings unable to penetrate my reality.

Since I hadn't showered today, I decided rinsing off would be the best method to pass the time. Not to mention, I didn't want to look like I let myself go in a matter of two days if Sebastian contacted me via video call.

I set a timer on my phone for ten minutes, so I wouldn't be in the shower at 9:45. Getting clean and putting on new clothes, even though they were only a step up from pajamas and basically the sister of the lounge clothes I wore all day was refreshing.

At 9:44, I sat on my bed, ready.

9:45.

9:46.

9:47.

9:48.

9:49.

9:50.

I stopped staring at my phone, willing it to activate, and picked up the book for the third time today in an attempt to numb my mind and pass the time. As planned, I waited until 10:30 to reach out to Sebastian. And I didn't have the guts to call, let alone face chat, so a simple message was all I'd send, seeing if he'd take the bait.

Three pages later, my phone *finally* illuminated with a connection—a call, ten minutes later than usual.

"Hello," I tried to sound casual like I hadn't been waiting forty-eight hours to hear from him.

"Hey." I heard a loud huff leave his lungs.

"You all right there?"

"Barely. My coach kicked my butt this weekend. I crashed as soon as I got home last night."

So that was the reason.

Relief poured down my spine. "You poor little fighter, you."

"Save it." He chuckled. "I can't take any more today. I'm officially tapped."

"Fine. I'll be nice then."

"You're always nice. What are you talking about?"

His words led me to believe he wasn't upset at how things were left between us—the last time he touched me. I didn't feel very nice.

"I hope you still think so in a minute." I chuckled, but it was majorly strained.

"Uh, oh. I don't like the sound of that."

"I've been thinking about what you said, you know, about transferring."

"Yeah?"

"Can we put a pin in that idea for now?"

"Sure." I thought I heard a sigh, but he didn't say anything else on the matter.

We didn't talk for long since he was exhausted. After a weekend full of mental exercise, so was I. Tomorrow had enough tasks of its own for me, so we called it a night. Although I would've loved to talk longer, at least I didn't have to roll into my workweek carrying emotional strain.

18

The stack on top of my desk Monday morning was dubbed the "Leaning Tower of Archives." One month's worth of invoices, statements, and payables climbed from the tabletop to the ceiling. Steve had a mischievous grin on his face as I walked in and caught a glance at my back-work. Although the hoard was daunting, I was up for the challenge. The first thing I did was take each file down, creating a new pile to get to the oldest statements at the bottom and work forward in time. Enter, balance, pay, file was the routine I entered with ease, mostly because I wasn't training anyone. I got in the zone pretty quickly, much to Steve's pleasure—precisely no chit-chatting—not that my office-mate and I were extra chummy or anything before I left either. From the look of things, maybe Steve should've taken a few more accounts from me.

What proved the most difficult in tackling the pile was new files were dropped on my desk as the day went on. Getting caught up on thirty days of data entry was a task all its own. Plus, I still had the normal amount of work coming in. *And* I was supposed to conference call with Tamika every day for the first week after I left.

Had I not talked to Sebi last night, I'd probably be in the ladies' room crying on a porcelain chair from the weight of my life. However, my mind was mostly clear.

When Steve gave his routine, "I'm out to lunch," in a neither excited nor disappointed tone, I found myself walking to Ralph's office, hoping he hadn't left for lunch yet.

"Come in," he answered after I knocked on the door. "Londyn. Welcome back to the Promise Land."

I knew he meant Texas, but the Northeast had held more promise for me in the recent past.

"Thank you."

"You getting your feet back under you after all your travels?"

"Working on it. That's why I'm here, actually."

"All right."

"You probably haven't seen my desk, but the mound I've been chopping at all day is still a strong cedar." I chuckled at my own joke, showing my lack of people interaction for the last four hours. "Anyway, I wanted to ask for permission to stay late today, and maybe tomorrow. I'll potentially hit overtime hours. With a month's worth of documents and new ones trickling in, I'm concerned how many days it'll take to catch up if I don't put in some extra hours."

"Granted. But don't work yourself too hard."

"Sure thing. Thank you, sir."

I turned to walk out when he continued.

"So, how was PA?"

Since he asked about Pennsylvania, and all of my good memories from the trip technically occurred in New York—*and* he was my boss—I kept all of my personal adventures during my off time to myself.

"Since my job is numbers, not much changed for me. The figures were larger, however." Ralph's eyes gleamed with profits. Since my friend wasn't here to give a report, I decided to put in some brownie points for him. "Donald had a bit more of a learning curve to natural gas. He works very hard for this company."

"He sure does."

"Anything else, sir?"

"That's it. Thanks, Londyn."

I left to grab a sub sandwich in the drive-thru—a footlong, so I'd have dinner later. In my brief moments of checking out of the office, I thought of Sebastian. His routine over the last month hadn't changed as much as mine. He still had work and slept in his own bed. Basically, he missed Sunday practices for a month. Which wasn't that big of a deal, in my opinion. He still went every night after work and all day Saturday. Sebi appeared to be in perfect shape to me. I shook my head like an Etch-A-Sketch to stop thinking about how good he looked every time I saw him.

Returning to the office, I chiseled away at the stack efficiently. Before I knew it, Steve clocked out for the day, and co-worker after co-worker continued to walk down the hallway past my open door, some popping their head in to welcome me back. Last of all, Ralph.

He walked into the office a little after 7:00 p.m. to remind me not to work too late. I was thankful he came by, so he knew exactly how large a pile I worked on. And that was *after* ten hours of effort. I reassured him I wouldn't stay much longer because I hoped to hear from Sebastian at 9:45 and wanted to be settled at home by then. Obviously, I didn't tell him all of that.

The office was so quiet all that could be heard was the clicking of my fingers on the keys and the whir of the air conditioner. I wondered how much cooler it was in the Northeast this first day of October and bet they didn't require an air conditioner.

When my phone went off in my drawer, I wondered how I managed to work until 9:45. However, when I pulled my phone out with a smile on my face, Sebastian wasn't the name at the top of the notification. And it was only 7:50.

Roman: Aren't you back in town yet?

My smile faded. Roman. I'd been so caught up in my thoughts concerning Sebastian that I neglected someone else who cared about me. I felt like the world's worst person.

Me: I am. First day back to work.

Roman: Sweet. I hope you haven't eaten dinner yet. Can I come pick you up?

In all of the possibilities that ran through my mind over the last several days, coming back to town and addressing my situation with Roman was not something I considered.

Me: I'm still at work, actually.

Roman: Bummer. I leave tomorrow.

This game of lining up our schedules used to be much simpler when I had nothing—and no one—else to fill up my calendar. However, had I already been home from work, I probably wouldn't have said yes anyway.

Me: Oh. Sorry.

Roman: It's okay. I'll let you know when I get back.

After our text conversation, I decided to finish out all the paperwork from the third week I was gone and call it a day. I hoped to catch up almost entirely during the typical workday tomorrow, but if not, I'd only have to stay an hour or so instead of four. I clocked out at 8:30 and walked out of an empty office into a dark and vacant parking lot.

On the drive home, I pondered my situation. Technically, I knew Sebastian longer, considerably longer. However, as an adult, I'd dated—or whatever it was called—Roman longer. Sebastian knew little details about my life even I'd forgotten, and Roman knew ... I don't know what he knew. Trying to recall if he knew anything about me made my brain hurt worse than the day filled with numbers. Roman knew how to have a good time, and he didn't seem to mind taking me along.

There was one major problem: I didn't miss Roman while I was gone, but I missed Sebastian every day. My bones missed him. Only three days had passed since I could touch Sebi, yet it felt like too many. The number was ten times as many for Roman, and the span didn't bother me.

I knew who I wanted, but that didn't seem to matter in logistics. Stupid logistics.

Last month, the *best month* of my adult life, only left me longing for Sebastian more but did nothing to actually change the circumstances. Here I was, balancing on a love beam, knowing my heart would break if I fell off. But just like a beam, my circumstance was risky to tread and not long enough to reach the distance I needed to travel.

Finally home after a twelve-hour day, I showered and got into comfortable clothes before my digital date, should a request come. With time to spare, I hoped Camilla could get my mind out of worry-mode and more into don't-overthink mode.

"Hey." I plopped down onto her bed.

"Come in," she said sarcastically.

"I've barely seen you at all since I got back."

"I know. My agent has been booking me in overdrive. I've been working nonstop, it seems."

Refraining from teasing with a comment along the lines of, "How hard is it to let people do your hair and makeup and look at a camera?" was harder than I let on.

"Rough life" was all I said instead.

"I know," Camilla said with a sigh. Her tone was serious, so I was glad I hadn't said any of the wise-cracks bouncing around in my head. "So what's up? You ready to chat now about your *boy* problems."

"Yes," I huffed and rolled onto my back.

"Spill it."

I told her how amazing and natural my time with Sebastian was, even said Sebi, and had to clarify his nickname. After recapping our dates and conversations throughout September, I waited for her input.

"So he made a comment about you moving out there, but you aren't sure if he was asking you to move to *be with him* or if it was like a casual suggestion so that you two could keep seeing each other every weekend?"

"Exactly."

"Did he ever use girlfriend, mine, love, or any words like that?"

"No. He did say, 'Getting to know you was even better the second time,' so I think he looked at our time together as more than casual."

"Did you kiss him?"

"Every chance I got," I admitted after covering my face.

"Way to go." Cam shoved my shoulder.

"*And*," I flipped over onto my stomach, "Roman reached out to me earlier and wanted to take me to dinner."

"Oh yeah, that guy."

I dropped my face down into her comforter, craving more comfort than she provided.

"And you said?"

"That I was still at work."

"Will you see him again?" she asked.

"Probably not. I think I need to officially end things with him." I spoke into the blanket, hoping she could understand me.

"Yeah, you need to figure all this out. Dating norms of this age aren't for you. Your eyes are looking haggard."

I was glad she finally saw the difference in how I typically functioned with the dating advice she'd been giving me. Perhaps settling down with Branch enlightened her. Camilla was right; I needed to figure out the course of my life because living in inner confusion wasn't something I desired long term. However, I didn't appreciate her jab at my appearance.

My phone, which I brought with me, rang. When I lifted it from the bed and found a face chat request on the screen, I smiled and showed it to Camilla before answering.

"I want to see him up close," she said.

"Uh, I don't know."

"Come on, I won't say anything."

I didn't want to leave the line ringing any longer, so I agreed. "Fine." Sitting up and swiping to open the call, I held the phone so Camilla could see over my shoulder. "Hey!"

"Hi, sweets."

"Sweets?" she whispered behind me.

I gave her a subtle elbow. "You just get home?"

"Yeah." He ran his hand through his post-shower hair.

"Hi! I'm Camilla." She popped her head into view.

What the actual heck?!

"Hi, Camilla. Nice to meet you."

"Same to you, Sebi," she replied, more flirtatiously that I appreciated, earning herself an unsubtle punch to her model thigh. "Ow," she said through a chuckle.

I rolled my eyes and stood up to walk away. "That would be my roommate. Consider yourself lucky for not having one."

"Bye," Cam yelled as I walked out and shut the door.

He laughed. "How was your first day back?"

"Long. I got home less than an hour ago."

"Ouch. Welcome to my world."

"Kind of. No one kicked or wrestled me for the second half of my day."

"Thank God. I'd have to come beat them up."

"So kind of you." I giggled. "I haven't finished either. I'll work late tomorrow also, hopefully not as late."

"For sure. I'm hoping that with you. Anything else going on besides work?"

For a split second, I was almost positive he attempted to ask something without asking it. Roman. He knew *about* Roman, but we hadn't discussed him hardly at all. Only twice that I could recall.

"Nope. Please don't envy my eventful life," I quipped.

"I'll try," he said with a smile. "What were you doing before I called?"

"Talking with Camilla. That's why she invited herself into our conversation."

"She seems lively."

"Ha! Living together is interesting. Calling us opposites would be quite accurate."

"Ah, gotcha. What were you gonna do if I hadn't called?"

"Wait for you to call," I said before thinking better of it. "Or read."

"Read to me then. What world are we visiting tonight?"

"A new one. I haven't been able to get into this story as much."

"I know what you mean. Sometimes, something grabs hold of you. Other times not so much." He smiled.

Were we still talking about a book?

19

The week went by equally fast and slow. Fast because I was so busy at work, and slow because I knew that Sebastian—in the flesh—wasn't waiting for me at the end of it. After staying late on Tuesday and working through lunch on Wednesday, I was all caught up and back to a regular flow on the second half of hump day. A highlight of my week was when Donald crashed my conference call with Tamika. He had me rolling the whole time. Tamika seemed to be smiling, too, though our connection was spotty. Parts of our video conference call were like a poorly dubbed movie translated from another language. I'd have to remember to ask him later if he asked her out or felt any sparks between them. The poor service didn't allow me to get a good read on their body language.

Camilla was on a location shoot in the electric blue waters of the Caribbean—rough life, remember—all weekend. My days off were looking long and quiet. The only thing on my mental planner was my nightly chats with Sebastian.

A whole week had passed, and he still kept our connection alive, unlike eight years ago. He probably misplaced my old home address in his move, and as time sat in, he forgot to write altogether. Our lifestyles now made it easier. One touch on our phones was all it took to connect.

We settled back into our normal lighthearted, easy, and fun conversations, much like they were before I traveled for work. That isn't to say I didn't miss him and think about him

~~practically non-stop~~ often. However, I was back to ordinary life. I knew the facts versus my dreams and could pretty much decipher between the two with clarity. *Time would tell*, I reminded myself.

Reluctantly, we navigated a course with an unknown final landing place. Had I not veered left back to Texas, that could've changed our destination, but the road between us seemed even longer and harder to navigate with each passing day. I feared as we spent more time apart, he'd slowly forget me again. Would the distance cause our lives to resume a routine closer to a few months ago—absent of each other?

After a long week that followed an emotional month, I unintentionally fell asleep in the grandma hours on Saturday. The chime for a new message woke me up. Only when I looked at my phone, not one but five messages awaited a reply.

Sebastian: How was your day, sweets?

Sebastian: I bet you are nose deep in a book. HELLO?

Sebastian: Hey, where you at?

Sebastian: Ummm, can you chat?

Sebastian: Message me when you're free.

I felt awful for sleeping through his messages that spanned thirty minutes and wondered if he already went to bed after a long day of MMA training.

Me: Hi, sorry. I was asleep. You up?

I waited without much hope, hating myself for the thoughts potentially running through his head.

Sebastian: Sleep? We're too young for that!

I smiled at Sebi's response, elated to still have some "time" with him in my day.

Me: Hush. I fell asleep watching TV.

Sebastian: Getting old, are we? What did you do today?

Me: A whole lot of nothing. Probably a good thing too. I needed a down day.

Me: Down like chill, not sad.

Sebastian: Right, right. I probably need one of those soon too.

Me: For real! You even more than me.

Sebastian: Since you're finally awake, now what?

It was almost 11:00, midnight for him. Sebastian had another full day of practice hours away.

Me: Idk, it's kinda late. You must be exhausted.

Sebastian: A little.

Me: Want to talk tomorrow?

Sebastian: I feel like yes is the smart choice here.

Me: You always were a smart one.

Sebastian: You would know. You were right there with me.

Me: I'll talk to you tomorrow. I won't fall asleep this time. Rest well.

Sebastian: Thanks, sweets. You too.

———————————

Sunday looked much like Saturday, filling up my day with activities to pass the time until I heard from Sebastian. I hoped we'd have more time tonight since over the last week, we had less interaction combined than one Sunday together in New York.

I was giddy when my phone rang, and I'd be able to hear his voice. As his name lit up my screen, I wondered what led to his decision on how he would contact me. The method was never the same consecutively and didn't seem to have any rhyme or reason. Sometimes he messaged me, sometimes he called, and sometimes he sent a face chat request. I enjoyed them all, accepted them all, but I'd be lying if I said I didn't have a favorite.

If my pulse was at sixty-five typically and seventy when he came to mind, it climbed into the eighties when we were in contact. And that was only digitally. I functioned in the triple digits when he was close enough to touch.

"Hello there, sir," I answered the call in a playful mood. "Finally free from the labors of the day?"

"Someone's in a good mood," he commented.

"It's a good day to have a good day."

"Oh, really?"

"Yeah. And maybe ... you're my first human interaction." I chuckled.

"Man, you should probably get out more."

"You think? I could leave now. I'll let you go."

"No, no. Not now, just sometimes. I guess. Or not. Whatever." Sebastian rambled.

"You survived another weekend of two-a-days."

"Barely. I'm beat."

"How much longer do you think you'll keep doing this? Both jobs, I mean."

"I don't know. Wish I did. I feel like I need a few more wins on my record first to prove I haven't had easy fights. My coach said I'm going to have to pull the trigger on it one day. He makes it sound like it's easy to just walk into the job I worked *so hard* to get over the last several years. Imagine me telling my boss, 'I'm out. I'd rather get punched in the face for a living.'"

I chuckled; he huffed. *Oops.*

"Well, there's no pressure. You're handling it now. What's the rush?"

"Yeah, I guess so."

"There you go. When it's supposed to happen, it will happen, right?"

"Right. Thanks for talking me down, sweets."

I applied the advice I gave him to our relationship and sighed in acceptance. No need to rush. No need to define the relationship.

We found a rhythm, somewhere between when we first started talking again and how we spoke while I was in the Northeast. Sometimes he called me sweets—and I tried not to let my heart skip a beat—and sometimes he called me Londyn—and I tried not to let my heart skip a beat. It didn't seem like Sebastian was going to push to take the pin out of the me-moving conversation, so I didn't feel the need to push either. We'd ride it out. Not that we had that actual conversation to confirm the aforementioned, I simply factored in all the data and came up with that result on my own.

Perhaps I needed to decide on a future month to take the pin out and reevaluate moving. We needed to have a conversation where I was open and honest, and he was open and honest, and this game of dancing around our commitment level would end. He was the stronger one, physically and mentally, but I didn't feel like he was capable of the task any more than me. So we danced some more. This time with no music.

As the week progressed, we only talked three times. I didn't feel the need to wait by the phone, though I still wanted to. One night, I went out with Camilla to meet the man of her dreams, Branch, when he came into town to visit her. He was a cool guy, definitely a step up from most of the men she entertained since we became roommates. Branch was a sports analyst, one in the making anyway, working on his Youtube channel and blog to submit to the major companies as a shiny application. Which made sense when I remembered he used my bedroom when he came to town for a football game. Sebi didn't call or text that night, regardless.

It appeared my fears were right; the newness was wearing off. Or possibly the distance settled in. Maybe Sebastian already let me go when I left New York on a plane without the response he'd hoped for?

I reminded myself of the words I used to encourage him several days ago: If it's supposed to happen, it will happen.

Right?

As time passed, surely my heart and mind would line up with further perfection. Plus, Sebastian's involvement—or lack thereof—would help solidify the conclusion.

20

The third Monday in October, after being back in my Texas office for only two weeks, Ralph informed me I'd be heading back to Illinois. Oddly enough, I didn't even get an option in traveling this time. Crystal, the woman I trained, turned in her retirement paperwork with a sticky note on top stating, *I won't be training my replacement.* I hoped whoever they hired would be more literate in technology and training wouldn't take long.

Seymour had done well and profited our company since the buyout three months ago, but I feared what kind of mess I'd find on my former trainee's desk upon arrival. I had a gut feeling Crystal was fed up and too far behind to care to catch up, and that's what spurred on her retirement. Then again, she did mention she was close to her eligibility marker. Perhaps she treaded water until the date on the calendar arrived—her rescue boat.

Just when I was back into a standard grind, I had a plane ticket in my hand. I genuinely hoped the rest of my week wouldn't be spent in another state. Ralph told me to touch base on Wednesday and see how much longer I thought it would take. It seemed my job had completely morphed into the traveling trainer without me signing the agreement. When I got back from this trip, I planned to ask for clarity on the matter. Had a plane ticket not already been purchased, I would've had that discussion before leaving.

I ran all of the payables checks that would go out on Friday in case I didn't come back and left them with Ralph for his John Hancock. However, I crossed my fingers I'd be back in time to be the one who dropped them in the outgoing bin.

When I got home from work, Camilla was in the middle of the living room floor doing her stretches. She had more flexibility in her ankles than I possessed in my whole body. Perhaps that's why she was able to stay in such good shape. That and the fact that she never ate anything that contained more than fifty calories, it seemed. Green things didn't really have calories. She actually gave up more in life for her job than I gave her credit for.

"Hey girl," I said as I dumped my laptop bag down onto the chair.

"Hey," she responded, extra airy through the breath she released.

"So, I'm leaving again."

"Already?" Cam contorted her body into a new pose I didn't know the name for, nor could I replicate.

"Yeah. But no need to reactivate the Airbnb. I'm hoping to be back in a few days."

"Sounds good."

"I'm gonna go pack."

Instead of packing, however, I fell facedown onto my bed and let out a sigh into the blankets. I wasn't exactly fond of this new traveling regime. The first time was exciting and fun, the second time was, well, Sebastian, but this third round was just blah. A blah cherry on top of a blah sundae. Then again, had I not ventured out with this opportunity months ago, I never would've run back into Sebastian. That was a deep thought.

After allowing myself a small pity party, I got to work. Since I hadn't done laundry in a hot minute, I didn't have enough clothes to take with me. Using UberEats before I'd be back in a tiny town without it, I ordered myself a giant burger and fries from Harley's before starting the first load of laundry.

The buzzer letting me know my dinner arrived gave me a burst of excitement for the first time all day. I bound down the stairs and was back inside in less than a minute—my own workout of the day. Camilla rolled her eyes as soon as she saw the greasy bag in my hand.

"Want some?" I winked.

"What did that cow do to you?"

"Make me smile." I felt like a murderer with some of her comments, but I reminded myself of her dramatic antics and paid it no mind.

My small suitcase rested open and partially packed on the bed, so I sat at my vanity to eat and read. The book I struggled to get into finally pulled me in. I blamed my own mental fog more than the story. The cadence letting me know the dryer was done resounded, so I put a bookmark in to save my place, took another bite of the juicy burger, and navigated back out to the main area. Camilla was no longer in the living room. I heard the shower running. Perhaps she had something to do tonight, or she was rinsing clean post-workout. *Did stretching cause actual sweat?* Heck, if I knew.

An hour and a half later, my bags were packed, and I was on the last three chapters of the book when my phone went off.

I swiped to unlock the face chat request.

"Hello, Ms. Londyn," he said as soon as both of our faces popped up on the screen.

"Hello, Mr. Sebastian," I replied.

"What are you up to?"

I pulled the book into view of the screen.

"But of course. I should've known."

"And you? All done with practice?"

"Yup." He hobbled backward and collided with his bed. "Got a new war wound too."

"Oh no! Where?"

He panned his phone down to show me his knee covered by an ice pack and wrapped in an ace bandage. I also didn't miss, even in the blur, that he wasn't wearing a shirt. I'd only seen him in such a state a few times, so I was still surprised as to just how many abdominal muscles he possessed. And tried not to care.

"My leg went one way, and my kneecap went the other."

I cringed as I sucked in air.

"Eh. The trainer popped it back in for me. He said to ice it, and I should be able to practice tomorrow."

"Be careful. You only get two kneecaps in life."

"Thanks for the reminder. I'll work on my grappling mostly, just to be safe." He situated himself on the bed. "What's going on with you?"

"All packed up and ready to head back for more training," I said matter-of-factly.

"Here?" He lit up as his crooked smile transformed his face.

Although his excitement made me feel good, great actually, it only confirmed to me how we could only progress if I was willing to move.

"Illinois," left my lips instead of no. It didn't feel as final. "Only for a couple of days, I hope. The return ticket says Thursday, but I'm supposed to check in the day before and let them know if they need to bump it back."

"Gotcha." Sebastian lost the bit of glow that illuminated his countenance seconds before.

"And this time, I'm traveling solo. *That* should be interesting."

"Nice. I predict lots of reading in your future."

"Hopefully so. Because crying alone in a hotel room sounds depressing."

"Crying? Why would you be crying?" His eyebrows dipped.

"I'm not too sure how keen I am on this traveling trainer thing. Thankfully this trip is short."

He was quiet for a moment. "You know what I just realized?"

"What's that?" I asked.

"We almost have the same things going on. We have jobs where we work with numbers and jobs that we travel for."

"Yeah. Only you have two separate jobs, and I don't get punched in the face."

"Good thing. You're too pretty for that!"

Blush colored my cheeks. It was apparent I was still invested in the what-could-our-lives-be path.

"I better get. Early morning flight."

"Be safe and have a relaxing trip."

I crossed my fingers in view of the camera.

"Later, sweets."

"Later."

After ending the chat, I tossed my phone down onto the bed and picked the book back up to finish the last few chapters. Taking a paperback book along only to finish it before the flight ended seemed pointless. But if I was honest with myself, I was trying to think about something—someone—else before falling asleep.

Forgetting to plug my phone in after my conversation with Sebastian wasn't ideal. Especially when my alarm didn't go off, thanks to a dead battery. Thank God Camilla's industrial blender woke me up before I missed my flight, but I was running behind. After getting dressed and securing my hair in the famous work bun, I threw my makeup bag in my suitcase and rushed down to the condo parking garage. Plugging my phone into the car charger would hopefully give me enough juice until I could charge it later. I couldn't be too late; the sun still hadn't risen above the tall buildings.

I parked at the office—where I'd leave my car without having to pay for parking—and ran inside.

"I called you a hundred times," Sammy said when I stopped in front of her desk.

Catching my breath, I replied, "My phone died. I just got all your missed calls when I charged my phone on the drive here."

"Are you gonna make it?"

"I think so. Let's go."

Sammy drove me to the airport thirty minutes later than we planned. If traffic wasn't bad, I'd still make my flight.

In the scattered morning, breakfast and caffeine weren't priorities. If I had time to spare, my first stop after passing security would be the coffee shop. I hurried out of Sammy's car and pulled my standard carry-on suitcase to my side, hollering, "Thanks," and I closed the door and hurried off.

For the first time all morning, I had a few minutes to halt my hustle. Fifteen minutes before I was scheduled to board, I made it to the line and ordered a giant cup of Help-Me and its sweet companion, Tickle-My-Tastebuds, to fill my empty stomach.

"Well, well, well. Fancy meeting you here. Looks like we finally get to see each other."

Before I could move, arms wrapped around me from behind. I tensed at the unexpected touch and turned around.

Totally taken aback, his lips brushed against mine before I said anything.

"Roman." *Oh no.*

"Good morning, sunshine."

"Sorry, I'm all kinds of frazzled today." I went to pull my hand through my hair only to feel the smoothed top and rounded bun—case in point. "I overslept and barely made it in time. You, uh, coming or going?"

"Coming."

"This early? Don't you usually have evening flights?" I scooted up in line.

"Yeah. I agreed to give up my seat last night for someone traveling for a funeral. The next flight out wasn't until this morning."

"That was very kind of you." It warmed my heart to hear. Not that I thought Roman was incapable of such a feat, he just always seemed in the zone and not as conscious of life outside of his work.

"Since we're both here, can I join you for breakfast?"

"Not really. I only have a few minutes to grab something and make it to my gate."

"Bummer. Where are you headed?"

"Illinois again." I moved up in line again.

"Ah, to the apple orchard city." He smiled.

"Yeah." Shoot. I shouldn't have waited this long to clarify where I was emotionally after my Pennsylvania trip. Roman had barely crossed my mind. *What do I say now?*

As if I hadn't already been inconsiderate with talking to Roman, I couldn't stoop even lower and give a this-isn't-gonna-work-for-me speech while in line for coffee at the airport after barely talking for seven weeks.

"Let's catch up when I get back."

"When is that?" Roman asked.

"Hopefully by Monday. Will you be in town?"

He looked up, considering his schedule. "I don't *think* so. I'll let you know when I get back." No telling when that would be.

"Okay." It was my turn to order.

When he came in for a kiss, I offered my cheek instead. More than ever before, in the split-second of deciding to let Roman kiss me, my heart was fully for someone else. His forehead wrinkled a fraction.

"See ya later," he said as I walked away.

As I juggled my breakfast and luggage and fell into my seat on the plane, I couldn't consume my latte fast enough. What a morning. The flight wasn't bad, and reading a new book on my tablet was the easiest strategy to checkout from the craziness.

An older man was in the aisle seat, I was in the window seat, and neither of us touched the middle seat as if it was laced with leprosy. We didn't even speak two words to each other. The seatbelt lights dinged back to life before it seemed like we had been at full altitude for five whole minutes.

I took one of the taxis waiting outside the airport and gave them the name of my hotel. Taking a few minutes to make sure my rushed morning look wasn't unprofessional was vital. All I needed was to meet the trainee looking like a disheveled mess.

Having the hotel room all to myself was the first time in hours I could stop and recharge without an audience. When it was time to head downstairs, I briefly expected Donald to come through the door across the hall before remembering he was still in Pennsylvania. After freshening up and waiting for the company car to pick me up, the day was already half over. I sincerely hoped I wasn't about to walk into another situation with a dated or inexperienced employee, not sure I could handle more today.

As the giant F-350 I once drove pulled to a stop at the curb, I didn't recognize the driver, leading me to believe they sent the new guy to pick up his trainer.

"Hi." I climbed in without clarifying who this person was. Did I just make a huge mistake? *God, please don't let me end up on the missing persons' list.* Of course, my fears were for nothing. It was the company truck, after all.

"Hey there. Welcome back. I'm Clay." He extended his hand for a firm handshake. Based on looks alone, Clay was a new graduate, excited about his first job. That alone gave me hope he knew his way around computer software.

"Nice to meet you, Clay, I'm—"

"Londyn, I know. I've heard all about you," he stated as he

pulled the giant gearshift from park to drive and pulled away from the hotel.

"From who?"

"The crew. Only a few of us, you know. Not much else to do in the office but talk while we waited for you to come train me."

"That I do. Who took over Blanche's spot?"

"Blanche?"

"The old owner. She was acting as the manager still, but after the buyout, she was set for her exit."

"Oh, yes. The new manager is Donald Wilkie. But he's regional, not local. They said he's supposed to come once a month or something. He hasn't been since I arrived, but my phone interview was with him."

"Really, Donald?"

"Yeah, you know him?"

"Yeah." I pulled out my phone to message my friend and thankfully had eight percent battery left. I shot him a congratulatory text and let him know I was on site for training and would update him later. "So who's running the office then?"

"Stan."

The sales guy. "Oh, really?"

"Yeah. Something about after the lady I replaced, he had the most tenure."

"Cool. So, tell me about yourself," I inquired when we were almost back to the office.

I was correct. Clay graduated in May, and after a short stint with temp-agency placements trying to find his niche, he landed a job at Seymour. Oh, and he was from Alabama. A good ol' southern boy. I should've known from his accent that didn't match our location.

There was no sign of Crystal at the desk we trained at, even though she occupied the space my whole life and then some. Homegirl was *done*. Sign the last check and cash it before the ink dried, see ya later kind of thing. I chuckled, happy for her. No doubt, she had a calendar full of grandkid playdates and blank days with her husband. I greeted Stan and asked about my favorite roughneck out in the field, Kevin. With Blanche and Crystal gone, Stan and Kevin *were* the team. And Clay now. We got right into training in a quiet office where Clay would most likely be alone most days. Not sure I'd like being the only one in the office or not.

To say I was pleased with how much Clay already knew was an understatement. Why they thought he needed to be trained in the first place was beyond me. I could've done this over the phone.

My nights alone in the hotel were filled with thinking. Unadulterated, uninterrupted, unbiased thinking. Roman, Sebastian, and I were quite literally spread around the country in an obtuse triangle. I knew my heart was with Sebastian. I didn't see that going away any time soon. Which meant I couldn't continue to see Roman when I wished it would be someone else looking at me from across the table instead. It made total sense that Roman wanted to be with someone when he was in town. His day to day, other than work meetings, was spent alone. Unfortunately for him, I couldn't fill that sliver of his time anymore. I solidified the exit speech I'd deliver soon. And perhaps, if I wasn't willing to move any time soon, I needed to prepare two exit speeches, not one. However, thinking about saying goodbye to Sebi literally made my stomach hurt.

21

The last nine days in October were the only ones yet to be crossed off of my calendar. Never in my life had a quarter of a year gone by so fast. No doubt it was due to all that occurred in one hundred and two days. I'd been on a plane six times, gone on a dozen dates with two different men, slept in three different states, trained three people, and taken on new accounts—*huge* accounts. I was tired, to say the least. With the holidays not too far away, I was hopeful for some downtime. The short two-hour drive back to my childhood home would be a breeze.

While on the office phone with Donald, discussing the new staff member in Belleville, my cell phone rang. I pulled it from the drawer to see who called in the middle of the workday.

Sebastian.

Why was he calling now?

"Do you have any other questions?" I asked, trying to end my work conversation so I could get to the personal one—hoping Steve wouldn't comment on it.

"I think that's it, Bridges. Thanks for going back out to Belleville and making sure all was well."

"You bet."

"You still miss me?"

"Just a bit." I laughed. "Talk to you later."

I hung up the receiver and accepted Sebastian's call before it went to voicemail. "Hey!"

"Are you sitting down?" he asked. Excitement decorated his words.

"Since I'm at work, always. What's up?"

"I just got off the phone with my manager. He booked a fight for me in Dallas. This Saturday." His voice indicated he moved around. No doubt, endorphins already surged through him.

My heart raced in my chest. I wasn't sure how much time he'd have before or after his fight, but the chance of even a few minutes together was exciting.

"Are you serious? That's great!"

"You, uh, up for some tickets?"

"Of course!"

"Fantastic. I'll have my manager put you on the list."

"Send me the info, please."

"You got it. I gotta go, still at work. Later, sweets."

Sweets.

In all the wondering about when I might travel to the Northeast again—work-related or purely personal—Sebastian coming for a fight hadn't crossed my mind. Which was naive since that's how we ran into each other in the first place. All progress I'd made to force my heart to proceed slowly evaporated in an instant. I was going to see Sebastian in five days.

Holy cow, I'm going to see Sebastian in five days!

Once again, I couldn't get to the weekend fast enough.

By Wednesday, I was so anxious I almost picked up the habit I kicked years ago: biting my nails. However, our conversation that night dialed me down.

Me: Are you nervous?

Sebastian: Not so much. More excited.

Me: What will your day look like?

Sebastian: The plane lands at 12:30, weigh-ins are at 2:00, fight card starts at 8:00. I'm the second fight.

From what I remembered, he'd be starving and ready to eat right after he weighed in. I wasn't sure what all he had to do to prep for the fight, but if he didn't mention getting together in that gap, I was confident it was because he couldn't. I huffed before concealing my emotions with words and exclamation points.

Me: Full day!!

Sebastian: Fight days always are.

Me: I'm excited! Hopefully, I get a chance to see you.

Sebastian: For sure. After.

Me: Okay :)

Sebastian: I got you down for two tickets unless you want more. I don't have anyone to give the other two too.

I hadn't even asked Camilla to come with me yet, let alone two more people. But I wanted Sebastian to feel like I was totally in his corner, cheering him on.

Me: Sure. I'll see if I can find some other people to come.

Sebastian: Awesome. I'll mark you down for all four then.

I went into Camilla's room after my chat with Sebastian ended.

"You up for another fight night this weekend?" I punched the air with my lanky arms.

"Umm, I don't know. Fights. Rhett. Rhett. Old news." She stated the workings of her brain while tick-tocking a small floret of broccoli in the air.

"What if I told you I had extra tickets this time? Four. I thought Branch might want to come. Maybe do a video for his sports channel?"

"Yeah?" Camilla sprang up, abandoning the vegetable on a plate.

"Yeah." I raised my eyebrows a few times, knowing my idea was good.

"Let me check."

I walked back out to get a drink of water from the kitchen. I was surprised the two of them, Branch and Cam, were able to keep things going long distance. Granted, it had only been a month, and my roommate could definitely be described with the word fickle. Give it another couple of months, and we might have a different story. Or was I simply in denial that long-distance couldn't work?

"He's gonna come." She ran into the kitchen in her tiny pj's, yelling, and clung onto me like a baby koala.

"Nice. Now I don't have to go alone. Being the third wheel is better than a loner in that crazy full stadium."

As if it wasn't already hard enough not to think about Sebastian in an endless game of what-if, now he was truly stuck in my head—there so much he should be paying rent. All day Thursday and all day Friday, The Basher consumed my mind. You know, in his fighting gear—without his shirt. It took me double the mental capacity at work to push through the distraction and focus. Perhaps I didn't need more time to decide? Maybe I was ready to take a leap of faith and move to be ~~with~~ closer to him. I hoped we'd have a substantial amount of time tonight to take the pin out and discuss our future face to face. And not on a screen.

Getting ready to head to the stadium, we waited on Branch to arrive. Camilla, getting ready in the bathroom, put a few final touches on her makeup. We were both amped as me to see our men.

I stood back to examine my look in my vanity mirror when the buzzer rang. I yelled, "He's here," to Cam before answering the bell. "Hey, come on up. We're just about ready." I mashed the button to allow him into the building and up to our door.

"Are we going to ride in his car or mine?" I asked as Camilla came into view, putting in her earrings.

"I'll let him decide. He already drove two hours to get here. He might like a break. Plus, how can we cuddle if he's driving? I'm feeling your backseat." She smiled and wagged her eyebrows.

"Is any of my stuff off-limits to you?" I rolled my eyes as the knock echoed on our door.

Camilla rushed around me to greet her man.

Only it wasn't her man.

"Surprise, sunshine. I'm back in town."

Roman. It was Roman. I stepped forward, utterly surprised indeed. "Hey. Um, we were about to leave, actually."

"Man," he chuckled, "our schedules just can't seem to line up, can they?" He asked as he walked in and hugged me.

I was so confused. He never came by without asking if I was free, had never even stepped foot inside my condo before. I looked at Camilla in terror while he embraced me. *What do I do?* I mouthed to her.

"Where are you headed?"

"We're waiting for my boyfriend to get here, then we're headed to a fight," she spoke up. I was glad for the help.

"Like at a sports bar?" he questioned.

"No. At an arena," I clarified.

"Ah. Gotcha. So, this is where you live, huh?" Roman asked.

"Yes. Not much, I know." I chuckled—pure nerves.

"No, it's nice. Give me a little tour. Which is your room?"

I didn't want to. The fact that he was already in my living space made my whole situation that much more complicated.

Buzz.

"There's Branch. We have to go," I said. "Can we get together tomorrow?"

"Can't. Leaving for work. That's why I stopped by. I'm only home for about fifteen hours. Just came from the airport, actually."

"When you get back then."

We made it down the stairs and out the giant glass door where Roman *typically* met me. Camilla looked like a sugar glider as she flew into Branch's arms. *All right, they're cute.* I turned to Roman to say bye.

"Hey, Londyn," Branch said. "Oh, you found someone to use the fourth ticket?"

I looked at Camilla and froze.

"You have a fourth ticket?" Roman asked.

Dang it. We were so close to leaving. "Uh, yeah."

"Well, why didn't you say so? Let's go."

"You aren't really dressed for it," Camilla said.

"That's fine. I don't mind. It sounds like fun." Roman countered.

"These things go kind of late. Are you sure you're up for it?" I made a last-ditch effort to get out of the situation.

"Hmmm, good question." He looked at his watch. "I have a morning flight."

My pulse jumped at the out presenting itself.

"Well, I'm already here. Besides, you look too good to walk away from." He pulled me into a hug and kissed my lips. I don't think my mouth actually puckered. So much for that out. "But I do think I'll take my own car in case I want to cut out early. I'll follow you."

"Okay."

I'm a coward.

How in the world did this happen? This was exactly why, no matter what Camilla said, one guy was all I wanted to date. If I got to see Sebastian, now I would've kissed two people in one day. That was not who I was.

The four of us made it into the parking garage and were en route moments later.

"CAMILLA!" I said, thankful the vehicle concealed my voice.

She jumped in her seat as if I scolded her for their entangled embrace in my back seat. When I brought my head to the steering wheel at a red light, however, I was pretty sure she knew it had nothing to do with her.

"Now what? I can't believe this." I pulled my hands through my wavy locks and gripped a hold at the roots. This was supposed to be Sebastian's night, where I'd commit to being all in for him. That would be difficult with Roman next to me.

"Stop that, first of all. You're messing up your hair. We'll figure this out. Take a breath."

"If I get a chance to see Sebastian, you're going to have to occupy Roman." Even the thought of it made me queasy. "Ugh, this is bad."

"It'll be fine. I got you."

"What's going on?" Branch asked. Camilla explained my horrible situation to her boyfriend. It sounded even worse as she said it.

"Ah. Sticky situation. Sorry, Londyn," Branch said with a grimace. "I have an idea. You tell me when, and I'll *need* a camera guy to help me with some footage."

"Genius!" Cam kissed him on the cheek.

"Yeah, okay. That can work." I still wasn't thrilled to be in this situation, but the game plan helped a little.

"I'll see to it. I helped create this mess, so I'll make sure to clean it up."

When we arrived, Roman ditched his coat and tie, opened a couple of buttons, and cuffed the sleeves of his pressed white shirt. He still wasn't properly dressed for the occasion, but he'd blend in better than if he didn't loosen his appearance.

He came up beside me and grabbed my hand. "I'm excited! I've never been to one of these. Have you?"

"Once."

I'd be a fool not to notice how much more he inserted himself into my world today. Showing up unannounced, pulling me for a kiss that wasn't a hello or goodbye, grabbing my hand as we walked. It was as if he knew something was up and tried to press in before I pushed away. Or at least that's how it seemed to me.

When we walked up to the ticket booth, I used the excuse of checking in to drop his hand before giving my name.

"Whoa! That was hot," Roman stated. "Look at you, all in charge. How did you manage that?"

"I know one of the fighters," was all I admitted.

"Score."

Like the other fight I attended, our tickets were in the front— the fifth row. Sebastian hadn't seen me in the crowd last time, so I prayed that'd be the case again. All I had to do was make it another hour or so. Then, I'd be able to check-in with Sebi after his fight was over. I whispered to Camilla, pointing out where I'd cut out if I went to the locker rooms so Branch could take Roman in the opposite direction.

Music echoed in the rafters, signaling the first fighter was walking out.

I'd yet to fully relax, but I kept trying. Roman hadn't let on that he sensed my tension, so I hoped he wouldn't. If Sebastian was by my side, he would've known long ago.

Thankfully, the room was so loud and energetic, I didn't have to do much talking with Roman. A bit of his childlike demeanor I witnessed a few times came out in the atmosphere.

The horn announced the end of the first fight that went all three rounds.

"Who do you think won?" Roman leaned over and asked.

Only I hadn't paid much attention. My eyes were in the ring. My head and heart floated somewhere else entirely.

"Uh, the guy in the green shorts."

"Really? I think the other guy took it." He spoke above the noise.

Five minutes later, the other guy was, in fact, declared the winner. Roman clapped and cheered with the crowd.

I only thought I was nervous before then. Because as the ring emptied out for the next match, my heart boomed in my chest. Sebastian was close.

"He's about to come out," I leaned over to Camilla to inform her. She grabbed my hand and gave me a supportive squeeze. We were in the middle, with the guys sandwiching us in. Branch had the end seat, hoping to get better footage at the aisle. Roman was farthest away because I hoped he wouldn't be seen.

The lights dimmed as a new song started, but it wasn't the tune I remembered for The Basher's entrance. I had a few more minutes to regulate my pulse before it peaked the limits. I dropped my head as I clutched the back of the seat in front of me.

"You all right?" Roman asked.

"Yeah, yeah." I stood back up.

Then his music played. My mind focused solely on Sebi.

He looked good as he shadowboxed down the entry lane. I hollered and clapped, not caring if I looked ridiculous. The ref stopped him diagonal from where we sat to apply vaseline, or whatever it was, to his face. He also checked for the mouthguard, cup, and made sure his gloves were done correctly.

Roman placed his hand on the small of my back and leaned in centimeters from my ear. "That's the guy you know?"

Distracted for a second, I turned to answer. "Yeah." I didn't realize his face was still so close to mine. "Sorry." I moved back.

Roman's eyes flashed over to Sebastian, then cupped my face and kissed me. I pulled away as fast as I could and turned back to look at Sebi. His eyes locked with mine.

No. NO!

That didn't just happen. This wasn't happening.

Only it did. It was.

Sebastian pounded his fists together with extra gusto and climbed into the ring.

I turned to Camilla, who apparently witnessed what happened. Her lips were pursed, her eyes sympathetic.

Maybe Sebi hadn't actually seen Roman kiss me. I implored it to be true. When the bell sounded and the first round started, Sebastian flew in with a leaping punch. He missed. My adrenaline thrummed inside of me.

The Basher was good, but the other fighter in orange trunks was too. Back and forth, they swung and blocked, a few blows landing on their intended destination.

I yelled and cheered him on, excited when he appeared to have the upper hand and mortified when he took a hit. It was as if I could feel the blows myself, watching the man I loved get beat. From what I remembered, it wasn't as brutal the last time I saw him fight. The first round ended with both men possessing a minor cut, or two, on their faces.

The trainers in his corner surrounded him as he sat on the tiny stool, tending to his cut and offering him water. One man ran a metal tool of some sort across Sebi's face, causing him to wince.

I looked down to take a few calming breaths. When my head rose, Sebastian looked right at me. And he wasn't smiling. He saw me. Saw everything.

There was no way I possessed the strength to handle all that occurred. It didn't appear as if he did either.

"What's going on?" His trainer hollered as he clapped against Sebastian's cheek to pull his attention back in the ring. "Get your head in the game!" The man demanded.

Sebastian shook his head and pounded his fist together as they pulled the stool from underneath him. The second round began.

He started off strong, landing a stiff kick to the ribs that caused the other fighter to double over. Taking advantage of the downed position, Sebastian rushed in to try for the win. Only his opponent anticipated the move and popped up with a massive uppercut.

The world seemed to slow down to half-speed as Sebastian fell backward like a giant tree, his limbs limp at his sides.

"NO!" I screamed. "Sebi." I covered my mouth in panic.

22

The ref stood over Sebastian, still down and motionless, and waved his hands in the air to call the fight.

My pulse raced so fast and hard, it was painful.

Camilla grabbed my arm. "He'll be okay. They know what they're doing in there." She tried to reassure me as a group of men hovered around the man I undoubtedly loved, blocking my view. More than ever, the leanings of my heart were clear. Thoroughly transparent.

On the verge of tears, I tried to gain sight of Sebastian again, holding my breath.

What felt like hours later, they finally pulled Sebastian to his feet. The crowd cheered when he was up. I simply sighed in relief while still covering my mouth. *He's okay,* I repeated to myself more than a handful of times.

Sebi stood in the middle of the ring with the ref, announcer, and his opponent. His head hung down as the announcer proclaimed the winner on the microphone. Blood dripped from his cut face and soaked into the mat. Seconds later, he walked out of the cage and back down the aisle his team entered less than fifteen minutes ago, never once lifting his head. How had so much gone so wrong in such a short amount of time?

I knew where he was headed, and there was nothing that could stop me from going to check on him. I gave Camilla the look as I tilted my head toward Roman. She tapped Branch's thigh with the back of her hand.

"Hey, Roman," Branch called out. "Can you come with me to see if we can interview the winner for my sports show?"

"Sure. I'd love to help." He turned to me. "I'll be back."

I nodded and waited until they were out of sight to talk to Camilla. "That was brutal. I have no idea how I'm holding it together right now. My insides are trembling."

"He's fine. You saw him walk out, remember?"

"Yeah. Right." I pulled out my phone to see if Sebastian messaged me, but I seriously doubted I'd find anything. And I didn't. The team was probably tending to his cuts and taking off his gloves and hand tape. Lucky for me, I knew exactly where they were. "I'm gonna go see him."

"Totally. If the guys get back before you, I'll say you went to the restroom or something."

"Thanks." I sidestepped out of our row and exited the giant arena, noticing the drops of blood that marked the floor.

Trying not to run through the halls and catch any unwanted attention, I headed back to the door leading to the locker rooms. I wished I had that backstage pass with me from last time. I took a quick left-right-left glance before heading in and waited for the door to close behind me completely before advancing to the locker room. As I stood there, frozen, I pondered on what to say.

First of all, I wanted to check on Sebastian and simply be there for him after his loss. But secondly, and far more weighty, I had to explain that what he thought he saw wasn't really what it appeared to be.

With one more giant inhale and exhale, I started down the hallway. I hadn't noticed the last time I was back here how the locker rooms had the fighters' names posted outside the door, making my job of finding the correct room even easier. Some doors were closed, and others were open, but I walked quickly and confidently like I belonged there, my pulse still racing.

The sign with his name hung on my side of the open door. Touching the doorframe, I stepped into view.

I wasn't prepared for what I saw. I expected to find Sebastian much like the last time, sitting in a chair, having the athletic tape cut from his hands and wrists. The scene before me was nothing like what I anticipated. Sebastian stood in the middle of the room, throwing his gloves at the wall, fuming. Blood still ran down onto his cheek from his brow as someone lectured.

"Listen, man," one of the coaches said. "This is what happens when you take training lightly. I'm not trying to kick you while you're down, but you missed Sunday practices for a whole month *and* came in overweight today. Thank God we were able to cut the two pounds with the sauna in the hour, or you might not have been able to fight at all. You have to take this more seriously if you're going to make fighting your career."

I wished I hadn't already made myself visible, wanted so badly to disappear back into the giant crowd, but he saw me. Sebastian looked at me, dead on. His stillness caught the others' attention.

"Ma'am, you can't be here. How did you get in?" The coach addressed me.

"I, uh. I've been back here before." I swept my hair behind my ear. "I just wanted to check on Sebastian."

The man turned to Sebastian. I waited for Sebi's permission to let me in and ask them to give us the room, much like the last time.

However, "Close the door," was all Sebastian said. It was the harshest words I'd ever heard him utter. My stomach bottomed out, but I wasn't ready to give up.

Our eyes were still locked. "I only need a min—"

"Another time, I guess." One of the team in matching shirts escorted me back and grabbed the doorknob.

Before he could shut the door, I gave one more plea. "Sebi?"

He finally looked away from me, a split second before the door divided us.

To say I was broken was a gross understatement.

What just happened?

I wanted to blame his pent up fury from the post-fight loss, but his harsh exchange caused chills to bite my skin. The idea to sit down and wait in the hall until he came out was strong, but the potential risk of getting another dose of the cold shoulder was more than I could handle in one night.

Instead, I made my way down the corridor, headed to the bathroom so I could fall apart privately in a stall.

But before I exited the long hallway, a door behind me banged open.

"Londyn!"

I turned to discover the rage in his face hadn't settled yet and wasn't sure how productive a conversation would be right now.

"You had something to say?" He added as he approached me like he was with an opponent in the cage.

Tears slipped from my eyes. "Maybe they were right. This conversation needs to wait for another time." I couldn't move.

"No. I want to hear it now." He grew closer at a rushed pace. "I want to know why in the world you'd bring some guy with you to *my* fight on the one night we could see each other." His taped hand pointed out, then onto his heaving chest.

"I didn't really bring him."

"It sure looks like you did. He was awfully chummy to be some random guy sitting next to you." He paused. "Do you know the guy or not?"

"I do."

"Is he the guy you were seeing?"

My answers weren't helping Sebastian to defuse because it was more than a yes or no response. I didn't want to answer.

"Is he?" Sebastian pressed, no calmer than before.

"Yes. But—"

"Seriously, Londyn! After the month we had. Do I mean nothing to you?"

"Of course you do."

"I'm too far away, so you go back to that guy like nothing?" He wiped his bloody brow and ran his hand down his shorts.

"No, Sebi, it isn't like that at all. I care about you deeply. I was ready to discuss our future."

"Are you kidding me? NOW? Why not sooner?"

"I wasn't sure you'd stick around." I clasped my twitching hands, hiding my tremors.

"Seriously? Why in the world would I spend every night talking to you and miss all of those practices to spend the entire day with you if I didn't plan on sticking around? I just got my first loss because of how distracted I was between last month and watching that tool kiss you. Ugh!" He grabbed his hair and turned around, about to walk away, but then faced me again. "I asked you to *move*, Londyn!" The crack in his voice broke my heart even more. If that was possible.

It took every ounce of my non-existent strength to talk without falling apart.

"I know. Let's talk about it later." I attempted to be firm with my statement, but the emotions controlling my face surely portrayed how weak and out of control I truly felt.

"No, you don't have to worry about moving anymore. How could I have been such a fool?" He huffed. "I can't believe I thought I loved you." *What?* His words sucked the air from my lungs.

"Sebastian, please. Can we wait until our emotions settle and have this conversation another time?" Tears dropped from my face onto the tiled floor as freely as the blood from his.

"No. I think I'm don—"

"Don't! Stop talking before you say something you don't mean." I lifted a trembling hand.

He took a breath, about to speak, disregarding my request.

"No." I ran. Turned tail and *ran*. I didn't have to stand there and let all of our history crumble into pieces because I made a horrible choice by not telling Roman he couldn't come. The Sebastian I knew was far from the man in the hallway. I chose to extend grace, considering his emotions were magnified after his first loss. I despised that he saw Roman kiss me, frustrated at myself for allowing this whole mess, but it wasn't what he thought. Sebastian had to know the truth but needed to have a level head before we could talk. Otherwise, he'd only hear my responses as excuses.

I'd never been one to cuss, but those were the only words coming to mind as I broke down in the bathroom. Thankfully, the loud music covered up my sobbing.

How much time had passed, I was uncertain. My phone going off in my back pocket was the only thing that made me move.

Camilla: Might want to wrap it up. Roman's getting antsy.

As best as I could, I collected myself. *He will calm down. It won't end like this. Give him some time.* I drew a finger underneath both eyes to clear up the melting mascara, ran my hand through my hair a few times, and situated my clothes. Clearing my throat of any remaining quiver to my voice, I went back out to the arena.

But what if he doesn't?

The vile thought sunk in as I reached to push the bathroom door open.

I almost texted Camilla back to ask her to order an Uber and tell Roman I wasn't feeling well, but I knew if I didn't press through the pain head-on, it would devour me.

When I made it back to our row of seats, Camilla saw me before Roman did. I lifted an eyebrow and bit my bottom lip, doing my best to hold the sorrow at bay. Her electric-model smile washed out like the tide.

"Finally," she said quietly. "I text you forever ago."

I shrugged. "Weird. I came as soon as I got your message."

"It's okay," she said as I passed in front of her. "We'll talk later."

I nodded and sat in my seat.

"There you are," Roman said, sitting down next to me. "You good?"

"Uh, I don't feel so hot right now." Not to lie, far from the whole truth.

"Oh man. Want me to take you home?"

I didn't want to be here, but I also didn't want to leave with Roman. "I don't think so."

"You sure? I think I'm about to cut out before traffic makes it difficult." He pulled out his phone and looked at the time.

"Yeah. I drove my car."

"All right. See you when I'm back in town?"

"Yeah." But only because I still hadn't told I didn't think we should see each other anymore.

Thankfully, he didn't try to kiss me. Possibly because I said I wasn't feeling well. He said goodbye to Camilla and gave Branch a firm handshake before disappearing.

Tugging on the back of Camilla's shirt, I asked after she leaned down, "How many fights are left?"

"Uh, I think one after this." She spoke above the noise.

I nodded. Seconds later, the fight in the cage ended with a vicious choke. The loser was still limp on the mat after the ref peeled the victor off. Seeing the downed fighter only caused the mental picture of Sebastian out cold in the cage to flash before me again. The cheers echoed so loud I couldn't even hear my own gasp.

What-was-I-thinking? flashed before me as I conceived how truly entangled my heart was with the guy I caused to experience such tremendous pain simply because I was too timid to tell Roman he couldn't tag along.

I couldn't help but think how differently the night should've gone.

Camilla sat down next to me. "What happened?"

"Sebastian saw Roman kiss me. And apparently, he *was* very serious about us." I kept his past tense confession of love and rescinding of the offer to move to myself.

"Oh, Londyn." She ran her hand down my back.

"It was bad. I've never seen Sebastian so angry." Hidden in a sea of MMA fans, I let myself cry again. Camilla leaned in and hugged me, then stood to say something to Branch. He looked back at me and nodded his head.

"Let's go," she said. "Give me your keys."

I walked out like a wounded fighter and curled into the backseat of my car as Branch drove us back to the condo.

If it wasn't Sunday, I would've taken a sick day from work. But the day that used to light up and drive my week was equally painful. I did a whole lot of nothing, mostly cried in bed. Or the shower. Even though I was slightly insecure but prepared to plan a future for Sebastian and me days ago, I never thought there'd be animosity between us. He was someone I wanted and planned on having in my life forever after getting reunited. At least to some capacity. The loss of that reality hurt the worst. Even more than discerning I was utterly in love with him as he laid unconscious in the middle of the cage. We could've been something. Now we were most definitely nothing.

I was almost certain I wouldn't hear from him today or any time soon. After how everything went down, I didn't plan on reaching out to him yet either. I still owed him an explanation, but was he ready to hear me out? Whether or not I'd get that chance was a toss-up. I had a bitter feeling he could leave me in his past. He did it once before.

At some point, Camilla knocked on my door.

"Want some company?" she asked.

I simply shrugged my shoulders, uncertain of practically everything. What a mess I made.

Since I didn't say no, she came and sat down next to me. "I know this is heavy, and you feel like your whole world is falling apart, but maybe this is how it was supposed to happen. He kind of decided for you."

A tear spurred on by her words left my eye and soaked into my pillow. Maybe I didn't want the decision to be made for me. Maybe I wanted a say.

23

The next couple of days were agonizing. My eyes were still so puffy on Monday that I used a sick day after all. Seeing how I'd never taken a sick day before, I figured it was okay. Donald caught wind of my absence and called my cell. "What's wrong with my Bridges?" he'd asked. I glossed the situation over as best as I could. No need to give him all the gory details of my heart being dragged through the wringer. Ring. Octagon. Cage. All of the above. He told one of the stupidest jokes I'd ever heard. Something about why one side of the "V" ducks fly in is longer than the other, but it was the first time I even sort of laughed in almost forty-eight hours. For that, I was grateful.

On Tuesday, I went to work and kept my head down. Steve and I typically only talked if I started the conversation. He'd usually turn down his oldies station on the alarm clock radio—which was probably as old as me—with a sigh he probably didn't realize I could hear and respond. Today, his music was all that could be heard other than our fingers clicking on keys.

Wednesday, Thursday, and Friday were like multi-colored carbon copies of an invoice, identical but fading with each layer.

I auto-piloted through the week, relying solely on my number skills to carry me through.

And I almost made it unscathed.

"Londyn," Ralph said two feet from my desk, an hour before my weekend started. "I didn't think it was possible, but you finally made a mistake."

His words straightened my spine like a ten-foot flagpole.

"I did? What was the mistake?"

"You were about to give this lucky guy an extra digit on his commission check. Not that he would've minded, I'm sure."

I took the printed check Ralph extended. Sure enough, seven digits instead of six looked back at me. An extra "2" took the total from two thousand to twenty-two thousand. That would've been a *major* error for the books had it not been caught.

"Oh my goodness. I'm so sorry." I felt an inch tall and wondered what type of reprimand would follow.

Steve leaned over, trying to watch us, and failed at being discreet.

"No problem. I doubt he could've cashed it. The written number is correct, and they have to match."

Thank God.

I was relieved he caught it, but just as embarrassed he did. I should have noticed that myself.

"It won't happen again, sir."

"Seeing as how it took you this long to have one little blip, I was beginning to wonder if you were some sort of unicorn." He chuckled.

Twenty thousand dollars was hardly "a little blip." To me, at least.

I was pretty sure he tried to lighten the mood—and remove the frightened look from my face—but I was mortified past what some lighthearted banter could save. My head, and not only my heart, still suffered from the fight. Had the situation been a real altercation, with fists and legs flying without repentance, my emotional black eye would be in the nasty yellowish-purple phase. Far from healed.

If it wouldn't have made me look weaker, I would've apologized again before heading home.

My bed was all I wanted. Correction: my bed was all I wanted that I knew I could have. There was obviously more that I genuinely wanted. I was asleep by 8:00 p.m.

Camilla asked me to escort her to a shoot on Saturday. Leaving the condo gave my mind something else to think about.

Sunday was the day I dreaded. The nature of Sundays was still morphed for me. Six weeks had passed since our last Sunday date, yet they remained so tangible to me. I knew, with all of me, just like the previous seven days, I wouldn't hear from Sebastian today either. I pondered reaching out to him, but how would I even start? And was he any more ready?

Needless to say, I was glad to be back at work on Monday and return to mind-numbing numbers. By then, the breakup feelings, or whatever they were, had subsided a considerable amount.

That night, I got a call from Roman, who I also hadn't talked to since the fight night.

"Hey, sunshine!"

"Hi, Roman. You back in town?"

"Yes, and I need your help."

"How so?"

"I need you to be free tomorrow night and in a black dress."

I huffed, mostly to myself. "That's pretty specific. Care to fill me in on some more of the details?"

"Have you ever been to an opera?"

"Can't say that I have."

"Well, after tomorrow, that won't be the case anymore."

An opera. I relished in the fact I'd have something to do. Sitting at home every night, although that was technically what I did when I talked to Sebastian, was depressing. Getting out and doing something I'd never done before was a great course of action to move on. Not that I wanted to move on.

Ultimately, I had no reason to say no. At the end of the night, I could finally talk to him about us. Even though my dating options had gone from two to most definitely one, unfortunately, he wasn't the *one* I wanted. And because of that, continuing to see Roman wasn't right.

"Will you pick me up?" I asked.

"Sure will. Can you be ready by 6:00?"

"It might be pushing it from work, but I'll make it happen."

"Great! I can't wait. See you tomorrow."

"Bye, Roman."

I walked over to my closet and scanned through my dresses, trying not to let my heart seize when I saw the slip dress I acquired in New York. I didn't own many dresses, period, let alone one in every color. Camilla did, but she was as slender as the celery stalks she consumed. Her clothes would never fit me.

The only black dress I owned was several years old—the one I wore to my grandpa's funeral. I tried it on and wasn't wowed by my appearance, which wasn't surprising, seeing as how I wasn't trying to impress anyone on the occasion I bought it for.

———————⚓———————

My door was open as I got ready. Camilla passed by and saw me doing something other than lying in bed for the first time in almost two weeks.

"Are my eyes playing tricks on me, or is Londyn Adams getting dolled up?"

"Only a bit, don't get too excited." Apparently, it wasn't unnoticeable how I refrained from makeup as the puffiness in my eyes slowly receded. I hoped she was the only one to notice, part of her livelihood and all.

"Where are you going?"

"The opera."

"That explains your fancy get up."

She wasn't wrong. I tried my luck at a posh secondhand store during my lunch hour and found this gem. I'd be lying if I said the whole time I was in the store didn't remind me of my last date with Sebastian—Central Station. The black dress dipped in a v-neck and decorated my back with a twisted racerback. The gown fell softly to my mid-thigh. I felt beautiful. Broken yet beautiful. The best part about my look was it only cost me ten dollars—old habits die hard. I could've gone to a designer store with the recent steep increase in my bank account, and I would've if I hadn't found something at the discounted place.

The higher-end store would've almost kept Sebi from coming to mind. Was I unintentionally punishing myself?

"With who?"

"Roman."

"Oh. You two are still going out?"

"I was actually about to call it off with him. Just hadn't done so before that tornado of a night that left my life in shambles. Haven't seen him since then either. I'm planning on doing it tonight."

"Are you sure you don't want to keep your options open?"

"Yes. That's what led me here." I ran a dangling earring through my ear.

"Yeah, probably. You are a rare breed, Londyn. Still no word from—"

"Nope." I didn't think I could handle hearing his name.

"I know that hurts, but it also makes it easier. I hope it goes well tonight. You look great."

"Thank you." I agreed on my appearance, but my insides were as jumbled as when I wore sweatpants and no makeup, buried in my bed.

The buzzer filled the air moments later. I walked down to the lobby, not wanting Roman in my living space even though he'd been once before.

His smile was intrigued as he watched me through the giant glass doors.

"If you aren't the prettiest thing I've seen all day," was how Roman greeted me. The expression was something I heard many times. I tried to believe he meant it and the words weren't merely his go-to phrase, lacking sincerity each time he uttered them.

"Thanks."

"I like your dress." The added compliment helped me to believe he was genuine. Was I simply looking for holes to make my exit easier?

"Thank you. I got it especially for tonight."

"Wow. Don't I feel special." He brought his lips to mine. How I felt when Roman kissed me paled in comparison to how electric pulses surged through me when Sebastian brought his lips to mine. As if the world faded away, and even if nothing else made sense, we did. But I'd never have a kiss like that again.

"You don't look so bad yourself," I said. Roman always dressed like a well-paid businessman, but tonight he was in a full-on tuxedo.

"Thank you. There is one thing about tonight I haven't mentioned yet." Roman tipped his head to the side and gave a half-grimace.

"Oh, yeah?"

"Yeah. The event is considered an opera, but it's a benefit for keeping fine art programs alive in the public school system."

"Okay?" I wasn't totally sure what he tried to communicate.

"And my company bought a table."

Now he made more sense. "Ah, gotcha."

"I have to make an appearance. Do the VP thing."

"Does this mean I'm finally going to put a face to the names I hear you say while on important phone calls?"

"Indeed, you shall."

I nodded. *Maybe I should've spent more than ten dollars on my dress at a thrift store.*

And that was only the first awkward moment of the evening.

Roman dropped his keys in the valet host's hand and rounded the car to open my door. As I stood, I made sure my dress fell correctly and my footing was secure. He offered his arm. "Thanks for coming. Walking in with you on my arm feels pretty amazing." I smiled, but it only lasted a minute.

As we entered the grand hall, hundreds of people dressed to the nines circled the vast space.

"Roman," someone called out.

"Hey!" he replied as I turned to the sound. A man in a similar tuxedo waved us over. "This way," Roman whispered to me. "There's someone I want you to meet."

"Looking sharp, friend," the man said to Roman once we were close enough.

"Thank you. We should really stop shopping at the same place, partner." Roman chuckled.

So this guy was Roman's partner, making him the big man in the company. "And who is this?" he asked.

"Forgive me. Grant, this is my plus-one, Londyn."

Plus-one?

My smile melted off my face.

How long had Grant's hand been extended?

"Nice to meet you," I finally said as I shook his hand.

My mind was pretty hazy after that introduction.

Our night was pleasant—except for Roman's words I couldn't get out of my skull. I met more people than I'd ever remember names for, but I was more in Roman's world than I'd been the day—months—before. Which should've been a good thing, only I was no longer attached. And apparently, neither was he.

When he pulled in front of my building to drop me off, Roman had yet to pick up on my agitation.

He turned to face me. "Thanks for coming with me tonight. I like the way you look with all of my people."

"Sure. It was a lovely event." The time had come. Was long overdue, actually. I couldn't even tiptoe around it now. "Roman, what are we?"

"*What are we?*" He chuckled. What do you mean?"

"Are we friends, casually dating, exclusively dating, boyfriend/girlfriend?"

"Oh. You're going *there*?" He paused and fixed his glasses. "Asking for the DTR."

"Yeah." Defining the relationship, something I should've done months ago.

A sigh escaped his lungs. "We're definitely more than friends." He chuckled with a hint of nervousness to it. "But I'm not entirely sure. I don't see a point in labeling it, though. I think it's just fine like it is."

With a point-blank question, he still couldn't give me an answer. I ran a hand across my lap, fixing my dress and trying to not get overly emotional.

"Why do you need to know? Are you seeing anyone else?" He asked before I answered his last question.

"No. Or not anymore," I answered.

"Okay. But there was someone?"

I nodded. Had I been upfront about seeing other people long ago, I wondered if I wouldn't feel so awkward now. Or stuck with my gut and *not* dated two men at the same time even though everyone else seemed to be fine with it.

"I see." Roman's jaw tightened. "It was that fighter guy, wasn't it?"

"Yeah," I felt vile admitting.

The annoyed arch of Roman's eyebrow triggered a memory. He seemed jealous when I was on a trip with Donald, but I glossed it over as if he was flirting. Had he kissed me in front of Sebastian on purpose? I closed my eyes and replayed the horrible event in my head. *Yes!* He looked at Sebastian before he kissed me. Apparently, his jealousy ran deeper than I assumed. But what would be the point of calling him out at this moment in time?

"Were you seeing other people?"

"Well, yeah. We aren't exclusive."

I nodded, biting the inside of my cheek. This information, the result of one simple conversation, could've saved me a whole mess of trouble. Suddenly I questioned a bunch of things. Like did he really travel *that* often for work? When would he have had time to see anyone else? What was the truth? And why was he jealous when he was seeing other people too? Had I misjudged Roman all along?

"So now what?" he asked.

Asking for details of his life didn't interest me, nor did I feel the need to divulge into my personal life. Yes, I should have been upfront about Sebastian, but Roman should have too.

"I'm done with the vagueness of dating life. Whether I assume too much or too little, it's proving detrimental to me."

"What were you assuming about us?"

How should I say this? "That I was more than a 'plus-one' to you." I couldn't believe I had the guts to admit that. My fist white-knuckled around my purse.

"Ah, I see."

Silence.

"My lifestyle doesn't leave much space for commitment, though. You get that, don't you, Londyn?"

"Yes. But whatever this is," I motioned my finger back and forth between us, "doesn't work with mine."

I wanted a relationship that built equity. I'd enjoyed my time with Roman, but what had it equaled? Some upscale dates, a few fun ones, gifts I didn't ask for, and a whole lot of nothing in between.

Finding myself as the girl at the fundraiser benefit in a ten dollar dress when my seat at the table probably cost ten times that amount spoke for itself. I'd never be part of Roman's true circle—which was fine with me. How did I not see it sooner?

I already had a lifetime of feeling like I didn't fit in. I wanted to be with someone who knew me, complemented me, stretched me, and *wanted* to be with me: labels and everything. In the face of moving forward or ending it all, I wanted someone willing to move forward even though it was scary.

And that's when it hit me. What I wanted was what Sebastian wanted from me. He merely hadn't figured out how to voice it either. The revelation didn't change anything, however. Sebi no longer wanted me. Still, the idea of going on dates with Roman so I wasn't one hundred percent single didn't intrigue me either.

"Right." More silence. "Well, if you change your mind down the road, let me know."

"I don't think I will, but okay."

"All right. See you around." He faced forward and put both hands on the steering wheel.

"Bye, Roman."

I closed the door on his car—and our relationship—and walked away.

Camilla was gone when I went inside, which really stunk because I wanted to fill her in on my night. Too tired to wait up for her, I went to bed knowing I had work the next day. We'd have to find another time to catch up.

The blender woke me up, creating one of Camilla's superpower veggie smoothies that looked greener than a pool left un-chlorinated for months. Smelled about as appealing too. She must have an early morning shoot today. Even though I should've slept for another half hour before my alarm went off, I wasn't mad about losing sleep this time—good news for her. Now we could finally discuss last night.

The whir of the blades sounded again as I walked out in my PJ shorts and hoodie, securing my day-old curled hair in a topknot.

"Sorry, it needed more ice. You want one?"

"Hard pass. It's a bacon and eggs kinda morning." I enjoyed cooking a big breakfast on days my heart felt off. I also had extra time now that I was awake.

"Eww."

"Same," I responded as she chugged her green slime. Stepping behind her to retrieve my groceries from the fridge — the perk of my vegetarian roommate: most of the food I purchased was never swiped — I inquired about her night.

"Turns out ladies' night isn't as fun when you're in a committed relationship." Camilla reported.

"It must be hard being so beautiful." I winked.

"Painfully true." She took another gulp. "How was the *oper-aaaaaah*?" Camilla gave her best vocal, which was nowhere near the skilled voices I heard hours ago.

"It was ... interesting."

Her eyebrows climbed her forehead. After a pause to make sure she wasn't about to say something, I proceeded with the details.

"So the 'opera' was a bit different than I expected. Turns out, it was just a company event for Roman, but one he needed a date for."

"Okay. Not too bad then, right?" I puckered my lips in question. "Wrong," she added in a questioning tone.

"The actual event wasn't bad, but I planned on talking with him about *us* at the end of the night, so I was already sort of disconnected. Then, he started introducing me as his 'plus-one.'"

"Oh no."

"Yeah." I tossed three slices of bacon into the pan, filling the awkward silence between us with the sizzling of glorious fat. "Months of dates and texts and phone calls and altered flights had awarded me the title of 'plus-one,'" I said with heaps of sarcasm and threw one more slice of bacon down for dramatic effect.

"I mean, I don't even know what else I would've wanted him to refer to me as; I was about to end things with the guy. But surely something other than *plus-one*." Another strip of bacon hit the pan. "Titles seem obsolete these days, but I wish I would've known how he saw me sooner." I wielded my spatula in the air. "Want to hear the worst part?" I didn't wait for a response. "I think he kissed me in front of Sebastian on purpose."

Camilla looked bugged-eyed, listening to my spiel before setting her gaze down and taking another draw at her superfood breakfast in a cup. Mason jar; we were millennials, after all.

"Brutal," she said.

"Yeah." I huffed. "I should've followed my instincts sooner, with both of them. Had I known Roman considered me his "plus-one" almost three months in, I would have ended things with him before I even went to Pennsylvania. And if I would've asked Sebastian to define our relationship, I'd probably have an actual boyfriend right now." I rubbed my forehead. "Did Branch ask you to be his girlfriend?"

"Not really. I guess we just knew."

"Must be nice. Why didn't I ask like I always did? That's what led to what we are now—*nothing*."

Perhaps that's what bothered me the most. Sebastian had my heart, no doubt about it, but I couldn't have him now. And Roman only saw me as nothing more than a space holder, a dinner companion, an arm ornament, an occasional entertainer. He inadvertently took up space in my life. Space that caused a significant rift in the relationship I actually wanted with Sebastian.

I'd absentmindedly thrown down several more strips of bacon during my rant. The bottom of the skillet couldn't even be seen, and grease flew out, making quite the mess. Big breakfast for sure.

"All right, slow down now. I'd offer to take over for you, but I can barely handle the smell from here," she said from across the bar countertop, dividing our kitchen and living area. "I think my arteries are clogging from second-hand ingestion."

"No need to be dramatic, Cam."

"Agreed." She raised her almost-empty glass to me and walked away. "We'll talk when I can breathe in here again," she added as she disappeared down the hall.

Way too much bacon was prepared for one person. Thankfully, I loved bacon—enough to call *it* my boyfriend—and saved some for my sandwich, salad, burger. Whatever meals came next.

Attempting to clear the smoke from the kitchen and my thoughts, I turned the vent-a-hood on and stretched my neck as I retrieved the eggs from the fridge.

I stopped my nagging thoughts to focus on the challenge at hand: making the perfect fried egg with laced edges and an unbroken yolk. Unfortunately, that only cleared my mind for less than two minutes.

When I honestly thought about it, the reason I was so upset in general and with myself was because had I simply asked for clarity upfront like I had in the past from both men, all of this would've played out differently.

Sticking some bread in the toaster was the last step to completing my soothe-the-soul breakfast. By the time it popped, my thoughts were clear.

Once all of the sounds of cooking ceased, Camilla came back out from her vegetarian-safe room. "I'm pretty sure you ruined that skillet forever. Anything I cook in there will have a hint of bacon flavor to it."

"How glorious." I spoke through a semi-full mouth.

"You owe me a new pan."

"Fine."

"You gonna be okay?"

I shrugged. "I mean, I'm not okay with how things panned out with Sebastian, but what can I do now?" At least the bacon filling my soul with superbness halted the sting of my life for a brief respite.

"Sorry my advice didn't seem to work for you. I feel responsible."

"Don't. I made my own decisions."

"Are you sure? I can make it up to you somehow."

"Eat some of my breakfast." I held out my bacon and egg sandwich, yolk running down onto my fingers.

She rolled her eyes and walked away. "Gross."

"Fine. More for me." I savored the last few bites before I had to get ready for the day.

24

With the clarity of Roman completely out of the picture, it only made me miss—and think about—Sebastian all the more. The one I wanted all along. Just like the last time Sebastian was ripped from my life, I thought about him almost every moment of every day for a week straight. Then multiple times a day, and essentially, every night for every single second until my brain surrendered to sleep. And seeing how he hadn't left my thoughts eight years after the first time we parted, I feared I'd never *truly* get over him after he left the second time. I still hadn't reached out to him, though. Was it too-little-too-late now, or did he still need more time? Maybe rebuilding could come one day; *if* he wanted it. I certainly did.

I did what I knew how to do—work hard. I went to work each day and put my head into my tasks. With fewer distractions, I got the job done even faster than usual, leaving me with free time to fill some other way than counting how many days it had been since I last talked to Sebastian—nineteen. Or kissed him— forty-five. I couldn't help it; I was a numbers girl.

The thought of getting back on the dating app that introduced me to Roman wasn't appealing, even after Camilla suggested I move on. Her advice on my love life wasn't exactly coveted these days. I knew who I wanted. Until my heart fully healed from losing him or until he reached out to let me know we'd never be a thing, I planned to remain one hundred percent single.

Bored and single. Lonely and single. Whatever. It was hard, but ultimately what I wanted.

My laptop chimed with a notification at the exact same time as Steve's. Which could only mean one thing: company email.

I minimized my accounting software program and opened an internet browser to check the email.

MARK THE DATE!
Our Annual Company Gala Is Almost Here.
Attendance is not mandatory but encouraged.
November 25th
Black Tie.
Each employee is allowed a guest.
Please RSVP

A gala?

The event would be held a couple of days before I headed home for Thanksgiving.

"That time of year again," Steve said above the radio from his side of the room. I wasn't sure if he was happy or sad about it from his lack of enthusiasm. Then again, his tone was typical.

"It's a first for me. What should I expect?" I asked while still in my chair, but got up and walked around to look at him while we spoke.

"A whole lot of hoopla. 'We've increased profits by blah-blah percent and added X-amount of new people on board this year.' I'd totally skip out if it wasn't a reason to get a babysitter, see my wife in a dress, and eat a four-course meal for free." Steve fixed a button over his dad-bod stomach.

Not once in the entire time I worked here had anyone ever mentioned the gala. I wondered if the employees of the companies we bought out also got the invitation. Since they'd have to travel, I wasn't confident they could come unless their travel was also paid for. Needless to say, I didn't hold my breath on seeing my co-workers in Illinois and Pennsylvania.

As far as Donald, however, I was almost certain he'd come. It would be his first time back in Texas in nearly three months. I found myself excited to see my ~~co-worker~~ friend. Steve might not be too enthusiastic about the company event, but I was thrilled. I'd finally have something to do. Even though the guest I was allowed would be me, myself, and I.

"Sounds fancy."

"It is. I'm the one who gets the budget report. I'm pretty sure it's just a source for tax write-offs before the end of the year," Steve admitted as he raised his eyebrows once and held his lips in a pursed line.

Something I learned over the last year: our company sure didn't lack finances.

Since I'd only worn my new little black dress once to Roman's work event and hadn't posted any pictures from that night—I neither wanted to make a statement or document I was with Roman should Sebi scroll through my page—I was pretty sure I'd wear that dress again. Get even more use out of my ten dollar purchase.

Having an event on my calendar cheered my soul. In the last couple of weeks, my mental planner remained depressingly empty.

"Hey, Londyn." Our office manager walked in, causing me to stand tall from my leaning position against Steve's desk. Sasha was beautiful and powerfully intimidating, the first one to break the unreservedly male staff. Even how she stood there made me feel like I slacked off. After the commission check mishap, I worried I was on thin ice.

"Yes, ma'am?"

"Ralph wants to see you."

"Sure thing."

Here we go again. I wondered if this had to do with solidifying the traveling trainer position. Over the last few weeks, I hadn't actually thought about it much at all. However, more than ever, I didn't have a reason not to travel. No one waited for me, here or there. As I walked down the hall to my boss's office, I had no clue what to say.

"Londyn Adams, my star employee." Ralph buttered me up.

I chuckled. "Am I about to get some horrible news?"

"No. At least I don't think it's bad." He placed a hand on his high-dollar tie.

"Let me guess? A new buyout."

"Hey!" He pointed his finger at me. "You're good."

"If you say so. It's basically the only reason I've been called into your office. Not that hard to deduce."

"True," he stated as he tapped a stack of papers on his desk. "You've been requested."

"Requested?" Clay in Belleville or Tamika in Monroe must've screwed something up.

"Yes, ma'am. The dream team will be reunited."

The dream team: Donald and me.

Getting away might be useful right about now. But was I ready to sign an agreement to continue this traveling thing?

"Back to Pennsylvania?"

"Almost. New York. A tiny town called Friendship. The market in Bradford County is pretty saturated, so we're going to the edge of the underground reservoir on the New York side. In Allegany County. Donald will oversee it as part of his region, but he needs you to get everything set up the Aspire way."

New York! Most of his words failed to compute after mentioning the state. Had this news come weeks before, I'd already be making plans for my first date with Sebastian. Now, I didn't even know if I'd let him know I was coming.

"I see. What about the gala? I was actually pretty excited to go."

"You wouldn't leave until December second, after the gala."

"Do I have the option to say no here?" I chuckled through the nerves.

"Of course. You're not obligated to this. But I think Donald would be disappointed."

"About that, obligated? I still haven't signed an agreement for this traveling trailer position."

"I know. Are you ready to?"

"I don't think so," I said like a question, rising in pitch.

"The power is yours, Londyn. You can go on this trip or not, and you can take the position or not. I don't feel the urgency to make it official yet."

Really? Even at my job, I lacked concrete labels.

"How long will this trip be?" My out of town trips spanned from three days to thirty-one days. One thing was for sure, I didn't want to be away from my parents at Christmas.

"Donald suggested flying out together and not purchasing your return ticket yet."

Together. So Donald would be at the company event. *Awesome!* But an open-ended ticket? His open-ended ticket led to three months in the Northeast. I wasn't sure I was up for that. Unless Sebi and I....

I shook the thought from my head. I couldn't base my work decisions around any person but myself.

"I'll have an answer for you by the end of the week." Which sounded like I'd be thinking about it for a long time, but tomorrow was Friday.

"Deal. Look over these." He handed me the info packet detailing the trip.

"Will do. Thank you, sir."

When I made it back to my desk, I used my work phone to call Donald since using our cell phones during office hours was frowned upon. Besides, this was a work-related conversation.

"Bridges!" He answered almost instantly.

"When am I going to stop finding out about work trips from Ralph when you already know about them and should be giving me a *heads up*?"

"Does that mean you're coming? It's beautiful out here. Who knew such drastic seasonal changes existed? Not us Texans, that's for sure. You better pack for colder weather."

"Whoa, whoa. I haven't decided yet."

"Oh." His voice deflated.

"I told Ralph I'd let him know by the end of tomorrow."

"That's fair."

"Regardless, you'll get to see me at the gala."

"For sure. Dress to impress. All the big wigs are there."

"Eh, I'm fine with being me. Let my brain do the impressing. Numbers don't lie, Donald."

"Whatever. Leave me to dress up by myself then."

"How's it going out there? You ask Tamika out yet?"

"Everything's great, and no with Tamika. I'm so busy, there's practically no free time."

"So take her on a lunch date during the week. You both get an hour every day."

"Please. I have far more to offer a woman than a squeezed in lunch date. Don't insult me now, Bridges."

"All talk and no play, you are." I huffed in laughter.

"And you miss me!"

"Hmm, debatable. Some days more than others. Right about now, I'm not missing you all that much. I was just getting into a groove again, and you requested to have me shipped across the country."

He laughed. "A little dramatic there, diva."

"Diva? *Diva?* Hold on, I need to go tell Ralph to buy that plane ticket for Steve Schneider." The typing across the room ceased.

"No, no, no. Stop. You know I'm only messing. Besides, I did it for you so you can be out here closer to the fighter guy."

"Um, sure. Look, I'm slammed here at work." It was a fabrication. "I'll let you know what I decide *before* I tell Ralph because that's what *friends* do."

"Perfect. I'll see you soon."

"I haven't decided, bully."

"At the gala. Geez."

Oh, right. "Bye."

"You're leaving again?" Steve asked as soon as I placed the receiver onto the base with a *click*.

I wondered what he thought, overhearing my conversation, especially the part where I used his full name. *Oops.* "Uh, maybe. I haven't decided."

"I might've envied you on the first trip, a nice little getaway. But they have you bouncing around like crazy. My wife would've never been okay with that."

"I guess that's a perk of being alone." *Ouch!* It hurt even though I tried to joke around.

I wished I could say I looked through the packet and made a pros and cons list or came to an educated conclusion on whether or not I'd travel to New York in an adult-like manner, but I couldn't. Still no closer to a decision on Friday morning before work, I pulled a box of playing cards from the entertainment center in the living room, shuffled the deck, and said, "Red card I go, black card I stay." Fifty-fifty shot.

With the deck sitting on the TV stand, I picked up a chunk and slammed it down, face up.

Nine of hearts. Red.

I was going.

25

With so much to prepare for before the huge company shindig and the looming trip to Friendship—I wondered if the town name was some weird sign for Sebastian and me, but I guess friends was better than nothing—my days went by in a hurry. And with nothing, or should I say no one, to fill up my evenings, I'd read an entire series by the time the gala had arrived.

I rushed home after work, so I had a reasonable amount of time to get ready. Because for *once*, I actually agreed to let Camilla do my hair and makeup. After I consented, I instantly second-guessed myself. She was on the grander scale of life. While I was, well, on the blend-in side. Either way, it'd make for a memory. I hoped a good one.

"Take out that overused bun this instant," my roommate demanded as she walked into my room.

"Hey, now. I'm still going to wear my hair like this tomorrow—and the next day. No need to give me a complex."

As my full, coppery hair fell from the bun, my natural wave rippled to the tips of my locks.

Camilla gasped. "Why do you always hide your hair?"

"Because it's easier." My hair had decent volume, but part of the reason I frequented a bun was to keep it from getting A- too poofy, or B- tangled into a rat's nest.

"Let's see," Camilla gazed at my head with squinted eyes, the wheels in her mind visibly turning. "I think we're going to work with these gorgeous waves. You just made my job a whole lot easier."

She took a comb and parted my hair a smidge left of center and flipped the front over in an arch to the right. Then came her magic. A spritz of something here, a lather of something else over there, and refreshing of a few of the less full parts with a wide barrel curling iron. *BAM*. My hair never looked better.

"Wow, Cam! Not half-bad." If I gave her an honest accolade of my thoughts, she'd never let me live it down and insist on helping more often.

"Who do you think did my hair and makeup *before* I was picked up by an agency?"

"All right, I hear you. I should've let you do this long ago. All that about you being awesome and trustworthy and blah, blah, blah."

"Thank you." She took my sarcastic half-compliment like the Miss Texas crown. "Perhaps you wouldn't be single now had I been helping you out sooner."

"Ouch." Was she teasing? I didn't care for it. Sebastian liked me as I was, and Roman never seemed to complain either. Besides, looks had nothing to do with my singleness. Time and distance did.

"Just messing around. You'll find someone."

"Maybe I need you to leave for an extended time, so I can reactivate the Airbnb in your room. Perhaps my prince charming will come like yours."

"Or you could also get struck by lightning. Those types of things don't tend to repeat themselves, friend."

Didn't I know it? What were the odds of Sebastian and I running back into each other after all those years? And what kind of a moron was I for walking away from the only person I ever really loved?

"Speaking off," she continued, "Does he know you're coming?"

She must've seen Sebi in my eyes. I hadn't meant for my thoughts to be so evident.

"No." I sat up straight and brushed her comment off like it didn't pinch. "If he hasn't talked to me by now, I doubt he wants to. What about my makeup?" I changed the subject.

Graciously, she didn't bring Sebastian up again.

"Your eyes have *never* looked this good," Camilla said after working on them for twenty minutes straight.

I leaned over to look in the mirror. The outside of my eyelid was smokey black, and the inside was shiny rose gold. The two colors blended perfectly in the center of my lid. I'd never seen such lavish eyeshadow on myself before. Let alone metallic. I felt glamorous. Even after sliding into my discounted dress, I felt like a hefty paycheck.

"I better go. Traffic might be bad. Thanks for dolling me up."

"Any time. I take tips in —"

Before she could finish, I ended her sentence. "Celery."

"Haha." She wasn't really laughing.

On the drive to the event center our company rented, excitement to see how elegant the night would be bubbled inside of me. If Steve raised his eyebrows at the price tag, of which we both saw large figures, I was in for a lavish night.

Upon arrival, I saw the giant, decorated board for our seating assignments and found my name under the number sixteen. Thankfully, when I arrived at the table, it was comprised of my local co-workers. My introverted side didn't want to sit with a bunch of strangers. I found the place card with my name on it after offering polite *hellos*. A guy from sales was on my right, and Sammy, the receptionist, was on my left. I didn't look beyond those two cards at the round table, which seated eight.

Moments later, I met Steve's wife, Margaret, a woman with a quick tongue. No wonder he was so quiet all the time. He was used to it at home. Margaret was kind but a talker. *Super* talker. Anything and everything. Whatever popped into her head, it seemed. Work was probably the only quiet time Steve had. It made me want to talk with him even less, allowing him to have some time to decompress. He winked. I nodded a mere fraction.

The place settings were simple yet lovely. White and silver. *Everything* was white and silver—plates, silverware, napkins, candles. The only exception was the greenery that supported white flowers. I recalled the table at the event I tagged along with Roman. I was confident this one was grander. After all, an oil company had more funds than the public school creative arts department—thus their need to raise funds. Not that I loved that fact. I made a mental note to suggest to Ralph that we make a donation to that organization. He'd see it as another tax write-off. I saw it as securing a space for children to learn and be kids.

As the seats at the dozens of tables filled up, it brought an eye-opening visual to precisely how many people were a part of the Aspire conglomerate.

The hall was elaborately decorated, including an embellished stage with a podium and microphone. Yet again, after seeing the grand scale of the night, I was floored I'd never heard a peep of this event until recently. Perhaps all the planning happened while I was in Pennsylvania.

When the lights flashed ever so quickly, I wondered if I blinked until they flashed a second and third time, letting everyone know the night was about to begin. Two seats at our table remained empty, the name cards reserving the seats unknown to me, leaving me to wonder who was late or not coming.

"Good evening, Aspire." The room filled with light and pompous applause, sounding like a gentle fall rain. I was glad my "Woohoo!" hadn't escaped my lips yet, further showing the gap in poshness between my extended work family and myself.

"Welcome to the Annual Gala and Review. It's been a great year." CEO Robert Kingston, as he announced himself, went on with all the boring jargon. But as I tuned in, excited to experience a night outside of my condo, a *PSSSSST* came from the table diagonal from me.

I turned to discover none other than Donald Wilkie, my closest work companion. He did an exaggerated wave like he'd been trying to get my attention for quite some time. *Look at you,* he mouthed, motioning two fingers up and down.

Fake bouncing my hair under my open palm, I mouthed, *Thanks. You too!* and swirled my pointer finger toward his appearance. Our facial dramatics rivaled morning soap opera stars.

"Londyn Adams."

Instantly, I was back in school, getting called on in class when I'd zone out. Only this time, it was from giant speakers. My eyes panicked as I still looked at Donald, who motioned for me to go forward. As I stood, I caught sight of the screen containing my picture and name under the banner "Top New Employee of the Year."

What?!

Not once had I expected some type of recognition. I humbly walked up the two small steps of the portable stage. Once on the platform, I turned back to face the full, large room. Donald caught my attention in the massive crowd, whooping and hollering.

"Congratulations. Thank you for all you do," the CEO said as he handed me a plaque the size of many of the books I cradled over the years.

"Thank you." I chuckled, still in mild shock. As I made my way back to my seat, Donald continued his applause, extended in my direction. I offered him a curtsy.

"Way to go, London," Sammy said after I sat.

"Thanks. I had no idea there'd be awards. Let alone that I'd receive one."

"Yeah. They don't typically tell people they'll receive an award unless they haven't RSVPed."

"Maybe you'll get an award too."

She gave me a *please* look. "For what? I answer the phone."

"Which you do so well." I encouraged her.

Across the table, Steve's wife, not so quietly, whispered into his ear. I wondered if they had conversations about me at home. Surely at least once, on the day he found out he had to share his office. That was if he managed to get a few words in. I chuckled at my own thoughts and looked down, not wanting to care what she said. But still kind of caring.

In an instant, there was only one person I wanted to tell about my award. But considering I hadn't heard from him in two days shy of a month, I didn't know if he'd respond. Or even care.

Back in high school, the two of us became rather competitive. Whether it was a higher GPA, more awards, fewer absences, practically everything turned into a fun competition. That was the case for me, at least. He swore the times my GPA ticked a few decimal points higher than his was due to the fact I was a grade below and thus *easier.* I stopped pointing out the tests I scored above one hundred on with the extra credit questions. It felt like I rubbed it in, and there was only one thing I wanted to rub in his face: my face.

Memories flooded back in seconds, faster than I could pick my favorite.

Whether I was a hopeless romantic, repaired enough from the heartbreak, or a friend until the end, I decided to message him. With a valid excuse, his response, or lack thereof, would let me know more than I did for the last twenty-eight days—which was basically nothing.

Holding the plaque against my chest, making sure my glammed-up look was visible in the shot, I took a selfie and sent it before I changed my mind.

Me: Look what I just won.

Sent.

No turning back now.

I stared at my screen for several minutes, waiting to see if a "read" timestamp appeared.

"Donald Wilkie," left the speakers, filling the hall.

"What?" I said to no one in particular as I looked up at the projector screen and dropped my phone into my purse.

Top Grossing Sales Manager capped his picture on the screen. Now it was my turn to show my enthusiasm and emotional support.

"Yeah, Donald! You go, boy!" Okay, maybe that last bit was extra.

He nodded at me from the stage.

Donald, ever the one to exude confidence, leaned in and pulled the microphone too close to his mouth. "I'd just like to thank... Nah, just kidding."

Everyone laughed as the CEO's face flushed momentarily before Donald gave him a friendly clap on the back.

Donald worked hard; I knew that. However, I couldn't help but wonder if his numbers were mostly the result of being placed over the giant golden goose across the country. Regardless, I was glad he won. Plus, I'd feel bad if only half of the dream team was acknowledged.

I casually stuck my hand out before Donald passed me. He didn't miss a beat, reciprocating my high—make that mid—five before he sat back down.

"Thank you all for sitting through the formalities of the evening. At this time, the dinner will begin."

As the servers zipped around the many tables, delivering salads, then the main dish, the room resolved to the sounds of silverware clinking against porcelain plates and hundreds of conversations. When my food was gone and the plates were cleared, I scanned the room to see what other people did with the two dessert options that stared me down since I was first seated. Surely they didn't mean, *"Pick one."* Each person had two behind their name card. I was fairly confident whatever was left on the table would be thrown away. Besides, I was an award winner. The night called for celebrating *and* indulging. I ate both the smooth cheesecake and the savory chocolate cake. The coffee I requested was simply to help wash everything down, not that I needed another stimulant.

"For anyone who would like, the dance will start in fifteen minutes. If you're choosing not to stay for that portion, please make your way to the gift bag table before you leave."

"We get a gift?" I said to our table as my face lit up.

"It's mostly office stuff with the company logo on it, but sometimes there's an actual prize in there, depending on our profits," Steve answered. "I bet there's something inside worth being excited about this year."

"Awesome."

This was one of the best nights of my adult life. But as I swallowed that thought, the other nights it competed with contained Sebastian. I wasn't sure this trumped those events. Had he been here, it would stand in first place, no doubt.

Wondering if he'd replied or even opened the message, I retrieved my phone from my purse. Nothing. No response. He hadn't even seen it.

I tried to encourage myself it was because he was at practice, but it only made me feel marginally better. Deep down, I couldn't decide if he'd answer or not.

"We're out," Steve said as he and his wife rose to their feet.

"You aren't going to stay and dance?" I asked.

"Do I look like I dance?" he responded.

"One of these days I'll convince him," his wife said.

"Good luck." I encouraged her, hoping whatever poor image she had of me would change.

They weren't the only people to leave. More than half of the crowd filtered out after collecting their swag bag. I sipped on my coffee, trying to decide if I wanted to stay or go. Dancing might not be so fun for people like myself, who attended alone.

"You sticking around?"

I turned over my left shoulder. Donald stood there with both hands in the pockets of his expensive navy suit. Pretty sure it was custom-tailored, if not custom made altogether.

"Not sure yet. You?"

"Yeah, I'm gonna stick around for a bit. Can I introduce you to someone?"

"Sure." I wiped my mouth and hands on the cloth napkin before standing to follow him, excited to meet his guest.

"I almost didn't recognize you, Bridges. You look incredible tonight, friend."

"Thanks. I finally let my professional model roommate play dress up with me."

"My compliments to her, too, then." His gaze left mine and fell on who I was about to meet. "This is Londyn."

She stood to shake my hand.

"Londyn, this is Natalie."

Natalie. Aka: the one Donald couldn't get over even though she'd been dating his best friend for years.

"Nice to meet you," I said. Then looked up at Donald, who winked the eye she couldn't see.

"Likewise. I've heard about you, so it's nice to finally put a face to the name," Natalie stated.

"Oh, have you now? Not sure I like that." I chuckled.

"Only a few stories about his travel buddy." Natalie clarified.

"That I am." I turned to Donald and gave my eyes a slight squint, showing I didn't fully believe that was all he'd told her. "Looks like we're about to head out again in a few days, actually."

"Yup." Donald agreed. Just then, the lights faded, and the music began.

"Wanna dance?" I asked, desperate to get him away and ask the questions running through my head.

"With you? Uh, fine. But only one song."

Donald looked over to Natalie, who hadn't finished her dessert. She only ate from one of the plates. Which wasn't surprising from the looks of her petite frame, crowned with gorgeous burnt-red, curly locks. "Is that okay, Nat?"

"Sure. I'll polish this off." She lifted a bite and pulled the fork from her mouth in a tight smile.

"I'll be right back. Don't you think for one second you aren't dancing with me next," Donald said.

Natalie nodded her head, looking more gorgeous than I ever would. No wonder Donald couldn't get over her.

In pure excitement, I drug him to the dance floor. For a moment, I felt like I was in the fifteenth century, and everyone was about to spin around the room in a dance we all knew from childhood. Unlike the last dance I attended, the music was soft and slow.

"Wow. Natalie," I said as Donald took my hand and framed me in a dancing position with plenty of space between us.

"I know, right? Ridiculously gorgeous."

"She sure is. What's the story?"

"Turns out David broke up with her right after I left for Pennsylvania. What a chump. She called to catch up and fill me in on everything. And I told her."

"That you loved her?" My perfectly crafted eyebrows rose in glee.

"No. I'm not that lovesick. Fine, I am. But also smart enough to know Natalie was most likely not ready for something else after being with David for so long."

"What did you say then?"

"I took my shot. Told her that I knew she was in a rough spot emotionally, but I was here for her. And when she was ready, I was the first in line to pursue her heart."

"Donald," I smacked his shoulder. "That's an amazing line! I bet she melted right into the floor."

He shrugged. "I hope so. This is the first time I've seen her in person since that conversation weeks ago. She seems to be doing fine. It's so hard not to push when I have all these years of emotions rushing to the surface."

"I know what you mean." Perhaps I didn't know how to handle everything that went down with Sebastian because our history clouded my future. I wasn't sure how they could coexist.

"Why didn't you invite someone? You had two guys to pick from last I knew."

"A lot can happen in a short amount of time I'm learning."

"Ah."

"Yeah. I'm finding myself pretty single these days."

"What happened? I mean, if you want to tell me. The non-detailed-guy version will be fine."

"Uh, the fighter guy got mad when the local guy came with me to his fight. That ended things with Sebastian. Haven't talked to him since. And it turns out the other guy wasn't the settle down type. Ever."

"Dang."

"Yeah."

"So, you want to be single then?" Donald asked.

"I mean, yes and no. The one I want doesn't seem to want me. We haven't talked in weeks. I sent Sebastian a message tonight after I got my award. He hasn't responded."

"I know all about that. Sorry, Bridges. Give it some time. It worked for me. You aren't chump change, you know?"

I huffed. "I'm not sure I can wait around as long as you did."

"Waiting was hard, but it's feeling mighty worth it right about now." He looked across the room to Natalie and smiled.

I already waited for eight years, wasn't that long enough? Afraid my sentiments were visible on my face, I didn't want my emotions to deflate his night.

"I'm most definitely the third wheel tonight and not going to keep you away from that lady another minute."

"Thanks." Donald smiled as he leaned in closer for a hug.

"Um, personal space, please." I used the joking banter he once said to me.

He laughed. A solid, full-of-life laugh I never heard before. "Good one."

"I'm so happy for you. Don't mess this up," I said as we walked back to the table where Natalie sat.

"No kidding."

"Sorry to keep Donald away from you. It was so nice to meet you, Natalie. I wish I could hang out longer, but my comfy clothes and fuzzy socks are calling my name."

"No worries. I was thinking the same thing."

"Sorry, Nat. She can leave, but you can't. I drove you here, remember?"

"How could I forget?" She smiled.

I literally held back a cheer as loud as when Donald won the award. Natalie was an even better and longer awaited prize.

26

After the gala, the rest of the week flew by. I only had two days of work before the four day weekend, thanks to Thanksgiving. Being back in my childhood home, where Sebastian frequented, was equally comforting and challenging. As I scanned the living room, my bedroom, the backyard, memories with him filled them all. Trying to think back to a time before Sebastian entertained me in my home was near impossible. Practically all my other memories involved only myself and a book, leaving them almost unreachable and indistinguishable. I drove home Saturday night in order to have a full day to do laundry and pack for yet another traveling training job. And during all the days that passed, I wished I could say I hadn't looked at my lonely unread message an insane amount of times, hoping one time I'd find a reply. Or at least see that Sebastian had read it. However, the only thing that would've hurt worse than not getting a response was if he read it and didn't reply. At least that's what I told myself.

The work trip was a welcome distraction, to say the least. I looked forward to hanging out with Donald and hearing more about his time with Natalie.

Now that he was finally able to pursue her, I wasn't sure how our relationship would function. What if, out of respect for Natalie, he barely talked to me at all anymore? I couldn't lose someone else. I allowed myself to be a mopey teenager for all of ten minutes as I packed the night before. Donald finally got what he wanted, and though I was entirely thrilled for him, jealousy pricked my heart.

What Donald didn't mention during the flight: If I heard from Sebi.

What I didn't mention during the flight: If I heard from Sebi.

Instead, I insisted he tell me how the last few days went with Natalie. Boy, did he light up. As he talked, all I could think about was how unfair it was that he finally got his girl, and now they lived in different states. Just. Like. Me. Only I didn't have my guy. Adulting was no fun. It was evident I couldn't apply my book smarts and hard work mentality to my love life. If only I could.

He went on and on about the woman he was infatuated with, and though it was sweet, my heart couldn't handle anymore.

"So, Regional Manager-slash-Top Grossing Salesmen of the year, where are we sleeping this time?" I asked when the seatbelt sign came back on, indicating we'd almost arrived at our destination. I never actually read the packet Ralph gave me. A fact I told no one.

"This team is already rolling. I bet we'll only be out here one week, ten business days tops. That being said, a hotel is all we need. Then I'll drive back to the house in Pennsylvania in a rental car, and you'll head back to Texas in an airplane."

"You mean I don't get to make your coffee every morning?" I feigned disappointment with a pouty lip.

"Not this trip, Bridges. Sorry to take that pleasure from you. Maybe next time."

I shook my head. But at least I knew our entertaining banter wasn't completely gone. At least for the time being.

"I still haven't decided if I'm going to sign the position agreement to fully become the traveling trainer, actually."

"Oh, you haven't? I figured by the fourth trip, you would've solidified it or told them no."

"So did I, but they keep coming so quickly. Ralph originally said they wouldn't be that often." I chuckled. "I don't think he foresaw the rapid growth tapping into the natural gas market."

"For sure. I already hired three new people in Monroe to help with sales. I can't imagine what adding this location into the fold will do."

"My head hurts just thinking about it." Not truly. Figuratively, for sure.

"I know how to help you decide," Donald said.

"Shoot," I inquired.

He held a hand out like Vanna White. "Isn't it obvious? More time with me."

I laughed. "Yeah, yeah. But sometimes I have to go alone."

"True. You should probably decide before the new year rolls around."

"Good suggestion, thanks." My mind couldn't wrap around the fact it was already December. Whether we'd be in New York for one week or ten days, by the time I got back to Texas, everything would be in full swing for Christmas. Soon, I'd travel again to see my parents, and then the year would be over. The first trip we went on five months ago felt like it had barely happened. But my life was pretty different, to say the least.

Oddly enough, we flew into the same airport we did in August, only this time we didn't have to drive to another state. Also, this time, Sebastian wouldn't be waiting there for me.

After getting our rental car and confirming our hotel reservation in the next town over—Friendship was too small for a hotel—we were on our way. The temperature dropped fifteen degrees as we walked outside. Donald and I carried on during the hour-plus drive, much like we always did.

By the time we made it to our hotel—more like a motel, it was small but still had free breakfast—the business day was over after our six-and-a-half-hour commute from Dallas. The building sat in the middle of rolling hills. Though they were bare, I knew the landscape would look lovely and full of color in the spring. We checked into our neighboring rooms that shared a conjoining door inside. The whole complex was a giant row, like the world's longest single-wide trailer. There weren't any across-the-hall rooms.

We ate, we slept, we got up for work the next day.

Thankfully, Donald was right. Even though the town was small, the people were immensely equipped. Some of the sharpest people I'd worked with, in fact. I trained the finance department, which was one person, and Donald trained a sales team, which was two people. The owner, Todd Stapleton, agreed as part of the buyout to remain the manager with a chunky pay. He gave us Texans the debrief before we taught the crew the Aspire way.

Todd took over the family business after his father retired. Thankfully, he already brought the company into the twenty-first century—unlike our other northeast buyout in Monroe—which made everything much easier.

I wasn't drained when I returned to the hotel on Tuesday night.

Wednesday night either.

On our drive "home" on Thursday, Donald informed me my flight would leave Saturday morning. He wanted one more full workday and was kind enough not to book me a trip that arrived back in Texas after midnight.

My time in New York was smooth and pleasant, but cold. I looked forward to the slightly warmer temperatures I'd experience when I arrived back in the Promise Land. I also had such a fun time goofing off with Donald after our months apart that I didn't have much time to dwell on Sebastian.

Until Sebastian finally messaged me back.

Sebastian: Congrats on the award. I'm sure you deserve it.

Now what? Should I respond? Let it slide? He basically answered a two-week-old message. Should I start up a new conversation? Or simply say thanks and see where he took it? That's what I decided on.

Me: Thanks!

Aaaannnnd wait.

When did I crack my phone case? I pondered as I stared with copious amounts of energy at the digital tether I'd thrown back his direction, wondering if he'd grab hold.

Then the dots. The three glorious, bouncing dots let me know Sebastian was typing. Hope that we wouldn't end as enemies sprouted in my soul.

Sebastian: What else have you been up to?

An open-ended question! Another good sign.

Me: Work, work, and more work. You?

Sebastian: Same. And practice, practice, practice. Ha!

Me: Such exciting lives we lead.

Our conversation wasn't as fluid as the hundred we'd previously had. We also never fought before, so navigating our first conversation after fighting proved challenging. As I tried to think of something else to say or ask, he beat me to it.

Sebastian: You traveling for the holidays?

Me: Yes. I went home for Thanksgiving and will go for Christmas too. You?

Sebastian: Nice. I didn't go home for Thanksgiving, not wanting to regain all the weight I finally cut, but I will go this month.

More than ever, a huge part of me wished my "home" and his "home" were the same city, even the same state. Now his home was in Maryland, where his family lived for the last nine years. I also felt a quick, one-two jab to the stomach after he mentioned his weight loss. He didn't have to point out the connection to our month together—and his first loss. I already knew that much and despised my role in the equation.

With how this conversation was going, there was only one other safe topic: the weather. Even though our conversation was basic, it was a conversation nonetheless. One with my favorite person in the world who I hadn't heard from in six weeks. It meant we were working on putting the tainted past behind us. That was my desire, at least.

Me: Is it as cold in Maryland as it is out here?

Sebastian: Than in Texas? It's much colder.

Me: No, I meant New York.

No indicator of activity filled my screen. Immediately, it registered that I gave myself away. I prayed he didn't pick up on it.

Sebastian: Wait...

So much for that hope.

Sebastian: You're in New York?

Me: Um, yeah. Actually, I am.

Sebastian: You're joking with me.

Me: If you say so.

Sebastian: Go outside.

Me: No. It's cold. I'm already in my pj's, and … it's cold! Lol

Just then, the screen morphed into a request for a video chat. I declined it and snickered.

Sebastian: See, you aren't serious.

Me: I'm dead serious. But there's no way I'm going outside right now.

Sebastian: Do it! Or I'll never believe you.

Me: What does it matter?

Sebastian: It matters!

The call request came again. Before I answered, I put on my coat to cover up my pajamas and slipped on my work shoes. I almost looked like I was headed out for work if I didn't have to open my jacket. And it wasn't past 10:00 p.m. The call connected as I walked down the only hallway.

"Okay, I see a hotel, but you could be anywhere." He assessed, then added, "Hi," causing me to laugh.

Seeing his face and hearing his voice was everything I longed for. My heart raced at his digital presence. "Hi. I can't believe you're making me do this." I flipped the phone to the other camera so he could see what I saw. "It's practically black out. What do you think you will see to let you know I'm here?"

"I'll be able to tell. Flip it back to your face, and tell me again where you are."

I did as he asked, slightly annoyed but ecstatic we were talking. He could've asked me to do a dozen jumping jacks or rolled in the snow, and I probably would have.

"Sebi, I'm several miles outside of Friendship, New York. And I'm freezing." I didn't mean to call him Sebi; it just slipped. Even though our connection started all of ten minutes ago, the month of silence already started to dissolve from my mind.

"Seriously, Londyn! Why didn't you tell me you were here?" His tone was excited yet irritated. So were his eyes.

"How'd you know? I didn't even show you anything recognizable."

"I only needed to see your face. You could never lie to me."

"Why did I have to walk outside then?" I laughed as I ran back in, shivering.

"Just because. It added more excitement, don't you think. Plus, I wanted to see if you would."

"You're a punk!" I exclaimed as I made it back to my room and closed the door.

"When did you get here? When do you leave?" His honey-brown eyes lit up.

"Monday. And I leave Saturday morning." I almost took off my coat but thought better of it when I remembered my current attire.

"I can't believe you didn't tell me all week." His expression wasn't exactly mad, his voice either, but I sensed the disappointment.

"We weren't exactly talking." I hated to admit aloud.

"I don't care. I would've told you if I was in Dallas again." I cocked my head and squinted my eyes. "I would," he added.

Donald knocked on our adjoining door.

"Hold on." I walked to the door and unlocked it, causing it to swing open on its own.

He took in my coat and shoes with a question mark resting between his eyebrows. "You all right?" Donald asked frantically. "I heard you call someone a punk."

"Yeah. I'm, uh, on the phone." I flipped the screen to show him Sebastian but also so I could express my excited face to him without Sebastian seeing. My eyes and mouth exclaimed, *Eeeeeeeek!* sans words.

"Oh. Cool. Hey, man." Donald greeted Sebastian with a "sup" nod.

"Hey! Welcome to my state again."

"Thanks." Donald's eyes left the phone and landed on me. "Let me know when you get off."

I had a feeling he was uneasy.

"Okay." I closed the door and also turned the camera off, going to an audio call. "Sorry about that. What were we talking about?"

"Why did you do that?" Sebastian asked.

"Because I needed to. It's late, and I'm getting in bed, and," *I can't look at you right now and think straight,* "other reasons."

The video chat request came through again. I declined it.

"Seriously, Sebastian, I can't video chat right now. I'm about to go to bed."

"Where are we going to meet up tomorrow?"

"What?" There was no discussion of it, no question of if I'd even like to. Just *where.* I was pleased I already shut my camera off. My face surely wore shock like a heavy winter parka.

"If you're here, I'm gonna see you. Maybe we can have a better conversation than our last one."

"I'd like that. But we can have it now."

"Nah. I need to see your face."

"*Fine*! I'll switch."

"I want to see you, Londyn. In person," he added.

Holy mackerel! My heart froze, then sped up to catch a regular rhythm. How did he do this to me so effortlessly?

I spent the next two minutes trying to regulate my pulse, hoping that seeing him wouldn't cause that much more damage to my freshly mending heart.

"I'm looking it up right now." After a moment of silence, he spoke again. "Seriously, Londyn? You're barely over an hour away." He chuckled. "I can't believe you didn't tell me sooner." *Click, click, click.* "Look at that. There's a cute little bookstore/coffee shop smack in the middle of us. A forty-minute drive each."

"Send me the location and time, and I'll be there. I'm going to bed. See you tomorrow."

"Goodnight, Londyn."

What I didn't miss: he didn't call me sweets. Not then, not once in our conversation. Which I tried to convince myself I was ultimately thankful for. I had to continue letting the feelings that erupted for him again after lying dormant for eight years cool into hardened rock. God knew I couldn't handle the lava anymore after getting burned.

What was I going to say? What would he say? Would we resume talking after tomorrow, or would this be the last time I'd speak to Sebi? I paced incessantly.

I *Ugh*-ed with ferocity as I slammed backward onto the bed, with my coat still on. No surprise that led to a knock on the door again. I opened it to Donald, leaning against the frame with his arms crossed over his chest.

He started when I said nothing. "You don't exactly sound happy to finally hear from the guy."

I walked back to the bed and repeated my dramatic "timber" onto the mattress. He took my body language as the invitation it was and followed me in, sitting at the tiny desk chair in my room.

"I am. It's complicated. At least now I know Sebastian doesn't totally hate me if he's willing to meet up."

"Anyone who hates you is an idiot." His comment was bold, his annoyance evident. I looked at him. "What? It's true."

I didn't address his statement. "Seeing him is going to be hard." I covered my face, so the tears that bubbled over my lids wouldn't be seen and hoped I could force them to stop. I'd been doing so much better with this crying thing when Sebastian came to mind before tonight. Another sign I still walked on hot coals.

"You're going to see him?" Donald asked with doubt in his voice.

"Yeah. Tomorrow after work. If that's okay. I'll need the car." I didn't want to watch what my answer did to Donald's face; his tone was already enough to decipher. I prayed he could sense my tense emotions, floating over me like a smoke cloud above the volcano, and wouldn't joke around.

"If you *want* to go, you can totally use the car."

I finally lowered my hands after I was able to suck the tears back in. "Are you sure?"

"Totally. Remember, you aren't chump change. Don't let him play with you."

"Thank you. I don't think Sebastian is playing me. I think he wants to discuss what happened. I'm pretty sure he's convinced I cheated on him. But it was more like I went on dates with two guys. Kind of, but not really. It's a mess. At least I'll get to clear my name."

"Good. I'm here if you need to talk it through and figure out what you want to say."

"I think I just need to sleep. Thanks, though."

"Sure. Goodnight, Bridges." He high-fived my limp hand resting on the mattress before he walked away, solidifying the protective brother role he took up months ago.

27

Donald caught a ride with someone from the office because our hotel was seven miles in the opposite direction from where I was headed. I thanked him again and apologized for leaving him alone. He encouraged me not to take all of the blame for something I hadn't actually done when Sebastian and I discussed *that night*. Which was good advice. I probably would've eaten crow for this to all be over. On the drive, I said things to myself like: "This will be good to finally be able to let him know what happened," and, "Hear him out," and "Don't ramble," and "Don't forget to apologize," and, "If he calls it quits for good, don't you dare fall for him again." Even though I wasn't sure I'd un-fallen for him anyway.

Pulling into the little bookstore cafe's parking lot caused me to gush at the location he chose. Only one other car was there, and it wasn't the Batmobile, meaning I arrived first. The town wasn't big, but it was twice the size of the township I worked in from the looks of the area.

As I went inside, the smell engaged me first, redolent to my comfort zone in an instant. The scent of aged spines merged with coffee cocooned me in tight, helping to put me in a better mental space for what was to come. Too nervous to sit at a table and wait, I perused the bookstore. The majority of the books were older than me, leaving the scent that filled the room all the more potent.

One of my personal library's neatest details was the age or location of where my books were purchased. I was excited to add an old book from this tucked-away treasure in New York to my collection. The story would also always remind me of the day I met up with Sebastian, so I hoped our encounter fared well. Because ultimately, it would impact how much I enjoyed the novel. Whether I was willing to admit it or not.

As I tried to decide between two titles that intrigued me based on their description on the back cover, a gust of cold wind blew over my arm, letting me know someone opened the door, most likely Sebastian. With a book in each hand, I looked up to discover I was right. I tried not to let my face show how frantic my insides quaked after not seeing him in person for forty-one days—*bubble, bubble, ca-boom*—so I hoped the smile spreading across my face let Sebi know I was delighted to see him.

He walked over to me without hesitation, causing my heart to pick up a beat with each foot he closed between us.

"Hey there." His voice was slightly shaky.

"Hi, Sebastian. I'm just trying to decide between these. Then we can get some coffee." I held the books out, wondering if we would've hugged each other had my hands not been occupied.

He didn't even look down, his eyes firmly locked with mine. "This one." He touched the book in my left hand—good enough for me.

"Done." I slid the other choice back onto the shelf and walked to the register.

After paying for my book and ordering a drink, I walked to a free table as he ordered something for himself. There was no surprise his cup held black coffee, containing practically no calories. My dulce de leche latte looked significantly better— even though I saw the small town barista pour a heaping scoop of flavored powder into steaming water—but probably contained his dinner limit in calories.

Thinking of dinner, I almost wished we would've met somewhere where I could've eaten. However, wishing this wouldn't last long so that I could go eat didn't feel right. I never wanted to rush through my time with Sebastian. In the past, in the present, and hopefully in the future. Even if it was somewhat tense.

"I still can't believe you're here," he said as he enclosed the steaming mug in his hands.

"I know. This traveling thing is becoming second nature. Not sure I like that, though. I'm a girl who craves some roots."

"I know what you mean. But I also kind of like it when I get to travel. Only I usually return home with a few cuts and bruises. At least you return in one piece."

That's debatable.

However, I said nothing, taking a sip from my wide-mouth mug instead. Should I dive right into an apology?

"I tried to message you."

I assumed he meant he wanted to but couldn't bring himself to do so. Or something along those lines. "When?" I needed to know how much time he waited before reaching out.

"The night of the fight. My fight. Our fight." He clarified. Though I didn't need any clarity on the last portion. "I wanted to see you before I left so we could actually talk after I cooled off. The message bounced back three times and wouldn't send. I guess the cell signal wasn't strong enough. I took it as a sign to have our conversation another time, but then I let too much time pass. And when you never reached out, I figured I scared you to death."

"Oh." Shock rose within me that he wished to resolve the issue immediately, even knowing I was there with Roman. Had I got his message, I wondered how differently things would've played out. In an instant, I recalled how Camilla commented on how long it took for me to return after she texted me that night. "I was probably gone already, anyway."

"Like twenty minutes later?"

"Pretty much."

He nodded but didn't seem to know what to say.

I swirled my drink around with the wooden stir-stick.

We sat quietly for a stretch. "I just gotta ask?" he continued. "Why are you still seeing that guy? I thought after our awesome month, I held some kind of place in your life. I mean, I knew about him, but I didn't think you'd keep seeing each other when you got back."

"I'm not."

Sebastian furrowed his brows and pulled his head back.

"Seeing him." I defined.

"But you were at my fight?" he asked.

"Not really."

"It sure looked like it." He pulled a hand through his hair and rested his chin against the fist propped on the table. "You're confusing me. How about you tell me what happened?" He didn't seem upset, but his tone was heavy. His lips held in a line.

I let out the breath taunting my lungs. "The night of your fight, I was so excited to see you." The intensity of his eyes locking with mine trembled through me. I looked down into my mug, clutching onto the warm porcelain for strength, and chewed my bottom lip. I looked back up and continued. "I hadn't even seen Roman—"

"Ah yes, *Roman*," he uttered the name like a disease.

"Our last date was before my work trip out here with you. I think I only talked to him once after I was back home other than running into each other at the airport. So when the buzzer at my condo rang that night, I assumed it was my roommate's boyfriend and pressed the button to let him in without asking. But it was Roman at my door. I didn't know he was gonna show up, didn't ask him to come over, and actually told him we were about to leave." I sighed at how the next part set the horrible night into motion.

"When Camilla's boyfriend blurted out that I had an extra ticket, I clammed up and didn't know how to un-invite Roman. That was on me. I should've said no. Shoot, I should've told him we weren't going to talk anymore as soon as I got back from Pennsylvania. But when I failed to put my foot down, he came. I desperately hoped you wouldn't see him. I promise you, it *wasn't* a date." I fidgeted with my bun.

"Oh." His golden-chocolate eyes turned foggy, the left one squinting with unease like it occasionally did.

Finally letting him know the situation truly wasn't what he thought and owning up to my part was liberating.

"But I saw the kiss. Watching him kiss you *seriously* jacked with my head."

"He did, but I wasn't exactly a willing participant. I would've stopped him if he hadn't moved so quickly. I was there to see *you* and ready to discuss our future." There was one more thing I needed to admit. "Roman didn't know about us. I have a feeling he caught on to my affection for you and did it on purpose." I rubbed my temple. "But that's neither here nor there now. I should've told him about you sooner. Honestly, I should've ended things with him as soon as I knew there was something here. I hope you know I'm not the dating around kind of girl. Obviously. I can't handle that lifestyle." I wasn't sure if my words helped or hurt. Surely Sebastian didn't want to be a secret in my life.

"So you aren't seeing him anymore? At all?" he asked.

"No." I was pleased to offer him concrete clarity.

Sebastian smiled that crooked, heavy on the right side, grin.

Unsure how to respond to his pleasure, I remained silent.

"I had it all panned out rather differently."

"I figured as much." Only I didn't ask for details because I wasn't sure I could handle the specifics of his impression.

"Yeah. I thought since I was in New York and you were in Texas, I was 'out of sight, out of mind.'"

"You've never been nor could ever be 'out of sight, out of mind,' Sebastian." Once again, I couldn't look up. I scratched my nail against the grains of wood in the table.

"Does that mean you still thought about me?" he asked.

"A little." I bit my lip and finally raised my head, knowing full well it was more than a little. Sebi grinned.

I knew this could go sour, but I had to know. "Did you think about me?"

"Every day," he uttered. "But I didn't want to."

Ouch! I looked away at the bookshelf.

"Because I was mad," he added after my eyes twitched at his comment.

"I was mad too. You kind of shut me down. No. You literally shut me down." The half-hearted chuckle I wanted to release got trapped in my chest.

"Sorry about that." He reached out and touched my hand that rested on the table. I tried not to notice how his touch ran up my arm and down into my toes like an energizing shockwave. "No matter what, I shouldn't have yelled at you like that."

"Apology accepted." I pulled my hand back in the guise of lifting my large drink to my mouth, so Sebastian wouldn't feel how much his touch affected me, putting space between us while despising every inch.

"Thanks."

"In case it hasn't already been clear, I'm sorry too. I can't believe I let my timidity hurt you so badly."

"Forgiven. So now what?" Sebastian didn't miss a beat.

"What do you mean?"

"Where do we go from here?" He clarified.

"I'm not entirely sure. We still live halfway across the country from each other."

"Which I already had a suggestion for." He downed the rest of his coffee and tapped the side of his cup.

"One you also retracted." I smirked.

"Maybe I want to retract my retraction?" Sebastian rubbed his chin.

"I'm not sure making such a huge decision fresh off of a fight is the wisest choice."

"That's what my coach says." He chuckled. "Do you want me in your life, Londyn?"

"Always."

"Then the distance isn't a deal-breaker. There are other things we can do, like weekend visits. We have the money that we never did in the past. Plane tickets aren't gonna break our banks."

"Lots of life happens between trips, though. I want to be able to do life with someone. All of it. The sad days, the fun days, the nothing but listening to me read days." *Don't cry. Don't cry!*

"Don't get ahead of yourself, sweets." He reached across the table and held my hands in his. "Can we promise to take it slow and work our way back to where we were?"

I'd be a fool to let him go. Weeks ago, I'd decided I was ready to move. I had to put faith in us that we could figure this out and make it work. "I'd like that. Slow is a good plan, don't you think?"

"I guess. It depends on who you ask." He chuckled. It wasn't exactly candid.

Drawing this conversation out was risky. If there was one thing I knew about Sebastian, he could always talk me down and get what he wanted. If I spent another hour in this coffee shop, I'd be looking at listings for apartments in New York.

"I'm glad we met up and got everything sorted out. Fighting with you was brutal, and you didn't even use your fists. I feel bad for your competitors."

He shrugged. "That's an entirely different kind of rage."

I had no response to how my actions affected him. The ache of a phantom black-eye pulsed on my face. The desire to apologize again was vast. Instead, I went ahead with my plan to close out our night.

"I'm gonna go ahead and head back. I need to eat and get everything packed for my morning flight."

"Let me take you to dinner," he suggested.

I blushed. "I'd like that. But no more talking about all of this." I circled my finger around the table where we spilled our issues.

"Deal." He scooted away from the table and stood.

I picked up my new book, looking at the cover and locking in the memory of the end of tension with Sebastian and the promise of a future, tying the two together forever.

We got in our cars, and I followed him to a restaurant. Like he said he would, Sebastian left all heavy talk at the bookstore. Our dinner was what I needed for months. To be with him, laughing, talking, touching. Being with him was amazing and challenging. I already hated our paced commitment.

The hardest thing I had to juggle now was forcing myself to move slow when I still loved Sebastian. Facts are, I probably could've moved already, but I knew it was a decision made by my heart and not my head. We were with each other again, and long-distance was working for Camilla and Branch. This was enough.

Time evaporated. As we walked out to our vehicles, I had no clue when I would be able to see him again. Touch him again.

"Thanks for coming to see me. Even though you didn't let me know you were here earlier." He squeezed my upper arm.

I laughed. "You're welcome. Thank you for letting me explain and hearing me out."

"You're welcome. If only we'd done it sooner, huh? I'm so glad we are back together."

Together.

It didn't matter if I had any other title. Sebi and I were together.

"Me too." I bit my bottom lip.

Sebi opened his arms for a hug.

Apparently, taking it slow meant a hug would end our time together instead of a kiss. I doubted my choice for the tenth time when I looked up at his inviting lips. I hugged Sebastian and pulled in his scent.

"There's just one more thing," he said.

Before I could conceive what he was about to say, his hands enclosed my face, and his lips parted mine. Even though we agreed on slow, here he was, flooring the gas pedal and giving me the best kiss of my life.

Cue the lava flow, in three ... two ...

He eventually pulled away since I never did. Sebastian looked at me, straight-faced, his hands still embracing my cheeks, taking in every line, freckle, and unspoken thought I possessed. For a few seconds, it was total silence.

Finally, he asked, "You sure you want to take things slow?"

"Yeah." I smiled, though it was shaky.

"Funny. You never could lie to me. Talk to you soon, sweets." He kissed me once more, smack dab in the middle of my forehead. With a gleam in his eye and a spring to his step, Sebastian got in his car and drove away.

Myself, in contrast, must've been cast into a slug by a wizard. I didn't even have my seatbelt on, or the engine started before he was so far down the road, I couldn't hear the roar of the Batmobile.

"What just happened?" I shook my head and entered the return address to the hotel on the map in my phone.

I used the drive back to think. Sebastian was smart, smarter than me, so he no doubt had a plan. The person who knew me the best in the world could read my face as plainly as a children's book. No matter how much I said I wanted to take things slow with Sebastian, my heart would always crave more. And my face would never be able to hide it. He called out what I wasn't willing to admit. I underestimated Sebastian. Only problem for him was, my head and my heart weren't on the same page yet.

However, what he thought would come next was as much of a mystery to me as the roads I drove on if I didn't have a map coaching me. I was set on establishing our connection again, for now, but I'd be lying if I wasn't charmed that he wanted to pick up right where we left off. Well, before the fight.

Seconds after the main door to my hotel room swung shut behind me, Donald knocked on our private, conjoining door. I almost pretended not to hear him so I could finish packing. But Donald's input and opinion could prove valuable if I wanted to discuss my night.

"You engaged," he teased, "or can I take you to dinner?"

"I already ate, but I can go with you and get a dessert." With my purse still on my arm and my shoes on my feet, I let the adjoining door swing shut behind me and walked toward the exit of his room.

"This isn't a date, though. I'm spoken for," Donald clarified.

"You're the worst." I rolled my eyes even though he couldn't see.

Ten minutes later, we sat in one of the two diners that serviced the town. Had it been in a bigger city, it might be considered a hole-in-the-wall place. For the locals, however, it was merely a restaurant.

"Do you miss Texas?" I asked. It had been close to half a year since he officially lived there.

"A couple of weeks ago, not so much. Now? Tremendously. But, I have one of my favorite parts of Texas right here." He lifted his glass to me.

"Thanks for being kind, but I know I'm not the Texan you wish you shared dinner with tonight."

"Can't disagree. Sorry, Bridges. So, you going to tell me how your meeting with fighter-dude went earlier or keep me in the dark?"

"Um, still processing. We can talk about it later."

"Later, when? This is our last night together for who knows how long."

"How sad for you. I'm going to run to the ladies' room really quick. If the waitress comes, get me two scoops of ice cream."

When I looked in the mirror as I washed my hands, the heavy weight of the last few weeks no longer pulled on my face and weighed down my shoulders. I looked forward to the future, whatever that might look like. *One day at a time*, I encouraged myself.

Donald had a smirk on his face as I approached the table.

"What?"

"I couldn't let you head back to Texas without some *apple* pie. One last time, before I retire the joke."

After the swaying emotions of the day, laughing was sublime.

A plate of warm apple pie, melting the scoop of vanilla ice cream on top of it, sat in the middle of our table with two spoons. We devoured it in less than two minutes.

"I seriously can't take you anywhere." Donald threw an extra napkin at me.

"Everyone knows food is more enjoyable when you don't care if it gets all over your face," I said.

"Is that so?"

"I don't know. Might've just made it up."

"Does that mean your shirt has to enjoy it too?" He pointed out a glob of ice cream seeping into my sweater.

"Oops." I laughed.

28

If only getting my head and my heart on the same page proved easier, life would be great. I was back into a nice little routine of work, reading, and nightly conversations with Sebastian. One thing I had finally managed to do, however, was make a decision on the traveling trainer job. I walked into Ralph's office, confident and firm, declaring I'd only take the position if I never had to be away from home for longer than ten workdays. Likewise, I was only willing to travel once a month. If needed, we could utilize video conferencing like I did with Tamika and screen sharing, like how I helped Crystal months ago when she still worked in Belleville. I figured Ralph would say no, considering that wouldn't be enough time based on previous trips' length, but even though I wasn't pinned down to Texas, I also had to plan personal weekend trips with Sebastian between Dallas and Rochester. After working my whole life to gain myself opportunities, I finally decided to be bolder in which opportunities I took. Much to my surprise, Ralph agreed to my terms.

The first trip was already on my calendar, back to the Northeast—our new milk cow—for the last week in January. A few days shy of six months as an Aspire accountant, I held an improved and higher-paid version of my previous job title.

I was thankful my job would take me close to Sebastian again since our holiday plans had already been made before we were back together—spending Christmas with him would've helped the crazy year end on a high note. But since the trip was scheduled to be a short one, I figured I'd only see him once, tops. At least I wouldn't have to pay for this plane ticket personally.

On the Saturday morning between Christmas and New Years, I woke up feeling confident in my life choices. Even though my inner hopeless romantic teenager still nagged one thing was missing in my daily routine. Make that *someone*. How long would taking it slow still feel right? For once, I was up before my roommate, meaning I was either awake super early, or she had a late night. Whatever the reason, her blender wasn't my alarm clock today.

I hadn't seen much of Camilla this month since she spent the holidays out of town with Branch. Plus, she left the week prior for some fashion week. Which was apparently a huge deal for her career. I didn't rent out her room like I joked about. If Sebastian wasn't the one who came to stay, I didn't want anyone else in my space.

All I wanted to do was wear layers of comfy clothes and spend a day in a book—the one I bought in New York and hadn't been able to start yet. But before that, I had to eat. Two slices of bacon sizzled in the pan, almost ready to be pulled out, so I could use the grease for my eggs. The coffee pot sputtered out the last few drops as Camilla rounded the hallway into the open kitchen/living room.

"Good morning. How was your huge fashion trip?"

"Someone's chipper this morning," Cam said as she pulled her hair into a ponytail. "Is there a man in your room?"

Whether she chose to forget our differences in relationship standards or slowly tried to implement her ideals into me again, I never let her comments affect me. I simply brushed her dramatics to the side as usual. "Please. I'm just happy to feel like I know what's going on in my life. By my choice, nonetheless."

"Good for you. Now we don't have to have a repeat of you cooking a whole pig and stinking up our condo again. It still smells in here. Move it." Camilla bumped me with her teeny-tiny hip so she could pull out her industrial juicer/blender from the lower cabinet. The motor in that thing could probably support a car. Maybe only a two-seater, but still. I was surprised she was able to lift it onto the counter. Her non-effectual bump didn't move me, but I kindly took a step to the side.

"I think you're just smelling today's ration. But I wouldn't mind if the scent lingered." I inhaled deeply. "It's better than the garden aroma you bring in with those chlorophyll drinks." I waved the spatula in her direction.

"Not even close. Your arteries could probably use a good detox with a few of my smoothies."

She told me about her fashion week after our herbivore versus carnivore banter died down. I asked her about her first Christmas with Branch, trying not to be jealous. *Next year* I hoped. *And not just a visiting trip.* I hadn't spent Christmas with Sebastian since high school. The gift he gave me, which I still owned all these years later, was one I treasured.

The present was a book from the eighteen hundreds. He saved up for months so he could buy it off eBay. The novel would always be one of my favorites. We didn't trade gifts this year, which was useful for my heart's navigation down the slower-traffic-keep-right lane.

More than jealous, however, I was happy for Camilla. Branch seemed to be able to handle her. Not that there was much to handle physically; it was all the other stuff she brought to the relationship most guys couldn't seem to deal with. Like working a career that meant millions of people would ogle over your appearance and her over-the-top dramatics.

Camilla disappeared to her room, probably to escape the aroma of the scrumptious meal I devoured. I sat on the couch and set my plate on the side table since we never bought a kitchen table. I wasn't what you'd call a slow eater, but when I read, I didn't always get to the last bite before it was well past room temperature.

The majority of the day passed by as I consumed three-quarters of the book. Not much changed other than my location. When Camilla came to sit in the living room for better lighting with a webcam interview, I went into my bedroom to give her privacy.

My phone went off earlier than I expected. His practice schedule must've been altered with holidays capping the week.

Sebastian: Are you home?

Me: Yeah.

Sebastian: Good. I sent you something. It should be there soon.

Perhaps I was wrong about us not swapping gifts. I felt crummy considering Sebastian got me something, and I didn't reciprocate the gesture. Two seconds after his words filled my screen, the call button in our condo rang. *Before* Camilla's digital interview was over.

I popped my head out to make sure the coast was clear to walk to our door and not be in her shot. I looked far from a model. The only role I could snag in my current getup was homeless chic.

The slightest nod toward the door was blended into her graceful hair flip as Camilla urged me to handle the buzzer. *Man, she's smooth.*

"Hello?" I tried to be loud enough to be heard over the intercom but not loud enough to disrupt my roommate.

"Delivery for Londyn Adams," a deep male voice said.

Camilla waved her hand out of the sight of the screen, urging me to handle the call without interrupting her meeting.

"Uh, yeah, that's me. I'll be right down," I said between a whisper and my usual volume. As I descended the stairs, I tried to tame the flyaway hairs that made me look like I had stuck my finger in a socket.

The man stood at the glass barrier with a large vase of flowers consuming his upper body. I felt better that the gift Sebastian sent was something less tangible. The bouquet would only last a week, tops, so it wasn't like I'd be reminded daily that he bought me a present, and I got him nothing.

Pressing the door open caused the delivery guy to take a step back.

"Hello. I'm Londyn Adams."

"I know," he said in his deep timbre as if no one else had exited. But when he turned sideways to pass me the vase, it wasn't a delivery man. It was him—the one who sent my heart racing.

"Sebastian!"

"Hey, sweets." Whatever he did to mask his voice ended.

"What are you doing here?" I asked, full of excitement.

"Seeing you. I told you I'd let you know if I was in town."

"You have another fight tonight?"

"Not exactly. Can we, um, go back inside and talk."

"Sure." *Whoa, whoa, whoa, Sebastian is at my place. And I look awful.*

In the adrenaline pumping through me, I forgot Camilla was on an important call. We caught her attention with our lighthearted banter and my giggles as we walked in. Her eyes did a double-take when I wasn't alone.

"Is everything okay, Camilla?" rose from the computer speakers.

"Yes, sir. What was the question again?" She shooed us away below the camera.

Sorry, I mouthed as we tiptoed into my bedroom and closed the door.

"Nice place," Sebi said.

"Thanks. Had I known you were coming, I would've spruced up a bit." I tried to move a few things around my room as I set down the vase. When my hands stopped moving items, they landed on the edge of my bulky college sweatshirt and insecurely pulled at the hem.

"You look fine. Always do."

I blushed. "Thanks," I repeated like a broken record and sat on the edge of my bed.

"Hold on. I need a hug."

"Oh, right." I chuckled. "I'm kind of frazzled."

Sebastian smelled like home. Felt like it too. Or maybe it was because I *was* home and never had him here before. We stayed there for a good while, longer than any hug I remembered with him. Unless you counted the one he gave me before moving years ago. At least I wasn't crying this time.

"So?" I prodded, still not believing he was actually here.

"Where to start?" He chuckled.

"Out with it." I smacked his thigh as he sat next to me. It was even more solid than I remembered.

He left out a priming breath. "Before you came back to New York a few weeks ago, I knew I wasn't over you. But I figured I would be eventually. I'd managed to do it once before, more or less."

That stung.

"After you came, I *knew* I'd never get over you. Especially how you looked at me after I kissed you. Our decision to move slow bugged me for days. Okay, weeks. When I went home for Christmas, I still hadn't fully accepted it. And my dad noticed."

Sebastian grabbed my hand. My nerves jumped to attention.

"When he asked what was up, I told them about running back into you, our month in New York, our fight, all of it. My father was silent at first. Not sure if you remember, he isn't the biggest talker. Then he told me something that changed everything."

In the rush of all that occurred so quickly, my brain reminded me to breathe.

"When we said goodbye before I moved, I told you I'd write."

"I remember. Why didn't you?" After all these months after reuniting, I finally had the courage to ask when he brought it up.

"I did." Sebi pulled an envelope from his back pocket.

"What?"

"I wrote you a letter and asked my dad if we had any stamps. He said we didn't, but he'd take it to the post office for me. I was so excited to hear back from you. Days turned into weeks, and you never replied."

Picturing Sebastian eagerly checking the mail, only to be disappointed time and time again, tore through me.

"And now I know why you never did. My father never sent it." He passed me the old envelope with my name and parent's address.

"Why?"

"He said he thought I needed to stop thinking about you and my 'childhood ways' and focus on becoming a man who was about to enter college." The pain in Sebi's eyes extended to my heart. "Not only did he decide to move our family away, but he also took the decision of staying in contact with you away from me.

"I about lost it, ready to storm out of the house before my fighter's reflexes kicked in, and I'd regret it."

"Oh, Sebastian." Why would his father do that? He was always so kind to me?

"I don't think I've ever been more furious in my whole life."

I looked down at the small paper that was the real reason our history was altered.

"My mom heard us yelling and came in to break it up. I stayed quiet enough for my dad to apologize. He said he regretted it later, but so much time had passed, he didn't even know if you would still be at that house or away at college yourself. I'm honestly baffled he kept it all these years. But I'm thankful. Now you'll know."

"Know what?"

He nudged my hand. "Read it."

"Now?"

"Please."

"You're just going to sit there and watch me?" I tucked the hair that fell from my mess of a hairdo behind my ear.

"If you don't mind." Sebastian smiled that stellar crooked grin.

"Fine." I ran my finger under the seal and retrieved the notebook paper, unfolding the page carefully as if the parchment was aged far more than eight years.

Hey Sweets!

Man, I miss you. Which really stinks because it has barely been a few weeks. But guess what? I got into Johns Hopkins University. It's gorgeous out here. The only thing missing is you. So I decided you should apply here. You'd love it. The library on campus is huge, and they have a whole section devoted to super old books. But save up and buy a coat. Supposedly it gets pretty cold here in the winter.

It's worth a shot, right? Just in case, maybe you should apply to all the schools out here. You're simply too far away in Texas.

You doing okay? I can't wait to hear back from you and see your handwriting again. Who knew someone could miss handwriting? Sheesh. I love you. Write back as soon as you get this.

Sebi

I looked up with tears filled eyes. "You wanted me to come to school with you?"

He nodded.

Heat radiated from my face. The blush in my cheeks had to be maroon. Not only did he want me to move closer to him once, Sebastian wanted to be with me so badly he'd actually asked me to move twice, only I never knew.

"My dad said one more thing. He said, 'I thought you'd never recover from leaving that girl behind. I feel awful for splitting you two up. Don't lose her again, Son.'"

A tear rolled down my face. Sebastian reached up and wiped it with his thumb.

"So here I am. Telling you I'm not going to lose you again. I booked a flight here from Maryland. I haven't been back home to New York. My home is wherever you are. Like you said, even if you move to New York, we'd still have a commute that only allowed us to be together on the weekends, which isn't much different from how we are now. I'm coming back to Texas. It's been too long anyway."

"What?" I was shocked. "But your job, and your gym?"

"Both of which can be replaced down here. What can't be replaced there is you."

As if the slow-lane I traveled on came to a close with flashing arrow merging signs, all it took was a gentle nudge on the wheel to be back on the fast-lane paved with love and ended at Sebastian.

I squealed, every bit like I was sixteen again, and threw him back in a grand hug/headlock/grapple move, crumpling his letter between us. He didn't resist one bit. Didn't tap either.

"I can't believe this." I lifted my head and kissed him.

To make sure this was happening, that moving to Texas was what he honestly wanted, I pulled back and looked into his amber eyes. While I formed the question in my head, he opened his mouth first.

"I love you, Londyn. I think I have for ten years."

"I am off the charts in love with you, Sebastian." I kissed him with no concerns for our future. Not a single one.

The words we admitted meant so much more now. Not to say the love we thought we had for each other as teens wasn't valid, but declaring it again now, after all we'd been through—love, loss, reuniting, overcoming adversity—made it that much deeper.

"What 's all the ruckus? I almost bombed that interview," Camilla roared as she opened my door, discovering me pinning Sebastian to my bed. "Whoa, sorry." She pulled the door back.

"No, it's fine." I laughed. "Come back in." I sat up, giving Sebastian the freedom to move as well. Not that he couldn't have overpowered me like I weighed nothing if he didn't want me there. It appeared he had no desire to do so. "Camilla, this is Sebastian. And he loves me." I gleamed.

"Yes, I recognize him." She turned her question to him. "Is that right?"

"Madly," he replied to her though he looked at me.

"And he's moving to Dallas!" I blurted out, my eyes not leaving his face either.

"You are?" Camilla responded.

"Absolutely." As his word ended on his lip, he finally turned to her.

"In that case, welcome home," Camilla said.

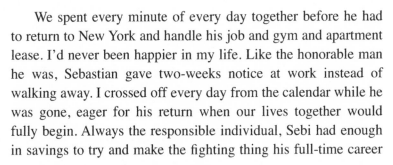

We spent every minute of every day together before he had to return to New York and handle his job and gym and apartment lease. I'd never been happier in my life. Like the honorable man he was, Sebastian gave two-weeks notice at work instead of walking away. I crossed off every day from the calendar while he was gone, eager for his return when our lives together would fully begin. Always the responsible individual, Sebi had enough in savings to try and make the fighting thing his full-time career for a year before looking for a corporate job in the metroplex. Thankfully, his former trainer had some connections in Dallas and was able to get him onto a talented training team with a former Olympian for a coach.

Sebastian's words were true: We hadn't won the lottery once; we won twice.

If you enjoyed Out of Sight, Out of Mind,

check out these other books

by Elle Ann Brown.

mental notes

S E R I E S

www.elleannbrown.com

amazonkindle

Maddison Miller is soon to discover the best life is actually
what happens after all of your plans have come crashing
down. However, choosing to let go and actually doing so is
the constant struggle she faces. And just when she thinks
she's back on the right path to achieving her optimum goals,
life comes along and scatters her Mental Notes.

ACKNOWLEDGMENTS

I'm so thankful for all of the support I've received over the last few years. Some pretty amazing people have helped me along the way. To my beta readers, fellow authors, family, and friends, I appreciate you more than you know. There are too many of you to name now. I don't want to miss anyone.

One special thanks to my editor, Aimee Ferguson, who helped me on a time crunch.

And thanks to you, my readers, who enjoyed my first series and asked, encouraged, and pestered (okay, not really) me until I wrote another book. I'm so honored by your love and support. I look forward to putting out many more books in the future.

Connect with Elle:

 www.elleannbrown.com

 instagram.com/elleannbrown

 twitter.com/elleannbrown

ABOUT THE AUTHOR

Elle (Leslie) Ann Brown equally likes to love and laugh. She does so with her family and friends in the great state of Texas, where she writes as she mothers her four children. Her first series, the Mental Notes series, was released in 2018-2019, and she plans on doing this author thing for a while longer. You can learn more about her and follow the journey on her website, Instagram, or Facebook.

If you enjoyed this book, please help me out by leaving a review on Amazon or GoodReads.